D0765216

The Usual Mistakes

FLYOVER FICTION

Series editor: Ron Hansen

The Usual Mistakes
Erin Flanagan

The Usual Mistakes

Erin Flanagan

University of Nebraska Press
Lincoln and London

Manufactured in the United
States of America

∞

Library of Congress Catalog-
ing-in-Publication Data
Flanagan, Erin.
The usual mistakes / Erin Flanagan.
p. cm. — (Flyover fiction)
ISBN 0-8032-2029-4
(cloth : alk. paper)
I. Title. II. Series.
PS3606.L356U85 2005
813'.54–dc22
2005004224

Set in Minion by Kim Essman.
Designed by R. W. Boeche.
Printed by Thomson-Shore, Inc.

To Charlotte Hogg

Contents

Acknowledgments

I'd like to express my gratitude to the Bread Loaf and Sewanee Writers' Conferences, the Vermont Studio Center, and the MacDowell Colony for the encouragement to write and a wealth of new friends; to literary journals for their hard work and dedication to new writers; to my dearest readers, teachers, and friends—Judy, Gerry, Hilda, Jonis, Charlotte, Talbird, Daryl, Renae, Kelly, and Naca—for their unwavering support and endless readings; to Ladette for keeping me sane and working; to my family—Judy, Ken, Kelly, and Olive—for their love and cheer; and to Mike, for everything to come.

The Usual Mistakes

The Usual Mistakes

The hospital where I work is actually a hotel—a renovated Best Western, just south of Omaha. The doctors kept much of the original décor, making only minor structural changes: the exercise room was expanded to include a pharmacy, the dank bar renovated into a chapel, although I don't think anyone's ever been there to pray. Check-ins sit on the same red and beige floral sofas vacationers would rest on while waiting for their sheets to be changed, in town for an Omaha Royals game or a trip to the Henry Doorly Zoo. Cora, the receptionist, stands behind the large, oak desk greeting patients and ringing the bell when their rooms are ready. The chandelier in the main lobby still glitters and tinkles when a breeze blows in, as if announcing the possibility of a wonderful time.

I worked for four years as night manager of this Best Western. When the hotel closed, I forged my credentials, created a pre-med degree from Creighton University with a 3.96 grade point, and voilà, I'm a medical assistant. I'm no more licensed to assist in medical procedures than I am to fly a plane, but I've been here almost eight months, and no one seems to notice.

Many of the patients look as if they're here for vacations, wearing what can only be described as cruise-wear: shiny fuchsia jogging suits with gold braided trim, khaki pants and pale golf shirts, an occasional visor. It's a private hospital specializing in reconstructive surgeries and prosthetics. We do plastic surgery, although I'm not allowed to call it that. Our patients like that the rooms are still decorated as hotel rooms. They say it makes them feel less like they're staying at a hospital and more at home, ignoring that, other than the car wrecks and burn victims, they don't need to be here at all. In truth, the linens, beds, and curtains were thrown in at such a ridiculously low rate when the hotel foreclosed, that the hospital would have been foolish to pass on them.

I work banker's hours, nine to five.

Cora rings me in the nurse's lounge, room 143 next to the Coke and ice machines, and tells me the two o'clock is here. "Good thing you blocked a lot of time," Cora says. "She's a real code red, if you know what I mean." Cora is seventeen and last weekend, drunk on Zima, had her belly button pierced; I'm thirty-one, a dead husband not a year in the ground, and barely able to make my mortgage payment. I rarely know what she means.

In the lobby, standing next to a faux-antique red divan, is a girl no larger than a ten-year-old boy, wearing clean blue jeans and a long-sleeved green T-shirt, reading the bulletin board. She has straight, clean brown hair and an ordinariness to her features that could be feminine or masculine, depending on your attentions—a strong, block nose and long, soft lashes. Poking out of the cuff of her right sleeve on the underside of her wrist is a dark line that looks as if it were drawn with a thick, black, permanent marker. It corners at a perfect ninety-degree angle into another black line and I realize, with a start, it's a swastika.

The girl looks up and tugs at the sleeve of her shirt. Of course, how odd it is to see someone dressed in a long-sleeved shirt and pants in ninety-plus heat, middle of summer, Omaha, Nebraska. I wonder what other tattoos are under there and, when the girl turns to look at the clock, I'm sure I see the nickel-sized head of a snake coming out of her hair, a modern day neo-Nazi Medusa. I look down at my clipboard. "Abbie Nelson?"

"That's me," she says and picks up the army-green duffel bag at her feet. "You the doctor or what?" Over Abbie's shoulder, Cora leans her elbows on the oak desk and folds her hair in her fingers, wiggling the blond strands like snakes.

I hold out my hand as I've been taught to do; the patients, Dr. Stein believes, feel more comfortable dealing with a friend, as if they're here for lunch rather than a new body part. "Assistant," I say. "I'm Eleanor." Abbie slings the tattered bag over her shoulder and it momentarily pulls her off balance. Whatever's in there, it weighs a lot.

In room 217, Abbie Nelson looks around as if we've possibly been transported to the wrong building. The examination rooms still look like singles with king-sized beds and desks, although we've moved in exam tables. "Is this a hotel?" she asks.

"A Best Western."

She sits on the too-soft bed and I sit at the desk with the attached lamp and ask her medical history—any allergies, what medications, diseases running in the family blood. I'm anxious to get to it, to see what kind of damage has been done, but I follow the questions on the form. "How many tattoos?" I ask.

"Twelve," Abbie says. "I've got nerve damage from the one on the top of my foot." I write this down.

"Where are they?"

Abbie gives me a list that spans her entire body, beginning at the bottom of her foot, trailing up the left calf, jumping to the right thigh, right buttock, her pelvis, the knobs of her spine, left shoulder, right tricep, both wrists, the backside of her neck, and the snake, which curls around her scalp and down behind her left ear to the jawbone. "It's a lot of ink," she says.

We finish the form and I ask her to undress as I hand her a paper robe. "Right here?" she says. Looking around the hotel room it does feel illicit, the curtains drawn against the bludgeoning summer rain, the king-sized bed next to the exam table. The table, with the stirrups and pedals, gives the room an ominous bent, as if it is part hotel, part medieval chamber.

"You can go in the bathroom if you'd feel more comfortable," I say. "I'll be waiting in the hall. Just shout when you're ready."

A moment later she calls out, and I open the door.

Sitting on the bed in the robe, Abbie looks like she weighs less than a hundred pounds, maybe less than ninety, and she is covered like a billboard of hate. Her legs are crossed at the ankle, and on her left calf is a blood-red "A" dripping inside a circle. Her upper arms are ringed with barbed wire. Swastikas inside both wrists. The top of one delicate pink foot reads "FUCK" in gothic script, a smiley face is impaled on a stick on her thigh. I do my best to offer a comforting smile, although I know it's too late—she already saw the horror on my face.

"You did better than most," she says. She traces the swastika on her wrist with a finger; I wonder if for years to come she will trace that pattern long after it's gone, like those suffering from phantom-limb syndrome. "Wait," she says. "There's more. We might as well get it over with all at once." And she takes off the robe. Her back is covered with two crossed hammers, there's a closed fist circled by a laurel wreath on one buttock. Although I'm not sure what each symbol means, I know I've never seen so much rage. Her face is almost placid, and it reminds me of those games I'd play as a child where I'd match three tracing plates from pants, shirt, and hair to form an outfit. I never would have put this head with this body, and yet there's something in her face, maybe sorrow, that completes the picture.

"This isn't going to be easy," I tell her. "You need to know what you're in for with this kind of removal."

She points at the tattoo slithering down her neck. "You think I don't have an idea what I might be getting into?"

Over the next fifteen minutes, waiting for Dr. Stein, I explain how the laser works. It dissipates the ink approximately thirty-five percent, so the effectiveness will be less and less with each treatment—thirty-five percent of a hundred the first time, thirty-five percent of sixty-five the second, and so on. I can't stop staring at the wreckage. Abbie nods along, fingering the frayed strap on her duffel bag. "You might be surprised," she says, "but I'm good in math. I understand what you're saying." The procedure will take eight to ten treatments. In plastic surgery, we use terms like "procedure" and "treatment," words that sound medical, so patients will feel they're spending their money on something worthwhile. Abbie may be the first case I've seen in the past eight months that actually is. It's 250 dollars per treatment of a five-by-five-inch surface; Abbie's will cost up to 1,250 dollars a visit.

"I know," she says. "I've done my research."

I excuse myself for a moment and come back with the camera I keep in my locker. "I'll need to take pictures for your file," I tell her. Truth is, no one knows I take pictures of the patients. I focus on the skull and crossbones on Abbie's thigh, the winged butterfly that flutters from one end of her pelvis bone to the other. The artwork itself is terrible—blurred lines as if the ink were cut into her skin with a rusty knife. She holds up her hair and I snap a landscape shot of the ss lightning bolts on the back of her neck. I put the camera in my pocket as Dr. Stein enters.

Dr. Stein is in his mid-fifties and has eyes that turn down at the corners, so he appears perpetually sad. He recently put his dog to sleep and now walks the halls like a ghost, haunting the hospital staff with pitiful questions of whether or not he made the right decision, although he doesn't want our answers. He begins to tell Abbie the same things I have about the cost and effectiveness of the procedure. "We're talking about a chunk of change," he says. "And we don't take checks." Abbie doesn't look at him, and he doesn't look at Abbie. She keeps her eyes trained on me, nodding as he tells her, basically, he doesn't think she can afford it. I reach out and brush the hair from her shoulder as if there were a piece of lint.

"I've got some money saved," she says to me.

Dr. Stein writes "I want payment up-front" on his notepad and turns it toward me. We talk for five more minutes about follow-up, the antiseptic gel she'll need to apply to each treated area for two weeks, the six-week wait required between sessions.

I follow Dr. Stein to the hallway and he writes her name on a manila file, puts in his notes, and hands it to me. "I've never seen anything like that," he says. "With those people in the world, I'm almost glad Sheba's gone." Sheba was his dog, a reddish-tan Whippet with the sad, sleek face of a very thin woman.

As Dr. Stein gets in the elevator, I knock softly on the door until Abbie says, "Come in." She pulls the T-shirt over her white belly just as I enter then slings the duffel bag over her shoulder, stumbling a step before righting herself. We stand facing each other for a long, awkward moment.

"Do I need to fill out some more papers or something?" she asks.

"No, that's it," I say. "You're free to go."

She nods, and I walk her to the front desk where we make an appointment to start treatments the next day; we're never so busy we can't fit someone in on short notice. Cora comes back from break in time to watch Abbie climb into a rusted Chevy Impala. "What'd she want," Cora says. "A nose job?"

On the way home I stop at Walgreens on Ninetieth and Center, and wait in the car for the film to be developed. It's usually my favorite time of day—the sun beginning to set in a violent pink and purple—but this summer we've barely seen the sun. With the rains, I had to put a bucket down in my bedroom in late May, but there isn't a room on the second floor now without a minimum of three buckets or pans. The longer I hold out, the worse it will become, but Frank didn't have life insurance and, even with my new, better-paying career, I'm months away from affording a new roof.

An hour later I start home, the pictures in my purse in the passenger seat. I won't look at them until I'm alone, safe in my house. As always, I feel a tug when I round the corner and see my home—the original brick from 1912, a smattering of irises by the front porch, an oak with a trunk the circumference of a poker table. Frank and I bought this house seven years ago and lived here in a-little-below-average happiness. When I pull into the driveway there's a boy sitting on my porch. I assume it's the Enger kid from down the block, a fifteen-year-old punk who's shown up on my doorstep the past three Halloweens with a pillowcase bulging like an overgrown, obscene gourd. I pull down the garage door and walk to the porch, and for a moment I'm convinced I see his bag of loot protruding from behind the porch swing. I look closer and see that under the cap it's not Mark Enger but Abbie, her duffel bag behind her, the tattoos covered under a button-down blouse. My breath catches; I'm sure she knows about the pictures, that I'm going to be called up on some kiddie-porn charge. I reach into my purse and feel the cardboard of the envelope, relieved that the pictures are with me, not loose at Walgreens or nailed to the front door of my house.

"I got your ad," she says and holds up a tiny sheet of paper with my phone number on it. "From the bulletin board at the hospital." I've been running an ad for a tenant the past three weeks. I swore when Frank died it wouldn't come to this, but ten months later I do what I can. It's four hundred a month plus split utilities, no separate entrance or private kitchen. I haven't gotten many calls—two actually, one placed from inside a prison, the other from Cora seeing if she could rent the space for keggers.

I'm not sure what to say to Abbie. In the context of the hospital I'd felt bad for her, but out here in my real world, on the porch of my house, I feel bad for only myself. "How'd you get my address?"

"Reverse directory at the library." She scratches at the hat she's wearing, and I see the rings of sweat collecting in her armpits, the damp neck of the long-sleeved blouse. The rain has done nothing to alleviate the heat.

"I don't have air conditioning," I tell her, and she shrugs. "Besides, it's rented."

"I doubt that," Abbie says and continues to stare at me.

"Even if it weren't rented, it'd be unethical—me living with a patient."

Abbie picks at the ring in her nose. "We're not treating AIDS here," she says. "I just need a place to live." I remember our brief contact—my hand brushing her shoulder—and wonder if she's built that into compassion, or if only I do that: redefine the purposeful bump of a thigh on the public bus, the swoop of flesh on flesh while counting my change into a cashier's hand. "I've got a steady job," she continues, "and I'll pay on time. Even early if you want, up to two weeks." She holds out a sheet of paper and turns it right side up so I can read it—a pay stub from Super America. "See," she says and shakes the paper.

I smile in what I hope is a sympathetic manner. "I would, but it's already rented. I told you."

Abbie gets up and puts the pay stub back in her pocket then reaches behind the porch swing. She pulls out the duffel bag, and I wonder if she's got no place to stay tonight, if she's going to sleep at the Greyhound station, or Denny's, or in the back room of Super America. "I know it's not," she says and swings the duffel onto her back. It takes a lot of control to not rescue her as she walks off the porch, as she trails that duffel bag down the middle-class street I'm about to be kicked off of, but I don't.

Upstairs, only after I've poured a glass of iced tea and stripped to the bare essentials so I can sleep in the heat, do I finally look at the pictures. They're taken too close up so all I can see is the runny color on a doughy background, although the ribs give away that it's a person. In the pictures, the images are even more striking, although removed. It's as if I could be looking at a picture cut from a prison magazine, not a girl I'd met earlier that day. The lines and curves are so blurred on her skin you'd think they could be smudged off with a little spit and Kleenex, not cut into her skin with needles and ink. It's amazing seeing one clean calf against the other, what Abbie must have looked like before.

I open the nightstand drawer and put Abbie's pictures in with the others—a woman's stomach so fat it looks like the landscape of the moon; a seven-year-old boy who fell from a three-story building, crashing the cartilage of his nose to within two millimeters of his brain; a man's foot with only one toe, the other four removed by the man himself.

I'm fascinated by these patients and what they've endured, all those visible mistakes.

At the hospital the next morning, I watch a woman pass outside in a skirt so short, for a moment I think she's wearing nothing but a tank top and panties. She turns to open the door and I recognize Mrs. VanRockel, a sixty-eight-year-old patient who had her breasts done for the third time just last month. "Ooh la la," Cora says. "Lock up your grandsons."

Mrs. VanRockel rushes over and puts her fingernails in my shoulders and kisses the part in my hair. At least when this place was a hotel, I was able to avoid direct and extended contact with the same customers. She's had so much work done that, compared to her, I feel almost *un*natural in the skin, bones, and mortar I was born into. "I'm in for a follow-up," she says and pats her breasts on the outer sides. "Checking the girls," she calls it. Her breasts don't jiggle but move forcefully side to side as if caught on a train track.

I pick up my patient files for the day from an erratic filing system Cora's organized on the floor. It's pretty straightforward being a medical assistant; Dr. Stein won't let anyone else do important stuff, so I basically fill out forms, check blood pressure and pulses—all the basic medical tasks that I learned from a video I rented at the library. Mrs. VanRockel passes again and gives me a high five.

Cora dings the bell, a lollipop rolling suggestively in her mouth. "Creep-oid's back at 3:20," she says. "I hope we don't short-circuit the joint keeping the laser on that long."

"You shouldn't be so rude to people," I say, although secretly I enjoy it. I was raised in a household that didn't express rudeness, that discouraged blatant emotion of any kind. Three years ago when Frank and I began having problems, we tried to sugarcoat our way through, each of us making a list of ten things in our lives we loved. Out of desperation I wrote down *my husband* and *my job*, both of which I have since lost.

Abbie arrives around noon with her duffel bag.

"She just sits there," Cora says when she calls me after lunch break to tell me Abbie's three hours early. "It's like she's in some kind of white supremacy trance."

"How can you tell it's a white supremacy trance and not just an ordinary trance?" I ask.

"Don't get smart with me," she says. "I'm not the one zoning here like some sideshow freak. I'm just doing my job." Cora hangs up on me.

At 3:40, I usher Abbie to room 217, glad to be walking in front of her, not staring at the Nazi lightning bolts on the back of her neck, peeking below her hair. I don't know if she'll say anything about last night or how long I can hold out without bringing it up, apologizing for forgiveness, yet at the same time not offering her a place to live.

As she goes into the bathroom to change, I hand her the salve we use to slightly numb the areas we'll be lasering. It's basically a psychosomatic drug; I've put the gel on myself and could feel clear as glass as I slammed my toe into the door. When Abbie comes out, she says, "I can't reach my back," and hands me the tube, half her body already shimmering with the grease.

I open the back of her robe and rub the salve over her spine, every vertebrae detectable under her skin. It's like petting a dog that's too skinny, gross with those protruding ribs but still a dog, something you want to love. She looks over her shoulder at the work I'm doing. "Eleanor. How much is it going to hurt?"

I look at the right side of Abbie's face, the side without the snake. Although she wrote down her age as nineteen, her cheekbones have a smooth coating of baby fat, her hips are slender as if she has not yet hit puberty. "It's going to hurt a lot," I tell her. "I'm sorry." I want so badly to ask how this happened, if she believes what she's had blazoned on her skin. It's hard to imagine this tiny girl hating anyone, but no matter what her beliefs, she's going to have to come up with approximately ten thousand dollars to right this wrong. Not to improve herself, but to get back to square one.

I leave her alone with a copy of *Modern Maternity* for twenty minutes while the salve supposedly activates, then Dr. Stein and I come in wheeling the laser. "Are we ready?" Dr. Stein says as he pulls the yellow goggles over his eyes.

I hand Dr. Stein the laser gun with a queasy stomach. Up until now all we've done for tattoo removals have been short names and Greek letters—Delta Tau Deltas and Sigma Nus trying to cover up a past that admits they were spoiled. These procedures have taken no more than a minute to three each, nothing like the expanse of Abbie's body. Dr. Stein's wearing a gold Star of David around his neck, something I'm certain he's never worn before. "We'll start with the foot and work our way up," he says.

Abbie and I put on our goggles, and I flip on the laser as Dr. Stein points the gun at the top of Abbie's foot and pulls the trigger. She barely flinches, and I remember the nerve damage she suffered from the tattoo; what should be the most painful, she can barely feel. Dr. Stein traces the "F" and moves to the "U." Abbie has her eyes shut to squints and is gripping the sides of the examination table but for the most part is holding still.

Dr. Stein stops when he reaches the bottom of the "K." "How you doing?" he asks.

She releases the exam table and shakes her hands a few times before gripping the edges again. "Let's keep going."

Dr. Stein points the laser at Abbie's calf and presses the trigger. This time she screams and pulls back her leg, squirming onto her side. Dr. Stein keeps going and I rush over to push down her shoulders as she doubles up at the belly like she's in labor. Dr. Stein stops the gun and looks at me. "I'm not going to be able to work like this. You're going to have to hold her still."

Abbie inhales deeply. "Just a minute," she says. "I had no idea." Dr. Stein stands, tapping his foot. "OK, let's do it." I offer her my hand.

We go over much of Abbie's body—the butterfly, the fist and laurel, the crossed hammers on her spine. After one of the barbed wire rings on her upper arm, she says, "Stop. That's all I can do today."

"We've only got four left," Dr. Stein says. "And no openings the rest of the week." I know he has no idea what the schedule looks like but don't dare call Cora to ask her.

We've already been going for over forty-five minutes, the heat and sharp, needling pressure of the laser on her body constantly. "We're so close," I tell her. "It'll be over in no time." She lays back down and Dr. Stein points the gun at her other arm, finishes that area, and moves to her right wrist. I can see the veins tinted yellow through my goggles, her skin so thin it looks as if the blood coursing through it is green. A racing pulse is detectable under a corner of the swastika, like the heart of a tiny animal. Dr. Stein finishes the left wrist and stops. "Only one left," he says, but Abbie shakes her head.

"I can't do the face," she says. "Not today." She has already decided not to shave her head to remove the body of the snake, and we will only treat what's visible.

Dr. Stein puts down the laser—"We'll start with it next time"—and steps out of the room.

Abbie is breathing in jagged gasps. Sweat wets her hair as if she has run a long race, and tears pour from the corners of her eyes. "We'll try it for a month," I tell her. "You can move in today if you need to."

She nods and points to the duffel bag. "That's all I've got. Shouldn't take me long to get settled." It's already after five, so I gather my purse as Abbie gets dressed, and we meet in the lobby to go home.

It takes two months before I'm able to sleep through the night with Abbie in the house. When she's home, I'll wake around two in the morning and trail down the hallway, listening for signs of what, I don't know—a noise downstairs, maybe a dull, unidentifiable thud that signals trouble. I never hear it. When Frank first died my sleep habits were altered from dreaming until the alarm went off to waking at odd hours, listening to the sound of no one else breathing. In the past ten months, between the hours of two and five in the morning I've taught myself tarot cards, regrouted my bathroom, preserved my life in scrapbooks. Most nights Abbie's not at home but working at Super America. Even though she wears long-sleeved shirts and pants, and heavy foundation on her face and neck, the shift manager figured out her secret and usually schedules Abbie for the graveyard. I wonder some nights just how big a mistake I've made asking her to move in. There are two Abbies—the one I see with her body of threats and the one I live with, who, for all I can tell, is a tentative and nervous girl. I know my house is only an object, a possession that holds more possessions, but I've put the past seven years into restoring these twelve-hundred square feet with unattached garage, and I'm protective of my house the way many are protective of their children and pets.

When Abbie's at work during the night, and I'm up wishing I could afford cable, I'll look in her room, justifying that it's not snooping if I don't touch anything. She sleeps in Frank's study, a room I've always disliked. Frank insisted I not clean it, and when he died there were stacks of rubbish piled to the short ceiling by the dormer—*National*

Geographics from the '80s, copies of our 1996 taxes, old work schedules from his job at Drastic Plastic Records on Howard Street. In a corner, I found a petrified orange, furry and green like an exotic, unopened flower. I feel guilty looking around the newly painted white room, as if by Frank's death I've finally gotten my way. Abbie keeps her makeup on the cardboard dresser I bought, her duffel bag under the bed. Most nights there's not so much as a sock on the floor.

On a lingering night, in which I've stayed up until dawn studying the patient photos, we pass in the kitchen in the morning. "How long have you been up?" Abbie asks, shedding rain from her hair.

"Not long."

She sniffs the coffee pot and rubs a kitchen towel against her head. "You don't sleep much," she says and pours the rest of the bitter, three-hour-old coffee down the sink. "Let me make you some breakfast." Abbie, it turns out, is a wonderful cook. She's able to take any three cans out of the cupboard, some rice, and with a little cumin or cilantro, make something extraordinary.

"I used to work at an ethnic restaurant on Fort Street before all this," she tells me, motioning a hand toward the tattoos on her body. "Any kind of ethnic food you wanted, we'd make it. I had over thirty cookbooks on hand and a spice rack as big as a bank." It's not as exciting as the version I would have guessed—cooking for a houseful of brothers and sisters, a mom strung out on heroin, father unemployed and split—but it makes sense. She tells me about all the jobs she's had: chef, assistant at a tanning salon, three weeks as a Wal-Mart greeter. I want to ask when the tattoos came into play, when in the midst of being a responsibly employed adult she had the time to become a skinhead. "I got some good news today," she says. I savor a bite of eggs—she's prepared them with salsa and dehydrated black beans from a box. "A raise for my six-month evaluation. It's a quarter more an hour."

It occurs to me that the reason Abbie cooks and cleans so much is she doesn't want to be asked to leave. I sip the coffee. "Abbie, how are you paying for the treatments?"

She coughs into her hand. "That's almost fifty bucks a month." It's only forty—I've already done the math in my head.

Abbie peels off her red work vest and long-sleeved shirt down to the sports bra underneath. After two weeks she finally gave in and began wearing shorts and tank tops in front of me at home, rather than her usual long-sleeved garb. She catches me every now and again staring at the circled "A," the barbed wire, but doesn't acknowledge it. "You don't have to tell me," I say. "I'm just curious."

"It's cooled down a bit with the rain," she says, rinsing the frying pan. "You want to sit out on the roof?" It bothers me that Abbie's keeping secrets, while I'd spill my entire life from birth until now if only given the chance. She doesn't know that I've been married, that Frank died in the car I was driving, that I have no right to be assisting in her laser surgery. It should be easy to confess to someone who's done worse than you.

We take our coffee upstairs and climb out the dormer window to the roof and lie on the upward slant, the wet shingles rough against our backs. It never occurred to me to do this, but I came home one day after work and saw Abbie up here, her feet hooked in the eaves. My first thought was she was going to jump, until I saw the lazy elbow crooked over her eyes, the gentle way her knees swayed in the breezeless evening.

On the roof, my life feels quiet, the water misty on my face. Even at work, we've hit a lull. It's the end of August, and it'll be another nine months before this much skin is exposed on a daily basis. Around January we have another, shorter busy season as couples prepare for trips to Jamaica, the New Year's resolutions more impossible year after year without a little help from the outside. Abbie holds out her wrists and swastikas. "Any chance you can't tell what they are now?" she asks me.

I look at the pale blue skin, the dots of rain coming down on her wrists; the tattoos have begun to dissipate a bit, as if they've faded over the years, but not enough. "You can still tell."

She nods. "I thought so."

"The snake does look a little lighter," I say.

She puts her hand to her jaw. "It's the makeup." We sit in silence, day six and counting of the rains. Abbie cups her hands until her palms hold an inch of water. "Dr. Stein doesn't like me," she says.

"I doubt he doesn't like you," I say, although I suppose she's right. He only sees the shell: a girl with signs of the Third Reich tattooed all over her body. But in the past few months I've grown affectionate toward Abbie. How could I not like someone so repentant? I wonder, if given the chance, if we'd live our lives differently or go on repeating the usual mistakes. Maybe not with tattoos or dead husbands but different errors, the same results.

"He told me he'll take my money because it's his job and he thinks I'm doing something to better myself. He doesn't really think that, though. He thinks I'm trash."

I slept with only one other man while I was married to Frank: Don, the Coca-Cola distributor at the hotel. He was a lot stupider than Frank, but his body was smooth, almost hairless, and taut like a fresh sheet pulled tight across a mattress. He wore his name sewn above his heart, almost as good as his heart on his sleeve, and I slept with him three months before I drove my husband into an embankment, run off the road by an eighty-nine-year-old man who had not had a driver's license in over a decade. Frank died, and I walked away from the accident, and three months earlier I'd slept with Don. "You're a lot of things, Abbie, but you're not trash."

"I suppose not," she says. "But it wouldn't kill him to try and be nice to me."

Sometimes what I regret most about Frank's death is the chance to make it work. With all the bickering and emotional blows we'd gone through, it was obvious to me that, had he lived, we would have been divorced within a year. I spent six months in mourning eating neighbors' casseroles, but what I really mourned was the chance to resurrect my marriage.

"It might," I tell her. "Who knows what's going to kill us."

Mrs. VanRockel stops in for her next appointment dressed in bike shorts and a half shirt. "Let me see that pamphlet on liposuction again," she says. "Just for kicks." Mrs. VanRockel window-shops at the plastic surgery ward like it's a Crate and Barrel.

We're sitting with Dr. Stein in his office, a space bigger than my living room. "Abbie doesn't think you like her," I say, looking at Dr. Stein.

"Who's Abbie?" Mrs. VanRockel asks. She does an elongated bend at the waist as she reaches for another pamphlet on forehead tucks from Dr. Stein's desk. It's depressing to see a sixty-eight-year-old ass that much better than mine.

"It doesn't matter," Dr. Stein says and holds out the coffee pot as invitation to Mrs. VanRockel, who waves it away and then pulls her eyes toward her hairline. "Caffeine," she says.

"It matters to me," I say. "Abbie's my friend."

Dr. Stein puts down the coffeepot and takes out a pen, writes something on a piece of paper, then shoves it in his pocket. It's not letterhead, and I wonder if he's making a grocery list or maybe a list of things he doesn't like about me. I've snooped through his office and know there's a good chance we might go under. People in the Midwest don't care about their bodies enough to support a ninety-room plastic surgery ward. "She's not the type I would guess you to be friends with," Dr. Stein says. He looks at me until I look away. "And no, I don't like her. Not that it matters." There's an eight-by-ten photograph of Sheba in a Santa's hat on his desk. Every other day another picture of Sheba pops up in Dr. Stein's office—Sheba's first bath, Sheba wearing roller skates.

"I don't think you should be rude to her, no matter how you feel."

He stands suddenly and claps his hands. "I'm going to take the rest of the day off," he says.

I pick up a glossy photo of Sheba in a raincoat. "What am I supposed to do?" I ask.

He takes off his white lab coat, pauses a moment, then continues, removing his shirt. His nipples glow red like two recent lipstick prints above a smallish belly. Mrs. VanRockel looks up and giggles. "Some bedside manner," she says. Dr. Stein pulls a T-shirt from his bottom desk drawer.

"Straighten some files," he says and pulls the shirt over his head, all the hair he has pulled forward like some magnetic oddity. The shirt reads #1 DAD. He looks around his office—there's nothing out of place, and other than the dog photos, no clutter. It looks as if he has just moved in today or could be moved out tomorrow. "Take some blood pressure, what do I care." He laughs as he opens the door. "I'm off the rest of the day."

Mrs. VanRockel reaches over and pats me on the leg. "I don't know Abbie, but if she's a friend of yours I'm sure she's a fine person." Her skin puckers at the knuckles like stretched-out pantyhose.

"She is. She's just made some mistakes."

Mrs. VanRockel holds up her hands as if at gunpoint. "Who hasn't? You think I was born with a nose like this? We've all got a past." She sits for a moment, fingering the corner of the liposuction pamphlet. She smiles shyly. "My fiancé has no idea I've had work done."

"How can that be?" It strikes me as impossible—her body must look like a bad hem job, all those stitches and tucks in the fabric.

"I told him I was in a car accident back in my late teens. It was the sixties, everyone was crazy. That he believed."

I quickly do the math, knowing Mrs. VanRockel passed out of her teens in the early fifties. "Does it matter?"

She shrugs. "I suppose not. I just wish I'd been honest. I can't very well tell him now he's not getting the real deal."

"My husband died in a car accident," I tell her. "I was driving."

"We've all got to die some time," she says and pats my leg again, a few liver spots marking the backside of her hand. I give her two months before she investigates the bleaching process. "Why not get it over with."

"I killed my husband," I say again.

"I'll kill mine eventually," she says. "It's the way the world goes round."

I spend most of the afternoon snooping through Dr. Stein's office—real snooping, like pulling open drawers, reading medical-sounding memos I don't understand. He's got files on every patient we've seen—some files, like Mrs. VanRockel's, almost two inches thick. I've got pictures at home of about twenty of these people, the rest are run-of-the-mill nose jobs and skin grafts. In Abbie's file, Dr. Stein's drawn rough sketches of her different tattoos, something he hasn't done for the other patients. On the inside of the manila folder, in Dr. Stein's handwriting, it says, "Terminate treatments."

I go through his desk looking for his home phone number, give up, and page his number for medical emergency. "We need to set up the next appointment for Abbie Nelson," I say when he calls back.

"Who?" He sounds distracted, and I wonder where he is. There's a scratching noise coming through the phone that could be static but sounds like someone trying to claw her way out of a coffin.

"The tattoos."

Dr. Stein sighs as if he is very tired; there's a high whistle, and the scratching noise stops. "We're not seeing her anymore—she's done."

"No, she's not," I insist.

I hear the phone bang against something. "Listen, Eleanor. She's just going to have to live in the bed she's made."

"You're not being fair." I think of the medical term: "Or ethical."

Dr. Stein is quiet for a moment. "I didn't want it to come to this, but you should know. The girl's a liar. She says you took photos of her, illicit ones, the hospital didn't approve."

The air-conditioned room suddenly feels as stifling as the weather outside, but my head feels empty, surprisingly cool; I know Abbie wouldn't have asked Dr. Stein about the pictures, even if she suspected I shouldn't have taken them. "That's odd," I finally say, "but not criminal."

"Either she's lying or you are," he says, and the scratching noise starts up again. "And I won't work with a liar." I'm not sure if Dr. Stein is talking only of the pictures or if he knows everything: that my degree is from a community college in hotel-and-restaurant management, that my only training for medical emergency was the night of Frank's accident. I used to think what we did here was trivial, that there could be no lower form of medicine than plastic surgery, but that couldn't be further from the truth. We might not extend lives, but we do give people the lives they want to lead. If Mrs. VanRockel wants to be fifteen years younger, why not let her? Dr. Stein tells me he'll be in tomorrow but right now he's resting at home and is going to hang up. I say good-bye and shove Abbie's file into my purse before I leave.

When I get home from work there is a man sitting on my kitchen counter with track marks up and down his arm. I get closer, and he points to the scratches. "Cat," he says and holds out his hand. "I'm Sam, as in Son of." With a Mötley Crüe tank top and acne scars, Sam rides a fine line between repulsive and sexy. He pulls down the top of his shirt and points to a rose tattoo by his nipple. "This bud's for you," he says.

In the living room, a woman wearing a Canadian flag as a dress and a chain through her nose and ear picks through my CD collection. "Neil fucking Diamond," she says. When Frank died we had over three thousand CDs that he'd pilfered from the record store—I gave them away at the wake, to all his regulars who came to mourn. By the end of the afternoon, people I'd never seen before were lined around the block, and I was left with the handful that nobody wanted. "Where's Abbie?" I ask her. I hear a thump echo from the attic—it's this sound I've been listening for, moping through the halls at night—and I take the stairs two at a time.

Sitting on Abbie's bed is a man wearing the largest boots I've ever seen. They ride up his legs, past his knees, shiny strokes of black that appear to grow into his hips. He has muttonchops below his cheekbones and a moustache over unnaturally white teeth. The same snake as Abbie's slithers below the blondish-brown sideburns as if it is sneaking through long-dead grass. "Howdy do," he says. "You must be Eleanor."

It's now I notice Abbie. She's sitting in Frank's old rocker in front of the fan, her mouth opening and closing like a dying fish, her hair blowing from her face then settling to calm. We keep the windows open all the time, although the breeze is nonexistent, and we move fans from room to room depending on where we're sitting. The man stands up and moves to sit in Abbie's lap. Without the boots I would guess him to be no more than five-seven.

"What's going on?" I ask.

The man laughs and holds out his hand. "I'm Kurt," he says. "Abbie's boyfriend."

"Ex," Abbie says, and Kurt turns in her lap and puts a hand over her breast, squeezing until his knuckles turn white, although she doesn't flinch. Abbie's wearing more makeup than her usual cover-up—lipstick and rouge—although it's smudged and unnatural, almost bruised-looking, much like the tattoos.

Kurt turns toward me slowly, crinking his neck as if notch by notch. "We're on a break," he says. "Putting the spice back in the pudding."

A slight, cool breeze bores through the curtains, and Abbie and I turn toward the window. For a moment I forget Kurt's in the room; I listen to the sound of the incessant rain and can imagine for the first time the onset of fall. "You need to get out of my house," I say.

Kurt turns toward Abbie. "You heard her, pack up. It's time to get you back home." He lifts himself from the rocker and opens the closet door. He begins pulling Abbie's T-shirts and long-sleeved blouses from the rack. "You got a garbage bag, or what?"

"Abbie's staying here." I look at Abbie still sitting in the rocker. The bones in her face seem to have grown, her skin pulled tight at the eyes and mouth as if she has shed the baby fat of a few months ago. "I'm keeping the girl," I say. She looks up at me like she's found religion.

Kurt's face is textured like the rind of a cantaloupe beginning to soften and go bad. "Now that I've found her, I'm just going to come back," Kurt says. He kisses the sock in his hand, pulls out the waistband of Abbie's jeans and shoves the sock down her pants, carefully sidestepping a bucket of stale water. "As often as it takes."

I point to the door. "Sweet ride," Kurt says and licks a finger then traces it against my neck, curving it down like the matching snake on his and Abbie's jawbones.

Abbie and I stay in her room for the next hour until all of them leave—the woman in the Canadian flag, Son of Sam, and Kurt, who peers back at us in the dormer window and kisses his middle finger before shooting it at us. "He will be back," Abbie says. The swastikas on her wrists are covered by soft leather wristbands that look like a cut-up purse tied with twine. "Do you want me to move out?"

I can't imagine going back to an empty house again, another two months of not sleeping when I'm just beginning to make it until dawn. "Ab, how are you getting the money to pay for your treatments?"

"If it were up to me, I'd be on the next plane out of this town," Abbie says. "But what's the point, looking like this?"

"How?"

Abbie pushes herself out of the rocker, and her bones sound frail, as if they've lived more than their share of life.

I follow her into the kitchen, where she opens and closes the cupboards until she finds a box of Bugle crackers. "I'll make us corn horns," she says and grabs the chive cream cheese out of the fridge, fills a Bugle, and eats it. "My father died in a house fire about two years ago."

She smears another cone with cream cheese and sets it on a napkin in front of me like a dried, dead ear. I sit silently as Abbie explains how the case was chalked up to faulty wiring, leaving her with a settlement of eight thousand dollars, enough to start her treatment. "If they reopen the case and find something else," she says, "the treatment will already be done. At least they can't take that."

"Was it really faulty wiring?" I say.

"Well, no," she says. "But I don't know what you want me to tell you, Eleanor." She wipes the crumbs from the counter into her hand and throws them in the sink. "My dad was a real S.O.B. Then I meet Kurt. He's an asshole but looks like a better option, and he decides to take matters into his own hands. You figure it out."

"Why don't you turn him in?"

Abbie laughs, a genuine laugh, not something dry and cynical like I might have expected. "You honestly think that'll work?" She puts a spoonful of cream cheese in her mouth and sets her elbows on the counter, leaning in to whisper. "They'd take one look at me and throw me in jail. And the thought of threatening Kurt with jail, well . . ." She runs a finger across her throat.

I motion across the counter, up and down her body and the tattoos. "He did this to you, didn't he?"

She shrugs. "I knew what some of the symbols meant, I just had no idea I'd be taken so seriously." She wipes her hand on her jeans. "I'd never been taken seriously in my life."

That night I don't sleep. I spread Abbie's file across my bed—Dr. Stein's crude drawings next to the pictures I've taken, his notes on the laser procedure, including the intensity levels for different pressure points of the body. Her photos look different to me now from the others, as if her tattoos were inevitable, rather than an act of stupidity or weakness.

Dr. Stein calls me a little after six in the morning and wakes me from a shallow sleep to tell me, with a forced laugh, that he's calling in "well." "Eleanor," he says. "I just can't face it today."

I sink my head back into the pillow, holding the receiver. "Me either."

"Good," he says. "Stay home, have a barbecue. We're supposed to see the sun around noon."

"Dr. Stein?" I say. He's quiet. "I took the pictures."

I hear the kitchen door open downstairs; Abbie throws her knapsack on the counter as she comes in from her night shift at Super America. "Not much we can do about it now," Dr. Stein says. "Can't go back and not take them. I'll see you tomorrow morning."

Abbie knocks on my door ten minutes later, and I call for her to come in, remembering the first time I saw her on the bed at the hospital in the paper gown—all that ink. "You want some coffee?" she says and holds up a cup. I can smell the shaves of cinnamon she adds because she knows I like them.

I sit up and take a sip from the warm mug. "What if I told you I came up with a plan that would help you get rid of your tattoos and me get my roof repaired?"

She runs a finger over my dresser and checks for dust. "I'd say you were about to suggest something illegal."

That night, as we sneak through the parking lot, there's a part of me that believes what we're doing is lawful, or at the least, the right thing to be doing. Abbie's gone so far as to wear a denim jumper-dress—what she calls a suburban disguise, one I'd consider too matronly to wear overseeing a group of orphans. The night is unusually quiet without the rain, the air thin without the thick humidity we've grown used to like another layer of skin.

Abbie ducks behind the shrubs outside the hospital. "I hear a cop car," she whispers.

"You're paranoid," I say, but sure enough, a few moments later a black-and-white Ford pulls onto the street and shines a light down the sidewalk.

"I've got a key," I remind her. "We haven't done anything illegal yet." We've agreed that I'll perform the laser surgery myself, and she'll pay me directly, a fifth of the cost that she'd pay to the hospital. If I raise the pressure of the laser there'll be scarring, but most of what remains of the ink will dissipate after tonight. We wait five minutes then proceed.

Inside, the hospital looks even more uninhabited than it does during the day. Most of our patients are outpatients, and other than the nurses' station on second floor and a handful of cases, the hospital is deserted. The overhead lights are off, the couches empty, and there is nothing medical in sight. I've seen this room at night only as a hotel still bustling with latecomers or the drunk crowd, and now it appears as if the festivities have been abandoned quickly due to natural disaster, like the ballroom of the *Titanic*. I'm certain we won't be open much longer.

"Welcome to the Hotel California," I say, and Abbie stifles what should be a giggle but comes out like the caw of a wounded pelican. The sounds are eerily silent, absorbed by the carpet without a hint of reverberation.

"Maybe this isn't such a good idea," Abbie says.

"It never was," I tell her. "But we're in it now."

We climb the stairs with the help of my flashlight key chain, not wanting to activate the elevators. "We're breaking, like, four hundred laws," Abbie says. "I really, really appreciate this." She says it like she's the one who's asked the favor, like this is her idea and not mine. I want to ask if she's been planning this since we met in June, but it wouldn't make a difference one way or the other.

We pass the two ORs, round the corner to room 217, and there I see it: a light is on in one of the empty, unconverted hotel rooms. My heart flutters, and I shush Abbie as I point to the laundry closet at the end of the hall. I stand still for a moment, raising my courage to look in room 246. *I have a right to be here*, I tell myself. *It's my place of employment*. As I approach the door I hear something and hold my breath. Someone is humming in the bathroom.

I push on the slightly ajar door and there is Dr. Stein in a white terrycloth robe, a foaming toothbrush in his mouth. He lets out a little scream and turns to spit in the sink.

"Eleanor," he says and bends to wipe his mouth on a hanging towel.

We stare at each other, unsure who is supposed to speak and what he or she is supposed to say. "I'm here for some files." It's the worst excuse I can come up with but the quickest to come to mind.

"Yes, of course," he says. "That makes sense." We stand for a clumsy moment as if we're at a cocktail party, both of us looking around the room for better company. Only difference is, he's in a bathrobe.

"I'm going to get the files now," I say and turn to leave.

Dr. Stein holds out a hand. For a moment I think he might try to touch me, not inappropriately, but in a way so awkward and desperate, I'll be able to do nothing but let him. "You're a good assistant," he says.

I know now that Dr. Stein's aware I've faked my credentials, although for how long he's known, I'm not sure. "Thank you," I say.

I turn to go, unsure what I'm going to do with Abbie huddled in a laundry closet, daylight five hours away. "Eleanor?" Dr. Stein says again.

"Yes?"

He fiddles with the ties on his robe. "Is it possible we're all good people?"

I smile, thinking it's one of Dr. Stein's odd rhetorical questions, but he stares at me long enough that I know he wants an answer.

"Statistically, no. There've got to be some bad apples out there." Dr. Stein worries over this answer for a moment. "But if it's any consolation," I add, "I don't think any of them are in the building tonight."

He walks me to the door, his hand leading me by the elbow as if we are about to emerge on a dance floor.

In the laundry room I close the door behind me and shine my miniscule flashlight into the darkness. Abbie pops her head out of a cart of linens with a bed sheet partially obscuring her face. "You look like you're in the KKK," I whisper. "That's about the last thing we need."

I pull her from the cart and we head to room 217, walking softly so not to disturb Dr. Stein. Inside, Abbie undresses, and I adjust the settings on the laser. With only the bathroom light on, we rub her skin with salve and don our goggles. I raise the gun.

Over the next hour, we work quietly. The pain is enormous, I can tell by the struggle on Abbie's face, but she doesn't so much as whimper as I finish most of her body and move onto the fading swastikas. It's slow going without Dr. Stein's experience, but I feel I'm doing a good job and half believe I can see the ink breaking up in front of me. Partway through the first line, she stills my hand with her own and cocks her head to the side like an attentive animal.

A moment later I hear the siren. I'd guess the police car to be no more than four blocks away. "I'll tell them I made you do it," Abbie says.

She pulls her hand away, but I catch it in my own. "It's all right," I say. "We're in this together."

She nods and holds out her arm; only four tattoos left, and we're not leaving until they're gone. I remember when I climbed out of the car, Frank's body appeared asleep at the side of the road, his neck crunched far to the left. My first thought was how he'd bitch when he woke up about the headache that was forming. Abbie and I are willing to pay the penance for the crimes we've committed, although we don't consider this one of them. I look down. Her scarred wrist appears to glow and pulse with a strange light until I realize I'm still wearing my goggles.

I bow my head and resume the treatments.

Intervention

Harry's mom calls early Saturday morning to tell us she is planning an intervention for Gerald. This will be the third one in three years, and she is convinced it's the one that's going to stick.

Harry can tell by the grimace on my face and the sound of my voice that the Judith on the other end is undoubtedly his mother. "Tell her I'm not here," he hisses. "Tell her I'm out." I point to the clock by the bed: 6:43. How much does he think his mother is willing to believe? He grabs his stomach and starts convulsing, falls out of the bed, and writhes on the floor. I know from his pantomimes he wants me to say he's not feeling well, and I contemplate telling her something serious like a ruptured lung, something broken. Something that would have her on the next flight to Minneapolis to teach Harry a lesson about faking. I try to listen to Judith on the other end—something about a predicament and Gerald being a loose cannon in the air. He's been on leave from United for five months after a prolonged recovery from back surgery and will be back in the skies in the next few weeks.

"Kate," she says again, "I am convinced there is a problem." There is nothing Judith loves more than a problem. Harry is out of the room now, and I hear him brushing his teeth. She tells me how Gerald fell asleep on his boat two nights ago, "drunk as a skunk," with his head cocked back and a highball in his hand. Three sets of neighbors saw him before someone thought to call the police, convinced Gerald was dead. "It's a disgrace," Judith says. I hear the water stop in the bathroom. It starts up again with splashing, and Harry hums while washing his face.

"You tell that Harry I've got it planned for next Friday, and I expect him to be there. Gerald gets home around five thirty from his physical therapy, and I want everyone in that house by five." It sounds like a birthday party. She says nothing about whether I am invited. "This is it," she says. "You tell that Harry his father needs him." Judith hangs up without saying good-bye; she likes the drama of such actions.

Harry comes back in the room with his face clean and his hair every which way. "Your mother's planning another intervention for your dad," I tell him. He comes over and puts his hand on my breast; I can smell his toothpaste. "She wants you there by five on Friday."

"I'm not flying to Myrtle Beach for another intervention," he says, but already I know he will go.

At Harry's college graduation party Gerald got plowed and sang Janis Joplin's "Mercedes Benz" a cappella before the band had even finished setting up. I hadn't met his parents before; they lived in North Carolina, and we were in Minneapolis. Judith wore wool slacks and a sweater even though it was May and in the 80s.

Judith and I sat at a table together, and I tried talking to her about adult topics such as political reform and the tax bill, which she dismissed with a wave of her hand. She was an intimidating Southern lady who until that week had never been north of the Mason-Dixon line. The tables were covered in maroon paper, and I ripped off small sheets, tore them to pieces in my lap. She wore Shalimar and didn't seem to sweat. Harry came over with his tie wrapped around his head, two beers in his hand, and told her, "Kate and I got a place. It's right in the city. You can see Lake Calhoun from the bathroom window."

She turned her overwhelming, coiffed hairdo toward me and looked at my left hand—now streaked with maroon dye—where there obviously wasn't a ring. "Gerald and I didn't spend one night together before that wedding," she said. "You just don't do that kind of thing in the South."

I tried looking her in the eye but settled for the vicinity of her forehead. "Harry loves me," I told her, and it was true. He'd said so for the first time two weeks ago, before we signed the lease.

Judith turned away from me and watched the band do a horrible rendition of "Crocodile Rock," her clean hands crossed in her lap. A week later they had the first intervention. Harry went home for two weeks with his parents before starting his job as a copywriter at McElliott and Jordan. When he got back he told me it'd been "fun."

"How can an intervention be 'fun'?" I asked. He started unpacking his suitcase, dumping most of his clothes down our new laundry chute that fell to the basement, sticking his head in after to watch them drop. "What do you mean by 'fun'?"

"You need to know my mother," he said. "She can plan the hell out of anything, but it never goes how she wants. Dad ended up leaving with half the people to go bowling, and we didn't get home until after two."

"*You* left the intervention to go bowling?"

"Well, you know," he said. "It was more fun." He turned to me and smiled. I knew somehow his actions reflected badly on me.

Harry doesn't call Judith back until Monday, by which time she has left three messages and sent a telegram. "I didn't even know they had these anymore," Harry says, holding the paper from Western Union in his hand. The yellow slip looks to me like a warning call, a sign of severity, something imminent, yet from the past. I know this is the effect Judith is going for, and she's hit the mark. "You need to call her," I say and hand him the phone.

He comes out of the bedroom fifteen minutes later with a defeated look on his face. "You're going, aren't you?" I ask.

He tells me how Judith harangued him into it, used all kinds of familial guilt and coercion. There are relatives coming from as far as Seattle. "We'll go down on Wednesday, hang out, and relax for a few days."

"Your mom wants me there?" I ask. "She said that?"

"Hon, she's excited to see us."

I tell my women's group that meets every Tuesday evening at a coffee shop with framed Georgia O'Keeffe posters that Judith doesn't believe

Harry and I should be living together. Her main opposition to the relationship is a stodgy belief that "you shouldn't give the milk away for free" or "put the cart before the horse." I tell my group these sayings belong where they originated—back in the nineteenth century. This is just the sort of quip I prepare beforehand to sound witty and off-the-cuff. There are four of us who meet: Jane, who is divorced with two children and runs a day care; Sarah, who's nineteen, a college student, and a lesbian; Martha, whose husband left her for a girl working the counter at an adult video arcade; and me. After college many of my friends moved away with husbands or careers while I stayed with Harry and a job managing the gift shop at the Natural History Museum, where I've worked part time since I was a sophomore. In college I'd been lucky to find something even remotely related to my geology degree, but now the rocks we sell as paperweights and the laminated oak leaves we sell as bookmarks only seem silly and depressing.

Telling myself it was something of a joke, I answered an ad in the paper ten months ago. *Women's Lives, Women's Issues: The evolving role of the female experience.* When the group started, we only gave our first names to retain a level of anonymity, although now I know everyone's last name and have sent Christmas cards to their home addresses.

When we first began meeting, our agenda was to discuss important issues affecting our gender today. Issues such as independence, equal pay, and a modern version of equality that celebrates our differences. These are not the issues we discuss. We all cried when Jane's daughter told Jane she'd lost her virginity at the age of fourteen. We watched pornos with Martha and laughed to think what her husband had gotten himself into. We have talked about shoe sales and crow's feet, even though such discussions go against what we supposedly believed in, and we have talked about survival. I like this set of women even though none of us can imagine the others' lives, and we are far from where we assumed we would end up.

At group they tell me they believe I'm doing the right thing by living with a man first. Harry and I have been together for four years now and own furniture together although we still rent. I wonder about their notions of living with Harry "first" when there's been no indication of what might be second. Martha tells me to write my name in all my books and CDs, just in case. "When Gary left he took my Motown collection. I'd been working on that collection a lot longer than my marriage." She smiles. "Harder too." She says after a break-up it's important to retain a sense of humor, and I wonder if like my quips about independence, these remarks are planned beforehand.

When I tell them Harry is taking me to Myrtle Beach, they agree this is a positive sign. Jane says it is "important movement toward resolution." Even four years into the relationship, I am constantly looking for signs.

I lie to my boss and tell her there is a family emergency, something with a close aunt, rather than my boyfriend's father. Weary of all the excuses she gets from college kids and high school students, she tells me to be back no later than Monday, that the days missed should be recorded either as vacation time or without pay.

Martha comes over to help me pack. She lies on her stomach, her knees bent with her feet in the air, tracing the design on the bedspread as I load the suitcase. "Is Harry's dad sick?" she asks.

"I don't know," I say. "I can't discern how much of this is Gerald or just Judith overreacting again." I say it with an air of knowing, like Judith is someone I've dealt with for years. "She tends to do that," I add.

"Why is it mother-in-laws are like that?" I don't correct her. "Jesus, Gary's mom used to come over and steal vegetables out of the garden while I was at work. I hated that. I would have given them to her if she'd just asked me."

I come out of the closet with a black cocktail dress and khaki shorts; I have no idea how to dress for an intervention. "What happened?" I ask. "Between you and Gary. I mean, why do you think he left?"

Martha continues tracing with her eyes focused on the pattern. "I don't know, Kate. I think about it sometimes, not so much anymore, and I'm not sure if I ever really come up with anything. It just seems like something I should have been able to make work." She looks up as if startled. "I think he was lucky to have me."

I start folding Harry's boxers and putting them in the suitcase, counting out undershirts by the number of days we'll be gone. "I miss that, you know," Martha says, and she waves her hand toward the suitcase and looks away. Though I would never admit it to my women's group, there is a comfort—almost a smugness—in having these tasks to perform.

Gerald and Judith meet us at the airport Wednesday evening. He is wearing Bermuda shorts and a U of M sweatshirt while Judith is dressed in summer linen. Harry runs to them with a "whoop!" hugs them both, and says, "I brought Kate. She's been dying to see Myrtle Beach," and I am angry, yet not surprised.

Gerald hugs me and says, "Damn glad you could make it, Katie," while Judith looks at me severely. I can smell sweetness on his breath, something like rum and curacoa.

Judith drives the twenty minutes back to their house, Gerald beside her, Harry and me in the back seat. Gerald stays turned around for most of the trip, talking to us about changes in the airlines, the price of gasoline, what he likes best about his new boat. When a car passes, I see Judith's mouth stiffen, and I remember it was there the need for the intervention had originated, with Gerald passed out on the boat. "She's got a Dead Rise of eighteen degrees," he says and leans over to pinch Judith's thigh.

Their house is by the ocean, which is barely visible in the darkness, but I can smell the salt water the moment I get out of the car. "Welcome home, son," Gerald says, and I hear his voice crack. Harry had warned me his father gets emotional over such things, and I wonder how much of it is from the drinking.

Gerald and Harry bring in our bags. As we get closer to the house Judith says, "Gerald, put Kate's bags in Missy's old room." She is afraid Harry and I will put up a fight about wanting to sleep together. It occurs to me there's about as much chance of Harry standing up to his mother on this as there was of his not coming in the first place.

"Righto!" Gerald says and hauls the bags through the front door. The foyer in itself is intimidating. Sprawling staircase, hardwood floors, a living room that seems the size of a street block. It is considerably more adult than the town house where we live, with the small breakfast bar and all white walls we're not allowed to paint. Harry hightails it up the stairs after his father and leaves Judith to show me silently to my room.

After I unpack, I find Harry alone and ask him why he didn't tell his parents I was coming, when he'd led me to believe that they knew. We are in his room, which is still covered with posters from his childhood—a red corvette, the Beastie Boys, a ludicrous picture of the Go-Go's straddling a motorcycle. "How could you not tell them?" I say.

"Kate, check this out!" He hands me a Rubik's Cube.

"How could you not tell them?" I am conscious of my voice rising and check myself, not wanting Judith and Gerald to hear us arguing.

He puts his hands on my shoulders, and I wince, feeling the right one may be bruised from Gerald's bear hug. "I just figured they'd know you were coming, seeing as we're together and all."

"That's not good enough, Harry."

"Well, then maybe I just wanted to give them a chance to get to know you since you've only met them a few times."

"Nope," I say.

"How about, I told them and they forgot?" He smiles impishly.

I set down the Rubik's Cube and cross my arms. "Harry, why am I here? Why did you lie to me?"

This change in venue has caught him off guard. "I didn't tell them, because I didn't want my mother to say you weren't invited."

I blink a few times, try to recover from his honesty. "OK, but why am I here?"

He smiles a sinister grin, and I can tell he's preparing a bullshit answer. "No Harry, why? You owe me that."

His face goes candid as a child's. "Kate, I couldn't do this alone," he says, and I pull him into my arms.

When we have finished unpacking Gerald takes us down to the boat to show us the ocean, as if water is something we don't have back in

Minnesota, back in the land of ten thousand lakes. Out on the dock I begin to think it isn't, that water is a thing inconsistent to all I've been taught and comparable, in size, only to the sky. Gerald climbs into the boat. "Katie, set your ass right here," he says and slaps the vinyl passenger seat, laughing at the sound his hand makes against the quietude of the ocean.

I climb in next to him; Harry gets in the seat behind me.

"Now this here's an Exciter 270 with a hundred thirty-five hp per engine." Gerald takes a sip of his gin and tonic. "Yamaha!" he says then slouches an arm against the back of my seat and gives me a wink. "Purrs like a woman."

"Jesus, Dad," Harry says, pushing his arm away. I'm not offended, even though I know I will fake indignation when I tell my women's group. There is something childish in Gerald's fumblings—maybe it's the Southern accent—that paints him as harmless. "It's a nice-looking boat," Harry says.

Gerald sits up and puts his hands in his lap, cupping his drink. "I'd take her out for a spin, but your mother won't give me the keys." He laughs. He knows nothing about the upcoming intervention. "She says I'm on probation after the incident." He raises his hands to make quotation marks around the word "incident." We sit for a few moments and listen to the waves. Gerald's ice clinks when he takes a drink, and I wonder if it has occurred to Harry his father seriously may have a problem.

Gerald barks out a laugh and says, "Listen to this!" hitting the horn with his fist. The sound is quacky and high in the darkness, like something a girl would win at a carnival. "Pussiest horn ever!" he roars. "Boat came with four life jackets and a damn good stereo, you'd think they could throw in a horn. Neighbors make fun of me as far out as Buxton Bay. It's a goddamn embarrassment."

Harry's in the back seat laughing, and Gerald joins in.

That night Harry sneaks into my room as I knew he would. "I can't get to sleep without you," he says. "I hate being in the dark without you."

I take this as proof that Harry loves me, this feeling of being needed so much. He snuggles in the twin bed with me, our arms intertwined in a hug, his sweet breath on my cheek. "This is every junior high boy's wet dream," he says. "Sneaking in to have sex with your girlfriend when your parents are right next door." He laughs softly and wraps his leg around my hip, begins stroking my hair.

"Does your mom usually like your girlfriends?" I say. It is embarrassing to refer to myself as Harry's "girlfriend" when we've been together for so many years. It seems insipid and childish, but I am afraid to use an adult term like "lover."

"God no," Harry says. "She's hated every one of them, ever since Becky Shinkle in the third grade."

"What was she like?"

"Jesus, she was something," he says. "Feathered hair, big brown eyes, the teacher always gave her stickers for her penmanship." He sighs. "I thought we'd be together forever."

"Why didn't your mother like her?"

"I can't remember why; I just know she didn't. Maybe her dad was a Northerner."

"Maybe she was threatened," I say.

"By what, her penmanship?"

"Just threatened."

Harry slips his hand under my T-shirt. "I've seen your penmanship, Kate. My mother has nothing to worry about."

In the morning I wake up alone, Harry having snuck out some time around three so not to upset Judith. Despite the sex, I am still angry at Harry for having lied to me, and now for leaving me forlorn in this gargantuan house. When I come into the kitchen, Harry looks up from the paper and smiles, tells me he's had a brainstorm.

"Where's your mom?"

"It's Thursday, I think she's got some book club. Now really, Hon, this is a great idea!"

"Why didn't you stay last night?"

He rolls his eyes. "Dad's gonna love this!"

After breakfast Harry and I go to a store called Dave's Rock Shock to buy a horn with "some balls." That's how Harry refers to it to the clerk—a horn with "balls." The clerk is seventeen if a day and greets me as "ma'am"; this reference makes perfect sense to him. They sell issues of *Low Rider* in a rack by the cash register.

Gerald will be at the airline all afternoon filling out paperwork for his return, and Harry gets the keys to the boat from Judith. She's kept them in her pants pocket for two weeks now, out of Gerald's reach. "I don't know what you're doing," she says, "but if you screw up his toy that father of yours is going to kill you."

In the boat, Harry leans under the driver's seat and fidgets with the wires. It is beyond me that he knows how to do this—that he feels confident installing even a horn into a piece of high-powered machinery without directions. I stand on the dock, passing him tools and feeling helpless. "Harry," I say, "do you think your mother likes me?"

He grunts under the seat. "What does it matter if she likes you?"

"I want her to. I want to make a good impression."

"Sometimes she doesn't even like me." He hands me two wires and the plastic horn he has removed from the boat.

"No, Har, she likes you." I squeeze the horn and it honks, inconsequentially, in my hand. "She loves you, you're her son."

He comes out from under the seat with a smudge of grease on his cheek. He looks even younger than the clerk at the audio store. "I aggravate her," he says. "On purpose. I like to see her get riled up and take care of things." He smiles and looks as innocent as sugar.

"Do you love me, Harry?" I have the tools in my hands, ready to pass him what he might need next.

"Yeah, I love you," he says. He snorts like it's a dumb question he's not willing to put too much thought into. Like telling me how much he loves the Minnesota Gophers.

"Why?"

He puts down the new horn and stares at me; the sun is hitting my face, and I can't see his eyes, and I am aware from the squinting my expression must be a scowl. "How could I not, Kate? You're so good to me." He swats me with the rag he used to wipe the grease from his face. "You take care of me."

"Well then, Harry, why do you think it is I love you?"

He seems bemused and is silenced by this question, and I feel like we are getting dangerously close to something. For a few moments, we stare at each other, and I can feel the muscles in my stomach contract, feel the heat of the day against my skin. It is as if the last four years have been leading up to this moment, although, of course, that isn't the case. Harry suddenly jumps out of the boat and does a manic version of the Charleston, legs and arms flailing, dissipating the moment. "Is that it?" he says, slightly out of breath with his hands on his knees.

In another minute we would have gone too far to turn back without answers, and I am hesitant, this time, to nod that it is.

When Gerald comes home, Harry tells him there's a problem with the boat—something with the stereo, possibly the equalizer. "Hell's bells!" Gerald says, and the four of us tramp down to the dock.

We all climb in—me in the back with Judith, Harry up front with his father. "It's just a funny noise it's been making," Harry says. "Something loud, like the bass is out of control." He tries unsuccessfully to look serious about the situation.

Gerald stops for a moment and turns toward the rest of us. "Does anyone know how much I paid for this boat?" he says. "Does anyone have any idea?"

"Sixteen thousand," Judith says.

"That's right!" Gerald says. He points his finger in the air. "This Yamaha's a pain in my ass!"

"Dad, look at the radio." Harry's hands pass over the stereo buttons, over the equalizer, and land on the horn where he presses before his father knows what he has done.

Gerald's head remains still, cocked at an angle as he listens to the cacophonous horn. It is deep and resonant and unexpected after the useless horn that came with the boat. It is so loud that Gerald looks around after a moment to see if perhaps it was another boat. "Jesus H. Christ!" Gerald says, and Harry throws his head back, claps his hands, and moves over to hit the horn again. "Jesus H. Christ!" They are slapping each other's hands away to try to hit the horn.

Judith starts to smile, rolls her eyes to the front seat, and winks. "That Gerald's a big goof," she says, and she seems happy with this prognosis.

The next afternoon, the day of the intervention, people start arriving as early as three; they've come from as far as Albuquerque and Des Moines. Judith tells me she's invited around thirty, but she isn't expecting that good of a turn out. "People have things to do on the weekends, especially on short notice." She rearranges crackers on a plate. "Bowling leagues, golf tournaments. I'm hoping for around twenty."

"What about an interventionist?" I say. "Isn't it supposed to be a small group?"

Judith waves her hand. "Gerald's got a lot of friends who would feel left out if I didn't invite them. Some go back as far as his Marine days. His family alone could fill a stadium."

"What about an interventionist?"

Judith looks at me. She is carrying a pitcher of orange juice and a pitcher of cranberry juice, both with masking tape on them where it is written "non-alcoholic." "Kate, this is my third intervention for this man. Do you really think I don't know what I'm doing by now?" She stands for a moment, the pitchers suspended. "Because there is a problem, Katie. Don't you think?"

I take the orange juice from her hand and touch her lightly on the arm. "There's a problem, Judith," I tell her and she smiles right back at me, before heading toward the living room.

When Harry returns from jogging around four, there are close to fifteen people milling about. He runs up and hugs his Uncle Reggie, bows mockingly to his Aunt Gertrude. A man in dress blues comes up, slaps him on the back, tells him he remembers when he was knee-high to a grasshopper, and calls him a pissant.

I follow Harry, who is running buoyantly through the foyer and up the stairs to the bathroom. He strips and climbs in the shower. "Harry,"

I say. "I don't like the looks of this. I don't think this is going to go well."

He sticks his head out from the curtain, his hair gelled up like a shark's fin with shampoo. "Dickerson gave me my first beer when I was eight," he says. "He's been my dad's best friend forever. He wasn't able to make it to the first two, and I bet Dad's gonna shit when he sees him."

"Harry, what about the intervention—what about the point of all this?"

"Kate, don't worry. My mom's got a handle on it."

By five the living room is packed. Judith has set up a buffet table with sodas and juices, little sausages. She is wearing a delicate turquoise pantsuit and circulating with a tray of hors d'oeuvres. "Gerald's going to be home in about twenty-five minutes, and he'll know something's up if he sees you all through the window." Half the people are banished to the kitchen; I don't point out the rows of cars lining the streets. When I offer to help, Judith hands me a tray.

By the time Gerald's Explorer swerves into the driveway I'm on my second round of stuffed mushrooms, and we're out of orange juice. He opens the front door and sees a crowd mingling in the living room. "Hell's bells!" he says, taking a look around. "Gertie? What the hell's going on here? Why aren't you in Tulsa?"

Judith gets up from the couch and walks toward Gerald, touches him on the arm. "Gerald," she says. "We're here to discuss your problem."

Gerald turns his head and looks at her, surveys the room again. "Marty Carlson? Hell, I don't think I've seen you since '95."

Judith takes a step. "Gerald, we're here for you."

A rumble has started in the kitchen and out bursts Dickerson singing "Semper Fi." He runs into Gerald from a tackling position, almost knocking him to the floor. "Jesus H. Christ!" Gerald yells. "Jesus H. Christ!" He and Dickerson slap each other on the back while Judith watches from across the room, where she jumped to avoid being tackled.

Harry is sitting next to me on the love seat with his arm around my shoulders. "You approve of this," I say. "You think this is OK."

"Hon, they haven't seen each other in a decade. Dick's been overseas with his third wife and just got back in the States."

I look toward his mother in the corner. She has recovered and is standing straight with her chin prominent, but the tray of canapés hangs limply from her hand. "There's a problem, Gerald," she says. "This is serious. Don't you understand that this is serious?"

Dickerson escapes Gerald's headlock, puts up his hands as if he is going to mime his way out of a box, and backs up. "Don't make the little lady mad," he tells Gerald. "'Member that time she cut all your trousers?" He is smirking on one side of his face. "She means business." I remember Harry telling me the story of Judith and Gerald as newlyweds, how in the service she cut the inseam of all Gerald's pants to keep him from going to the Officer's Club one night.

Gerald turns toward Judith. "Jude, the last thing I want to do is make you mad, especially after you threw me this party."

She sighs. "It's not a party, Gerald, it's an intervention. We're here because you drink and because I love you." She puts the tray under his chin. "I made your favorite."

Judith looks as close to helpless as I ever expect to see her, trying to show her husband why she would go to this trouble once again after two failed interventions. Gerald lifts his hand to chin-level and takes one of the canapés, places it in his mouth, and makes yummy noises as if he is tempting a child to eat. His arm encircles her waist. "My wife's a goddamn gem!" he yells, and Judith nestles her head into his side as he tousles her stiff hair and kisses her on the lips.

Harry laughs. "Get a room."

"Knee-high to a grasshopper!" Dickerson howls.

I wonder if Harry realizes why his mother does this. Why she throws interventions that have nothing to do with his father's drinking, although it obviously is a problem. I look up and see she has already been dismissed as Gerald charges again for Dickerson. She looks forlorn in the middle of the room—her hair flattened on one side from the weight of Gerald's chest—as the guests mingle about her.

When the buffet table is almost empty, it comes out that one of the neighbors was in the Third Battalion, and the men lunge for the door, heading to his house for a "real drink." Before Gerald leaves he comes over and puts his arm around Judith, says, "Sugar Drawers, I'll be home by midnight!" When he leaves he swats her ass; she doesn't turn toward him. Compared to the party guests, her profile looks tightened, resigned, as she walks toward the kitchen.

Harry stands when the other men head for the door. "Don't do it, Harry," I say. "You can't do this to your mother."

He turns around. "This one lasted an hour longer than the second one," he says.

"Don't, Harry. You can't desert her."

He leans over to kiss me, and I pull away. "Come on, Kate. It's not that big a deal. Dickerson's been MIA for the last decade of Dad's life. I want to be there." He is starting to whine, and I stand up, feeling an ultimatum coming, although even before I speak I wonder if it will be an empty threat, one I'm not willing to follow through.

"Harry, I'm telling you in all seriousness, do not leave this intervention." It seems a joke now, to even call it that, but I catch Judith's neck stiffening as she strains to hear what I'll say next. "I won't be here when you get back. I mean it."

Harry looks at his feet, over at his mother, scratches his head. He looks much like he did the day before, out in the sunshine, working on the boat. "I won't be gone long," he says and smiles a pleading sort of smile as he turns for the door.

By ten the house is empty. I bring the paper plates into the kitchen, wrap the hors d'oeuvres in Saran Wrap, and put them in the fridge. Judith has been missing for close to an hour, and I find her in the dark, out on the boat. I tentatively put my foot on the passenger seat, and there is the disconcerting feeling from the waves that I am suspended somewhere between solidity and the unknown. I sit next to her, wondering if she has been crying, and look straight ahead, rather than directly at her face.

"I shouldn't have invited Dickerson," she finally says. "Dickerson was my big mistake." She is quiet for a moment before declaring, dramatically, "I wonder sometimes if that man even loves me."

"I don't think that's the issue," I say and am surprised to find I believe it. Before I think to stop myself, I tell her, "He just loves that you try so damn hard." She snorts, and I glance over at her, surprised by the indelicate noise. She brings her hand to her face and covers her nose, but I can see her smiling. She snorts again, and I feel brave. "What it is, Judith, is that more than anything, he wants you to *keep* trying. He wants you to keep planning these damn things so he can know you care, but he doesn't ever want to change."

She turns her body toward me, and I can see the traces of tears on her face. "Do you think that's it?" she asks, and I nod—I do. She turns forward again for a moment, and I see her body relax, staring at the water lapping against the boat. I'm used to the feeling now, the disjointedness of not being on the land. "And what about that Harry," she says. "What does he want?" I am caught off guard by this question and remain silent, start thinking about Harry and his sweet teenage smile. His gift to his father and the innocent, childish belief everything will by itself mend.

"Or what about you?" Judith says.

I turn to my potential mother-in-law, who thirty years earlier had the spunk to cut the crotch out of her husband's uniform and now sits here alone waiting for him to come back from where he shouldn't be in the first place. It's so easy for me to catapult myself that many years into the future, into a silk pantsuit and an identical marriage, Harry's pants hanging whole and unchallenged in the bedroom closet. He will come home tonight, chagrined and apologetic, and I will take him in my arms as I did two nights before. It seems inevitable now, and I wonder at what moment Judith realized the same—at the first intervention, at the altar, on the bedroom floor of the officers' housing with a pair of scissors and a thirty-four waistband in her hands.

It is now I hear it: the horn, breaking through the silence. A deep, steady sound louder than anything I've heard in any time I can remember. It's like a foghorn, or a god, or a godlike foghorn, calling us home from sea. I look at Judith; the sound seems to have surprised her also, although her hand is square on the horn, and she has pressed it on purpose. It seems out of character for her, and out of character for the small size of the boat and the silence of the ocean. She begins to smile, and her hand presses again. I feel the unsteady boat shake from the force of the horn, although we are secured to the dock by ropes underwater; we aren't going anywhere. I cover her hand with my own and wait for the horn to sound into the night. I sit and wait for something more than just the inevitable echo to resound back.

Honda People

Mara's first thought was they were going to die, that they were about to land in a cornfield in a heap of flesh and metal. Their Honda did a three-sixty and ground to a halt fifty yards from the point of impact, with very little damage other than a large crunch in the driver's side back door. The '88 Nova fared far worse. Merging onto I-80, Ron had taken out the front passenger wheel and propelled the car across the ditch and through oncoming lanes, thankfully empty at 5:30 a.m.

Ron's hand shot out and touched Mara's shoulder. "You OK?" She turned to him, his voice so anxious she could taste it along with the blood on her tongue. "Mara, can you hear me?" He shook her shoulder.

"Ron," she said, "you're a terrible driver." She spat blood into her open left palm where there was a small laceration from gripping the compass on the dashboard.

They looked over at the Nova. "Jesus, I killed him," Ron said.

When the door finally opened, the man who got out looked like little more than a boy dressed in a ripped sweatshirt and jeans. In Mara's confusion, she assumed tiny shards of glass from his windshield had punctured his clothes and body.

Ron put his hand over his heart. "Thank God." He opened his door. "Are you sure you're all right?"

"Ron, I'm fine," she said and rubbed the blood and spittle onto her jeans. "Are you?"

Ron nodded and got out of the car. He jogged across the two lanes and ditch, waited for a semi to pass, and headed over to the driver, who was stretching his arms toward the sky then bending to touch his toes.

Mara knew she should have driven. Wiping up eggs Benedict at the slumber party she was catering for a twelve-year-old, she had heard it in Ron's voice, deadened and heavy, as he finished the last of his radio show. She hated to drive in the dark with no sense of what lay beyond two-hundred yards, but when he pulled up shortly before dawn she should have insisted he let her take the wheel. Mara got out and stood by the car, the sun now rising as Ron and the other driver headed back across the highway. The man waved a hand painted with black fingernail polish. "Nice to meet you, Mara."

Ron put his hand on the man's back. "This is Carly. He's on his way to California; he's got to be out there by—" Ron looked at Carly.

"By Thursday morning. Five days."

"Carly's an actor," Ron added and shot a smirk at Mara. He pointed to the Nova with New Hampshire tags, now dead on the other side of the interstate. "He's not going to be able to drive out there in that."

Carly laughed. "You guys really shit-canned me."

"I told Carly he could come home with us while we came up with a plan." Ron smiled nervously.

"Home with us?" Mara looked again at the black nail polish and then at Carly's face. With a bath and haircut, she imagined he would have the scruffy, blond, blue-eyedness that would get call-backs for the parts passed on by Brad Pitt's agent.

Carly stretched and cracked his neck, a sound that made Ron's shoulders tense. "I'm gonna get my bags," Carly said.

He jogged back to his car while Ron dialed 911 on the cell phone. "Mara, I had to invite him, his car's totaled. The last thing we need is him holed up in a motel in the middle of Nebraska thinking we pissed away his acting career. He'll sue us for sure."

She looked at Carly half bent in the trunk, a backpack slung over his arm. "He hardly looks like the type to have a lawyer on retainer."

Ron told the person on the phone they'd been in a car accident, no one injured, and was put on hold. "He's probably been watching *L.A. Law* since he was ten. Kids pick up things." Mara knew Ron believed all people would behave as he did in any given situation, and she looked at him accusingly. "One time," he bellowed. "One time I sued!" He drew in a breath and looked at Mara patiently. "Mara, we've been in a car accident, will you please leave me alone?"

Carly walked back to their car, dodging a pickup heading toward Omaha. He opened the back door and put a large suitcase and backpack on the seat. "You sure this is OK, Mara?" Carly said.

Ron hung up and dialed "A" Street Repair to request a tow-truck for the Nova. Mara knew there wasn't a way she could say no without coming off the heavy, although why this should matter she didn't know. "Mi casa es su casa," she said.

Carly smiled. "Spanish, cool. I took that in high school."

Ron put Carly's bags in the guest room and handed him a set of towels then came into the kitchen where Mara was washing a set of plates that looked like 45s. "You should have asked me first," she said.

Ron sat at the kitchen table and flipped through a stack of mail, settling on a catalog from Land's End. "Mar, there wasn't any way I couldn't invite him. We'd just smashed his car."

"*You* smashed his car, Ron, and we need to discuss these kinds of decisions." She handed him a towel. "Two-way street, remember?" This was one of the pat phrases they used to talk about Ron's affair eight months ago.

He stood up and picked one of the plates off the drying rack. "Hon, I'm sorry, but there really wasn't time. Besides, he's not dangerous." Ron opened the cupboard. "He's from New Hampshire."

"This is not about him," she said, and as an afterthought: "I've picked up tons of hitchhikers." She'd made out with one too, before she'd met Ron. A fireworks salesman on his way to South Dakota with hair like Jesus Christ. They'd kissed for an hour at a rest stop, shirts off, and even at the time she imagined what a good story it would make to tell her girlfriends over Coronas.

"He's not a hitchhiker. I hit his car, remember?"

Mara put down the dishrag and looked at Ron. "That's not the point."

Carly came into the kitchen with wet hair and sat at the table, picking up the catalog. He looked up. "Did I interrupt something?"

Ron smiled and flicked the towel at him. "Not at all. We were just talking about what to do with you." He looked at Mara then back at Carly. "Perhaps you'd be more comfortable at a hotel?"

"That's a nice shower you've got," Carly said.

They slept most of the day, Mara in the master bedroom and Ron and Carly dozing in and out on the living room sofa watching college football. She could hear them every now and again, whooping over a touchdown or an intercepted pass. For dinner Ron and Carly walked the few blocks to Vincenzo's for takeout, coming back an hour later with fettuccine alfredo congealing in a paper container. "We stopped for a beer," Ron said. "Spur of the moment."

"They didn't even card me." Carly laughed. "Must be the old man." A year ago when Ron started balding he'd shaved his head with dignity, never trying for a last ditch comb-over or, god forbid, a ponytail. Mara had shaved it in the bathroom and afterward stood staring at him in the mirror, thinking rather than looking desperate he looked dangerous and virile. At the time she'd thought perhaps she'd made a mistake, that she was letting loose on the world a man far sexier than the one she'd married.

"I'm not that much older than you," Ron said. "Hardly an old man."

Carly laughed. "You're six years younger than my mom."

"I wish I'd come," Mara interjected. She felt like she'd walked in on the middle of a conversation she wasn't invited to join.

Carly and Ron stopped talking and looked over at her. "That would've been cool," Carly said.

Ron put the fettuccine in a sauce pan and switched on the stove. "Yeah, I wish you'd come." He stirred the pasta. "It was pretty spur of the moment." He added pepper and milk, beginning to softly hum, then sing, "Ring of Fire." Carly joined in while Mara stood patiently until they finished the chorus.

"It was playing at the restaurant," Carly said. "That song."

Mara did a quick knee bend and came up clapping, singing "A Boy Named Sue" off-key. She trailed to a whisper partway through the first verse, her cheeks burning. "It's another Johnny Cash," she said. "The Man in Black." Carly looked at her then bent his head to pick at his nail polish; Ron went back to stirring the pasta.

Mara awoke at 2:30 a.m., Ron's side of the bed still empty. She walked into the hallway wishing for a distraction—a dog loose in the neighborhood or the television left on. After she found out about the affair, she imagined seeing Ron and the girl every time she rounded the corner to the living room, felt that small compulsion to check the sofa to make sure it was empty. And then it became so the living room wasn't enough. She imagined them on the washing machine, in the broom closet, until they were possibly everywhere: sneaking moments between the stacks at the public library, at the post office when she stopped for stamps. Mara began trailing Ron to ease her mind, parking her car across the street from the radio station and waiting. He usually went straight home, but stopped once or twice a week at The Mill, a coffee shop in the Haymarket full of young girls in tank tops. She tried to form it into a schedule—Tuesdays and Thursdays at the coffee shop to meet the other woman—but when she looked at the notebook she kept hidden in the glove box, she had to admit the pattern was random.

Watching him those afternoons from the safety of her car, she tried to turn Ron into a caricature of himself: bald, mid-thirties, playing soft rock at a radio station he despised, but that left her vulnerable to look at herself too: a woman who grew up wanting only to be a wife and now, scrunched low in her car, wondering what she had expected that to be. After two months of trailing him to the boring coffee shop she realized he didn't want to come home. That sitting alone had become preferable to sitting with his own wife, and she felt a sense of blame, then one of anger, at being made to feel guilty her husband had had an affair.

Now coming into the living room in the darkness she was surprised, again, to see the room empty. She opened the door to the garage and stopped suddenly when she saw the car was gone, Ron having escaped in the middle of the night. Mara looked down the driveway, out into the street, expecting to see tread marks, some sign he was really gone. Carly stepped under the porch light and smiled, Ron behind him in pajama bottoms and a parka. Mara hugged herself against the cold and remembered Ron coming into the bedroom during half-time to tell her he was taking the car to Williamson Honda for repairs.

"Your husband's been telling me about his days as a rock 'n roller," Carly said. "Pretty cool." Ron had been in a band his junior year of college twelve years ago, playing Deep Purple at fraternity parties to kids drunk on Pabst and the hope of sex.

Ron crossed him arms, and immediately uncrossed them; they hung limply at his sides. "It was nothing," he said. "Just kids fooling around."

When the band broke up he did everything he could to start another group, hanging flyers at the local bars and the Union on campus, advertising open auditions. "It was a good band," she said. "You guys were really good." They had mainly done covers of early Aerosmith songs, but she was glad she said it.

Ron's face swooned into the light, and he smiled at her. "We were not," he said. "We never even had a steady drummer." He stepped forward to wrap her inside his parka. "But thanks."

"How'd you guys meet?" Carly asked. Mara stood on Ron's slippered feet, elevating herself off the cold cement.

"We were on some committee together," Ron said. "Something for saving the dolphins."

"The whales," Mara corrected.

"Yeah, the whales," Ron said. "That's right." She could feel the warmth of his chest rising into her back through the nightgown. "I didn't really care, I just joined to meet her. I saw her in the Union—you were wearing some sweater with cows on it; I think it was purple—and I just followed her to the table and signed up." The sweater had actually been maroon, but Mara loved this story: the story of Ron pursuing her. "I could never resist a woman in a cow sweater." She felt Ron's cheek form a smile in her hair and knew they were flirting for the benefit of Carly, an old routine that felt familiar but now just short of natural.

It reminded her of the first few months after the affair when Ron had been awash in guilt. He sent cards to their home in the middle of the week, planned a surprise trip to Alliance to see Carhenge, a day full of silences and the solid, awkward beauty of the gray-painted cars stuck in the ground in the dimensions of Stonehenge.

Carly mimicked the motion of playing a violin.

Mara hummed along and squirmed in the coat, knowing Ron would wrap his arms around her chest to steady her.

The next morning Ron leaned over the bed smelling of Irish Spring and aftershave, his shirt slightly damp from his body after the shower. "Are you going to be home all day?" he asked. "I'm thinking someone should stay with Carly." He touched Mara's hair. "It'd be nice if I didn't have to work Sundays anymore."

She rolled over and put her head on his pillow. "Still afraid he might sue?"

"No," Ron said. "I think he's a good kid." She wondered what had been said last night to ease his mind about Carly. She wanted to ask if, in the camaraderie, he had mentioned the affair and was humiliated to think another man might know her husband had cheated on her, as if it somehow was her fault and not Ron's.

He was silent for a moment. "We still need to figure out what we're going to do with him, what we're going to do about his car." He caressed her head again, his thin fingers snagging in her hair as he looked at his watch. When he leaned over to kiss her good-bye she rolled purposefully toward his mouth.

Carly came into the kitchen as Mara was pouring coffee, his eyes bloodshot. She held up an empty mug, and he nodded, sitting at the table. "What do you usually do on Sundays?" he asked. "Do you go to church?"

"I need to make a cake," she said. "For a birthday party on Tuesday." It made her nervous, the idea of entertaining a twenty-year-old for an entire afternoon. Ten years younger and she could have sat him in front of a video game, ten years older and they could have comfortably watched CNN in silence.

"Yeah, bake a cake." He sipped his coffee and nodded. "That's cool."

Mara knew spending a Sunday baking was about the furthest Carly could get from cool but appreciated he would say it.

They rode the bus to the grocery store, all other seats empty except for a pierced, teenage couple in the back and an old man carrying a cat under his coat. The couple looked like they had been up all night and now, at ten in the morning, were kissing desperately. Mara was amazed at the naked way the couple groped each other—his hand on her breast over her coat, her arm shifting restlessly below Mara's view. She watched the couple with mixed feelings of revulsion and jealousy. Carly was sitting next to her, shifting uncomfortably, reading the newspaper he'd found on the seat.

At the grocery store they loaded a cart with almond paste, vanilla, and other items for the cake and stopped at the meat counter for a pork roast for dinner. The butcher handed the roast to Carly rather than Mara, and she was struck they must seem like a married couple, or more likely, a woman and her much younger lover. Carly looked at the wrapped meat in his hands then winked at Mara. She tried to imagine what the butcher would do if she pressed Carly against the glass, his denim buttocks smashed against the ice and pork loins, as she kissed him like the woman on the bus. Ron would get a call at the station saying his wife had gone insane, assaulted a boy at the grocery mart, and was pinned down in the back next to the lettuce crates until he could fetch her. It wasn't so crazy, she thought, that Carly would respond like the hitchhiker on his way to South Dakota, that maybe Carly would kiss her back.

"Mara, you coming?"

She picked up the closest item, Cajun seasoning, and threw it in the cart. "I never knew where they kept that," she said. She wanted to say something intimate to Carly to confirm the butcher's suspicions about her and her lover. Something about eating the seasoned meat in bed later that night, or buying oysters to complement the meal. It would be futile, like trailing Ron after work, but she wanted to all the same.

When she looked back at the counter the butcher was concentrating on his work, cutting salmon steaks for the next customer.

Carly bent over the wax paper with concentration, dolloping sugar flowers on the corner. “It doesn’t look anything like a rose,” he said.

Mara put down the eggbeater and looked at the yellow blob on the paper. He was right; it was a dandelion at best, a non-descript bush at worst. She took the icing nozzle from his hand and squeezed the flex bag on the left then the right, a perfect rose appearing on the wax paper. “It’s in the wrist,” she said and wiggled her hand to demonstrate. She looked again at the flower Carly had made. “Maybe you’d just better mix colors.”

Carly sat down and poured powdered sugar and green coloring, along with a teaspoon of warm milk, into a bowl. “You always do kid parties?”

Mara nodded. “Mainly. They’re usually more fun than adults.” At the few cocktail parties she’d thrown for a philosophy professor at the university, many of the guests had sniffed the food before eating it, wary of how fresh California rolls could be in the middle of Nebraska. “Sometimes I dress up depending on the theme, a lion tamer or a clown.” She added vanilla to the cake batter. “Two years ago I dressed as a robot.” She had worn an iridescent silver jogging suit and wrapped tin foil on her head. It was in someone’s backyard, an August birthday, and by the end of the party her face was shiny with tropical-looking burns. The boy’s father was sipping vodka tonics by the fence for most of the afternoon and laughed, telling her she looked more like a baked potato than a robot. She smiled congenially and charged him an extra twenty percent for the paper plates and napkins.

“I had a bank robber theme party when I was six,” Carly said. He poured more sugar and coloring, mixing the paste into a thick, bright green the color of Easter basket grass. “We had a cake with licorice whips that looked like a jail cell. My mom took pictures.”

“I think the parties are more for the parents,” Mara said. She spent hours cutting peanut butter and currant jelly sandwiches into the shapes of footballs and castles only to watch kids eat them in one bite or smash them into their neighbor's hair. "The parents just want to have something to look back on in the photo albums." She looked at Carly, who had stopped mixing. "Not that your mom didn't care about you." She peered at the green icing. "It's perfect, Carly, really. Can you make me some blue?"

Carly started another bowl.

"Tell me more about your acting."

"Well," Carly said, "I took some drama classes in high school, but they weren't that good. They wanted us to pretend we were different kinds of birds. Sparrows and chickens, shit like that." He stood up and struck a pose with his hands on his hips, arms akimbo, flapping like wings. "I don't want to play a chicken, I told them. I want to play a cowboy." He pointed his fingers like pistols and pushed down his thumbs, knees bent slightly. He held the pose a long moment until Mara looked away, uncomfortable with his childishness, although that's what he was: a child. She felt silly now that she had envisioned kissing him at the grocery mart, that she had wanted the butcher to notice them.

Carly squirted more food coloring into the bowl. "I'm auditioning for some action movie, that's all I know."

"What part are you reading for?"

"A cop, I think." Carly added more powdered sugar. "Maybe it's a drug dealer, my buddy wasn't too sure. Really, it's a bit part."

Mara opened the fridge and pulled out the pork roast, a tiny pool of blood melting under the meat. "Are you staying with him?"

"Naw, my dad's out there. I'll be living with him. He's close to UCLA, so it'll be easier for classes."

She was surprised to hear Carly would be taking classes, surprised too he would live with his father, and wondered if he had told Ron this the night before out by the garage. "What are you studying?"

"Mathematics." He looked down at the tablecloth as if embarrassed to admit this. "Can I do something else?" he asked. "Maybe try flowers again?"

She handed him the icing nozzle, and he began squeezing out flowers little improved from the first try. It was the way he held the flex bag—gripping in the middle rather than a rolling down motion like with a tube of toothpaste—but she didn't correct him. Mara felt a sense of pride she could keep Carly engaged for an afternoon, a small thrill she could never share with Ron, who entertained thousands of people via radio five days a week. Two years ago, six months after he'd started at the station, Ron had been stopped for an autograph at Gateway Mall by a woman who recognized his voice when he ordered a chicken taco at Amigos. He joked to Mara about it later, his "fans"—all middle-aged women shopping for yet another matching jogging suit. But for weeks after Ron sounded stronger on the air, making witty jokes between songs, almost flirting as he played a ballad by Chicago, going out to Charlotte. As the job wore on, the glory of the Gateway fan faded as did the flirting voice, replaced by the monotony of introducing the same songs over and over again, with little hope of sneaking something in by John Prine.

By the time Ron came home that evening, Carly and Mara had finished the sheet cake. It was decorated like a rose garden with a plastic blond girl sitting on a bench in the middle, holding a bouquet of flowers. Carly had spread the grass for the footpath with a butter knife and it reached half way up the bench, a steroid-size overgrowth, but was beautiful all the same. Decorating the cake, Mara had forgotten about the pork roast cooking on the grill outside, and they sat chewing the tough meat without conversation as Carol Burnett ran through her variety acts in syndication. It was sad, really, Mara thought, that she could create a marble cake in the shape of a fantasy but couldn't make a simple pork roast without burning it.

After dinner Carly went to his room and left Ron and Mara drinking beer in front of the TV. Ron had nudged Carly's shoulder and asked if he wanted one, but Carly smiled and declined, reminding them he wasn't of age. Mara smelled it a few minutes later, the sweet, dry smell wafting out from the back of the house. She'd suspected it earlier when she and Carly were baking the cake; she had put her nose near the oven to try and deduce the smell, convinced the cake ingredients were wrong.

Ron inhaled deeply and turned to Mara, slack-jawed. "Is he smoking pot?"

"Sure seems that way." She searched for the remote control and turned to the Weather Channel.

"Well, you're awfully calm," he said. "Aren't you going to say something?"

"Why don't you? You brought him home." She thought how naive Ron was to be surprised. Ron who had been in the rock 'n roll band and was in touch with the alternative side because he worked at a radio station and had affairs.

"What should I say?" Ron sat for a moment sipping his beer. He nudged Mara. "He likes you better. Why don't you make the bust."

"He's twenty years old," Mara said. "You want me to go back there and demand his doobage? Think about that, Ron." She flipped channels. "It's dope, not heroin," she said. "Lighten up."

Ron swigged more beer and laughed, holding his arms out like he was balancing on a beam. "Mara, walkin' on the wild side."

Mara looked at him; she'd wanted to tell him about the hitchhiker for years to let him know she was unpredictable and attractive to other men, or at least had been at one time. She set down the remote and walked back to the guest room and knocked on the door. "Carly?"

There was a rustling noise, like sand being shoveled into a plastic bag. "Yeah?"

"What are you doing?"

There was no movement or noise for five seconds or so. "Nothing."

"Do you want to come out here and do nothing?" She could feel cold air on her feet and knew the windows were open even though it was October. "You're going to freeze to death smoking pot in there. Come out in the living room."

She heard a scraping noise; the door opened and he stuck out his head. "Yeah?" She could see the dresser in the middle of the floor rather than against the wall and considered the ridiculousness of him barricading her out of rooms in her own home.

"Yeah." She walked back to the living room and sat on the sofa.

Ron tapped her arm. "You take care of it? What did he say?"

"He won't be smoking pot in his room anymore." Carly rounded the corner with a bag of Doritos and a red glass bong.

Ron looked from Carly to Mara. "No shit?"

Mara shrugged her shoulders. "On the wild side, Ron."

A half hour later, Mara couldn't feel her teeth. Ron had taken one hit and passed the bong back to her, content with the beer. He was on the sofa still, and she could feel him watching as she leaned over the bong, her hand on Carly's back as she held the smoke as instructed without coughing. She'd smoked before but not since college, and then only a spit-laden joint passed at a party.

Carly leaned back against the ottoman next to Mara and smiled, his eyes seeping shut. "What are we going to do about the car?" he asked.

Mara had nearly forgotten about the Nova: three wheels and a crunched frame down at "A" Street Repair. She remembered learning somewhere that the car wouldn't sell in Spain, although the executives couldn't imagine why. *No va*: it doesn't go. She waited five seconds and exhaled. "We'll fly you to California," she said. "We'll pay for it." Ron set down his beer, and she looked over at him. "You wrecked his car. We're flying him to California." She liked the feeling the marijuana gave her. She felt she could make any decision, as long as she concentrated and could remember the problem.

"We could do that," Ron said.

"I'm still going to need the car," Carly added.

"We'll get it repaired," Mara said. "Our insurance'll cover it." She wanted someone to ask her the quadratic equation or the capital of Indiana; she felt she could answer anything.

Ron picked up the remote for the stereo. "It's a sweet car, a classic. Mar, maybe we should trade him the Honda."

Mara wondered if Ron was joking or if he was serious enough to do something that desperate for the past. "We're thirty-three," she said. "We're Honda people now, Ron. You're just going to have to accept that."

Ron stood up suddenly. "Say! Maybe I could drive it out after repairs, take a week or two to see the country." Mara looked at Ron, airguitaring Steppenwolf in the middle of the room, and tried to imagine them tooling down the highway like in a British spy movie, the wind through her hair and the beautiful countryside.

Carly reached for more Doritos. "You guys could stay with me for a week or so, check out Cali. Beats hell out of Nebraska, I bet."

Ron turned to Mara. He smiled wanly after a moment's hesitation, and she knew he had envisioned going alone, roaring down the highway in an '88 Nova, his elbow hanging out the driver's window as he listened to the Dead. She remembered walking into this living room eight months ago and seeing Ron stretched out on the sofa like a cat, a nineteen-year-old co-ed scratching his belly.

"Ron, you couldn't just up and leave." She looked around the living room. "Who would play all those awful Phil Collins records for KLTE?"

Ron went over and took the Doritos from Carly, now slumped against the ottoman with his eyes closed. "I got fired," he said and smiled at Mara. "Shit-canned."

"Fired?"

"Three weeks ago. They said I wasn't, quote, invested in the music anymore, like anyone could invest in Dan Fogelberg. I finish my contract through November, and I'm out of there." He held his arms parallel to the floor like airplane wings. "We could go to Disney World—or is it land?—I can never remember."

"What do you mean you got *fired*?"

Carly smiled. "I think it's 'land.' The other one's in Texas."

"You mean Florida," Ron said, while Mara fought for control. She wanted to return to the moment when she felt she could solve algebraic equations, conquer the world.

"Jesus, why would anyone go to Florida?" Carly asked.

"Ron, what the hell are you going to do?" She stood up and crossed her arms. "Just what the hell?"

"Yeah, what the hell?" Carly laughed.

"You shut up." Ron pointed at Carly, his voice escalating. "You don't know a thing about this."

Carly stopped laughing, Doritos in his hand. "Hey—"

"Don't you yell at him," Mara growled. "This isn't about him." Ron turned toward Mara, his chin beginning to move right to left as he ground his teeth, a slow circular warning she'd begun to recognize over the years. She could feel him losing control, slipping away somehow, and she sat calmly on the sofa. She looked at Carly over by the ottoman and remembered how Ron had invited him into the house. "He's my lover," she said to Ron. "We're lovers." Ron looked from Mara to Carly and back again, his entire face expanding. It wasn't what she meant to say, but she felt she was getting closer.

Carly leaned forward and held his hands up as if someone had pointed a gun at him. "Wait a minute," Carly said. "Just wait a minute. Ron, that's not true—"

Mara looked at Carly and could see him childlike in the kitchen, pretending to be a bird. "It's not true, Ron," she said. "I was joking—" but Ron was already in motion, running across the living room toward Carly, when he tripped on the ottoman and kicked Carly squarely in the side.

"Jesus, man!" Carly yelled and stood up, holding the right side of his ribs.

Mara sprang from the sofa where Ron had fucked the girl and jumped on his back, forcing him to the ground, her arm around his neck in a stranglehold. Carly stood by the doorway. "Who the hell gets violent smoking pot?"

She eased her elbow from under Ron's chin, and he dropped in front of the fireplace, wheezing. He put his hand to his windpipe and looked at Carly. "It was an accident," he sputtered. "I tripped, swear to God."

"You kick like a girl," Carly said. Ron looked at his hands as if he expected them to be covered in blood, although he'd kicked Carly, not hit him, and in stocking feet. "And you!" Carly said, pointing at Mara.

"We're not lovers," she told him.

"No shit." He picked up his bong and chips and looked around the room. "I want cash for that ticket, and a hotel room for tonight, I mean it." He sat on the sofa, holding his possessions against his chest. "I still need to be there by Thursday."

Mara turned toward Ron and saw the imprint of her arm on his neck, the rest of his face losing color as if some essential blood was draining out. "I never would have done that to you. I wouldn't have done that to anyone, especially in my own home."

"It was an accident."

Mara remembered back in college when Ron was in the band, he'd been in a fight at O'Rourkes over a bar tab. Ron had placated the man until he turned away then tapped him on the shoulder and caught him unaware with a right cut to the jaw. She wondered now if she had been fooled all along, and the fight was really over something else. "And you're not going to California," she said. "I'm taking the car." It was a useless thing to say; she realized after seeing the wreckage the auto wasn't worth salvaging. But she had said it now, out loud.

Ron glanced up and snorted. "You don't even like to drive at night."

She looked at him, his shaved head glistening, and thought about the hours logged in the Honda, the notebook she'd kept in the glove box: *August 13: grocery store for apple juice and hot dog buns, then home. August 14: coffee until 6:40 p.m., ordered mocha.*

"And the house," she said. "I'm taking the house."

Ron stood up quickly, his brows coming together under the furrows of his skull. "I said it was an accident. The ottoman—," but Mara had stopped listening. She was concentrating only on what she would say next as she kept going, kept pushing, until she'd claimed not only the house but everything in it. The block, the entire street and city and state. She would claim everything she'd ever seen or heard just to see the look on Ron's face as she said it was hers.

The Story of Gladys

I found Dr. Gus on daytime TV. During the afternoon when Ted was at work and Sammy was finally down for an hour, I'd turn on the tube and flip though Oprah and Montel and Ricki Lake. In the beginning, I only watched the makeovers or the stories I felt concerned the community, but it became the bad ones I wanted. I stayed riveted to the screen when a sixteen-year-old told me she met her incarcerated husband through the mail. I wanted transsexuals to describe their dates with unsuspecting frat boys. The commercials, like the shows themselves, were different from the ones we watched at night; day commercials advertised fad diets as opposed to exercise equipment, sex as opposed to love. Dr. Gus's ad, in all its home-video glory, showed him sitting on the edge of his desk discussing his credentials: Ph.D. from UCLA Berkeley and a lifetime of knowing people. At the end he was quiet a moment too long, causing me to glance up from the *TV Guide* crossword puzzle in my lap. He leaned toward the video-cam, wrung his hands, and said, "I just want to help you people in trouble; I want to help you find what's missing."

I wrote down, on a whim, the number of the Community Center.

Ted came home that night trudging snow in the house and explained the latest glitch in his possible promotion: Deborah, an intimidating transfer from Seattle whom he'd met at the water cooler. In turn, I told a story about Sammy eating a bug at the grocery mart, about a woman who bought nothing but a cart full of five-pound bags of sugar. I didn't mention I thought our problems might be solved thanks to a commercial I saw while watching a show on ménage e trois. Ted and I hadn't vocalized there might be a problem; we're Midwesterners. Rather it was a feeling—the milky silences permeating the house as we watched sitcoms and listened to canned laughter; the mornings with mechanical brushing of lips to cheek, where before was a playful swat and the giddy possibility of a quickie.

That evening, we ate tuna fish casserole and watched the news. The newscaster wore a polyester suit coat and a face approximating woe, telling us about the twelve-car pile up on I-35, the unexplained fire in the warehouse district. I had grown used to the crazy outfits the guests wore during the day, the way a talk show host scampered from audience member to audience member, fielding questions without sweating through his makeup. I wasn't going to tell Ted about Dr. Gustafson. I couldn't bear the thought of him looking at me in a somewhat amused and glazed manner just like I watched the guests, who were there, despite their outfits, in a desperate attempt for help.

In bed that night, Ted fell asleep first, too exhausted again, and I lay there watching him sleep although I too was tired. I liked this idea of therapy. It seemed a scientific way to spread the marriage out and poke around inside for something that had failed. Possibly the heart, or something more obscure, like the trigeminal nerve.

Dr. Gustafson answered on the first ring when I called to make my appointment. "Dr. Gus, here," he said. His voice was boisterous and friendly, the voice most people use only when they recognize the caller on the other end. "What can I do you for?"

I held my date book in my lap, flipped to two weeks out, empty except for pediatric appointments and oil changes. "I'm calling for an appointment," I said. "For me."

"How's tomorrow," he said. "Can you make it around one?"

I thought for a moment about the talk shows—the fraught guests and their reckless need to get their stories out to millions of viewers—as I gave him my name and telephone number. "It could be Friday," I told him. "If that would be better, I don't know what your schedule's like, if you can squeeze me in." I was grasping. "It's not like I'm that desperate."

Dr. Gustafson was quiet for a moment, but I heard his breath coming through the wires. "Mrs. Klaasen," he said dramatically. "We're all that desperate."

I arrived at his office twenty minutes early wearing a navy blue suit left over from my job as a loan clerk and carrying a purse matching my shoes to inspire the impression of togetherness. The receptionist at the Community Center led me to a folding chair outside his office, and from the hallway I could see inside the tiny room. There was a metal desk in front of two plush, mismatched chairs that were divided by a coffee table with a potted silk plant and a fanned selection of *Psychology Today*. "He can't even nurture a real plant," Ted would have said. On a bookshelf to the right was a framed degree partially obscured by a water-colored sign reading, "THE MUCK STOPS HERE."

I heard sneakers squeaking down the hall in the gymnasium, a group of people reading poetry to each other one door down. Poetry readings, did they still have those? Back in college I had attended one with Ted for extra credit in an English class. Graduate students slouched on stage in a smoky bar, reading personal riffs from their lives, giving me more details than I ever thought possible from a stranger. I remembered in particular one woman reading a story about having her first baby, how the placenta oozed onto the table, combining with her own feces. It was one of those things—shitting on the table—that if you thought about, with all the pushing and grunting, seemed obvious, but if you hadn't, you were horrified to realize. The point of the poem was something life-affirming concerning the passing of generations, but I listened with equal parts astonishment and embarrassment. I thought at the time this image was reason enough not to have children, and it haunted me through my entire pregnancy with Sammy. When I finally delivered, I was so overwhelmed by the entire experience that the mingling of placenta and shit somehow was life-affirming. But all the same, the thought of reading this aloud to a room full of smug strangers mortified me.

Dr. Gus shuffled down the hall a few moments later and stepped inside the office, waving me in behind him. He was shorter than I imagined from the commercial—probably no more than 5'4"—and he turned to me, arms open. "Mrs. Klaasen," he said. "Let's hug."

Hug? There hadn't been anything in the commercial about hugs. I stepped tentatively into his arms and patted him once on the shoulders. This kind of contact hardly seemed legal in a first session, but I had no concept of therapy past what I'd seen on TV.

He squeezed back and released me. "There," he said. "Now I feel like we've already broken some ground." He went and sat in the chair behind his desk. "Now, what are we going to talk about?"

I wondered what Sammy was doing right then over at Marla Stamp's house, our neighbor three doors down who baked cookies as a side business and had perfect TV hair from the fifties. "I want to talk about my marriage," I said.

Dr. Gustafson slapped his hands together. "Bull's-eye! I've got a lot of experience with marriages. What specifically are we looking at? Adultery? Financial distress? Sex life down the tubes?"

I stared at him, gape-faced. "No, nothing like that. My husband's a good man, he just works a lot."

"Workaholic!"

"No," I stammered. "Just a lot. We decided when Sammy was born we wanted to have a stay-home parent, very diplomatic you see, so Ted's got to earn enough for all of us. He's under a lot of pressure. He loves me." I stopped and thought when the last time Ted had said that with conviction was and could only remember the passing endings to conversations, or one time drunk at a barbecue six months before, when the words had brought tears to his eyes. "He loves me," I said again.

"Who's this Sammy?"

"Our son, he's two." I thought about Sammy eating the bug at the grocery store. "He's an angel."

Dr. Gus took off his glasses and put one stem in his mouth. "I don't know much about kids, Mrs. Klaasen," he said. "We've got our work cut out for us."

Dr. Gus and I developed a routine over the next few weeks: he'd sit behind his desk and stare at me until I thought of something to say—usually a defense of Sammy just acting like a normal two-year-old or a story of how Ted and I used to stay in bed on Sunday afternoons for no other reason than we could. If I couldn't think of anything, we'd flip through his psychology books and look at the indexes to get ideas. There were chapters on things like "Schizoaffective Disorder" and "Freudian Sexual Hierarchies."

"Margo, you seem real normal," he told me. "Some of the people who come through here have got problems I've never imagined. This one woman keeps cutting her leg with a razor to stop herself from eating a bag of cookies. Eat the cookies, I tell her. They're not going to kill you." He seemed astonished that such things went on, and I asked him again where he got his degree. "California," he said. "I lived out there for six years. You think I'd be more in tune with this stuff." Sometimes I gave him advice based on what I'd learned from the talk shows.

One Wednesday, during a story about Ted and me shopping for lawn furniture, Dr. Gus said, "I've been married, three times. Barbara, Lana, and Gladys. All Virgos. I just realized that today when I was reading the paper."

I stopped for a moment and looked at him. "All Virgos?" I said. What did he expect me to say?

He came out from behind the desk and plopped in the seat next to me, crossing his short legs. "Every single one of them." I could barely see him over the plastic fern. "I checked one of those astrological charts, and it didn't say here nor there whether Virgos are a bad mix for me. Far as they know, I'm supposed to be all right with them."

I dug in my purse for a breath mint, wanting desperately to seem occupied with a task. "You can't really believe those charts," I said.

"No, I'm with you on that. I just thought it was odd, like they might be in some kind of a club against me." He splayed his hands and looked at his fingers. "Lana's just a cusp."

I moved aside my checkbook and sunglasses. "It's only a coincidence," I said.

"You really think so?" Dr. Gus said.

I held out the tube of Mentos. "I'm a Virgo, and I'm not in a club against you."

"But we're not married," Dr. Gus pointed out.

"Well, no." I looked at him. "I'm married to Ted."

Dr. Gus took a Mentos and thought about this for a moment. "And what's he?"

"Sagittarius."

He went and sat behind his desk again. "Margo, I can't think that's a good sign."

After that, Dr. Gus and I decided it made more sense if we used the $10 fee for an entire week—like an all-you-can-eat—rather than per session. I would usually bring Sammy along with me. There was a free day care at the Community Center, but the girl in charge didn't look a day over twelve, so Dr. Gus said it was fine if Sammy sat in. Dr. Gus wasn't a father, but he'd always liked the idea of kids. "Maybe it's because I never had them," he said with a sad smile. Sometimes if I came over the noon hour we'd go across the street to Wok on the Run and get takeout.

He abandoned sitting behind the desk even when I came in now and was usually waiting near the receptionist's area or sitting anxiously in one of the two patient chairs. We'd spend equal time on my marriage with Ted and Dr. Gus's past relationships, trying to figure where the problems lay. Up until then, therapy had reminded me of that woman in college, how naked she seemed reading her poems alone on stage.

We talked in depth about two of his wives: Barbara—whom he married straight out of college—and Lana, a brief eruption that was mainly a counterbalance to loneliness after the first divorce. Dr. Gus and Barbara remained civil, sending holiday and birthday cards every year since the separation. "Even though I was with her the longest, it wasn't love, not for either one of us. I can look back on it now and see that. We were together for twelve years in all, but the last five seemed more out of habit."

"And Lana?"

He waved his hand in the air. "I don't even know what Lana was."

Dr. Gus barely talked about Gladys, his third wife. They had been divorced now for almost a year, and the very idea of her still seemed sacred, as if to bring up her name somehow violated a long dead vow. "Gladys was my wife," he said with authority. "I loved her and I thought that she loved me." When I pressed for more information on the elusive Gladys, Dr. Gus was uncharacteristically quiet.

I still kept from Ted I was seeing a therapist. When he asked about my day I would skirt around the question by telling a simple anecdote about going to the library or taking Sammy to the children's museum. After a while these alibis became more and more explicit, with plots and subplots extending over a few days. There was the lie I told concerning a fender bender I supposedly witnessed at an Ace Hardware. How I had to go to the police station the next day to give my statement and saw a couple crying because their thirteen-year-old son was being held on charges of possession. It came out sounding like an episode of *Hill Street Blues*. I told Ted over the phone the mother had looked me in the eye (I was holding Sammy in my tale) and said, "You watch out for that boy. You raise him right!"

"A thirteen-year-old," Ted said. "Can you imagine?"

We sat in silence for a moment. "When are you coming home?"

Ted kept his voice low. "I can't leave before Deborah, and I know she's going to be here until at least eight." I heard papers shuffling on his desk, voices in the background. It occurred to me Ted could be having an affair. I considered this: Ted with another woman.

"What about dinner?"

"I'll pick something up on the way home." He covered the receiver, and I heard muffled voices. His voice came back, "Listen I gotta go, I'll call you before I leave." As I hung up, I imagined Ted kissing another woman, holding her face in his hands, running his thumb softly over the curve of her cheek. I thought about him at the office with Deborah. This Deborah person I knew nothing about, who shared moments by the water cooler and spent all her days with Ted.

When he came home that night, walking through the door with a pizza box and a haggard expression, I was struck by how absolutely handsome he was.

The next day I told Dr. Gus Ted might be having an affair. "I know it, I just know it," I told him, although there was no such conviction in my mind.

Dr. Gus took a bite of his chicken lo mein. "Well then, he's an idiot," he said. "If that man can't recognize the wealth of what he's got right in front of him, then he has no right to have it."

"Deborah works in his office; they must have a lot in common." I fished in the bag for a fortune cookie. "She might be prettier."

Dr. Gus wiped soy sauce off his chin. "Impossible. I won't even discuss that possibility. Barbara was a working woman, and she looked hollow-eyed as the day was long. Trust me, you're wonderful. We can beat her." He took another bite. "That's my professional opinion." It had become obvious to both of us he had no "professional" opinion. The very phrase had turned into a standing joke between the two of us—like when Ted and I were dating and used the word "lovely" as code in front of his parents to tell each other we were horny. As in "Margo, don't you think the beef stroganoff my mother prepared is just lovely?"

Dr. Gus had confessed, taking the degree out from behind the sign on the bookshelf, that psychology was only one of his minors; his degree was actually in botany. "Plants," he had said. "They were so much safer." He'd given up his research after publishing a distinguished book on energetic possibilities in relation to photosynthesis and had decided to retire on top. I pieced together his interest in psychology was piqued shortly after Gladys left. The Community Center didn't seem to mind as long as he paid his rent on time and didn't claim to produce miracles, and I felt much the same way. I wasn't angered by this divulgence, rather looked at it as a big step for Dr. Gus.

I blew on a bite of egg roll for Sammy and handed it to him. "I think your wives were all idiots to let you go."

"Lana was an idiot, I'll give you that." Dr. Gus looked thoughtfully at his chopsticks. "But Gladys. Gladys, she knew the right thing to do when she saw it." He sat there for a moment, chopsticks suspended. "You need to decide, Margo. You need to decide what you want this marriage to mean to you."

I determined I needed to go see Ted, storm into his office, and put a stop to this Deborah woman and her water cooler antics, and I called Dr. Gus to let him know.

"She's not going to give up easily," he said. "She's probably in love with Ted. Are you just going to let her do that? Be in love with your husband?" He seemed even happier than I was to finally have something to battle back against.

"I'm going to fight her," I told him, and Dr. Gus nearly squealed with delight.

When Ted called from his office later that afternoon and told me it was going to be another late one, I casually mentioned I might stop by. His company had moved offices three months earlier, and between the talk shows and Dr. Gus, I had yet to make it down to see the new building.

"Hon, that'd be great, but why?"

"I'm just curious, just want to see where you are all day."

He sat there a moment. "Are you going to have time? I thought you had to give another statement today."

I remembered the fender bender and the woman I had created at the police station, her thirteen-year-old son, and the suffering he'd caused her. "That's over," I told him. "The charges were dropped."

I wondered if all along Ted suspected I'd been lying.

His desk was in a white cube only slightly bigger than our bathroom. On the plain white walls he had tacked pictures of Sammy playing whiffle ball and one of me from the barbecue we had attended the summer before, two cold beers sweating in my hands. On the desk was his computer, too many papers for the counter space, and an old birthday card signed by the entire office. Ted spread his arms. "Here it is."

To see the closest window I would have to strain far to the left. "It's nice," I lied.

"Well, it's mine," he said and looked around, taking in the piles and the mess and the tiny, tiny space. He leaned in and whispered, "If I get the promotion it means an office."

A woman rounded the corner and stopped at the cube to give Ted some papers. She looked at me and Sammy and smiled. "You must be Margo," she said, and I knew instantly this was Deborah. She was wearing sensible gray slacks, and her hair was clean and plain.

Ted nodded. "Margo, this is Deborah, she works in the department."

Deborah grinned at me and leaned over Sammy who was sitting on the floor by the recycling bin eating paper. "And you," she said, "you must be Sammy." I could imagine Deborah's cube by just looking at her: a smaller, framed card like the Successory posters out front, an old picture taken with girlfriends she hadn't seen since college, all of the papers neatly color-coded by file.

A phone started ringing a few cubes down, and she shook my hand quickly and said good-bye. Ted leaned in. "That's Deborah."

"I know."

"*The* Deborah."

Ted suddenly seemed small. "She's not out to get you," I stated.

He sighed. "I know."

Ted walked me to my car at the Dayton's parking ramp, helped me strap Sammy in the safety seat, and opened my door. "I'm glad you came down and saw the office," he said. "You should try coming again some evening around dinnertime. Maybe we'll be celebrating the new promotion." He fidgeted with the seatbelt. "We could ask Marla to take Sammy for the night."

I got back out of the car and kissed him on the mouth. "That sounds lovely, Ted."

On the way home I stopped by Dr. Gus's to tell him I was ending my therapy. I knew after seeing the office, the cube where Ted worked, he wasn't going to get the promotion. It was the same part of me that knew, long before I saw the degree, that Dr. Gus was not a psychologist.

Walking down the hall of the Community Center I heard once more the people reciting their awful poetry. I remembered suddenly how after the reading in college Ted and I had gone straight home and made love in the kitchen, not taking the time to get to the bedroom, or even the sofa, the urgency so great. We'd been dating for almost six months by then, and the sex had been wonderful, but that night it was different, as if we both knew, although it was unspoken, that we were somehow committed.

"Margo!" Dr. Gus cried when I walked though the door. "I thought you weren't coming until tomorrow."

He was at his desk, building an elaborate pyramid out of the business cards he had printed at Kinkos. He had given me one on my first visit: *Dr. Gustafson, Trained Professional.* "Professional what?" I remembered thinking at the time.

"I went in and saw Ted," I told him. Sammy went over and sat companionably on Dr. Gus's lap.

"Yes, Ted," he said. "Did you meet that Deborah?" He motioned to my chair. "Sit, sit!"

"I can't stay," I told him and rattled the car keys in my hand, hoping this would pass for an indication of other obligations. Sammy had discarded his coat on the floor and was fingering one of the business cards as a possible snack. "Well, just for a second," I said, and I sat in my chair.

Dr. Gus ran his finger over his bottom lip. "You'll come back tomorrow?"

There was something hollow in his voice, and I fidgeted with the keys as I told him, "Tomorrow's a busy day." I went to Sammy, took the business card from him, and set it on the desk. "I think I'm better now. I don't think I need any more therapy."

When I looked directly at Dr. Gus he was nodding his head slowly up and down, contemplating my wellness. "Do you really think you're better?" he said. Dr. Gus came out from behind the desk, and I thought fleetingly of the first time we met—his arms open, the earnest way he had requested a hug. He sat in the seat next to me. "You're right,

Margo, I think you're cured." He smiled sadly. "That's my professional opinion."

We sat there a minute in uncomfortable silence, and when I got up to go, I stopped for just a moment to turn around and look at Dr. Gus, sliding one of the business cards between his fingers.

"Why Gladys?" I asked. He seemed surprised and glanced quickly at the solid comfort of his desk. "Why her, out of all of your wives? Why is she the one you miss?"

Dr. Gus looked at me as if evaluating my sincerity, searching for something in my face that would allow him to answer. I knew then that despite my resolve to leave, we were not yet through; Dr. Gus had not yet finished. I took off my coat slowly and placed it on the floor, motioned for Sammy to lie down, and settled into my chair, pulling my feet up under me. When I looked back at Dr. Gus I knew whatever he was searching for in my face would be there, and this one last time I would listen.

Dr. Gus nodded and began, slowly, to tell me the story of Gladys. As the room shaded into evening I leaned forward intently, knowing I mustn't miss a word.

Laws of Relativity

It's my turn to drive, and I am complaining softly about Palma, Mark's great aunt, who is asleep in the backseat slumped over her travel bag.

I look at her reflection in the rearview mirror, her chin tilted to her chest, a needle-thin string of wetness running toward her shoulder. "She told me I shouldn't be wearing shorts, even though it's almost a hundred degrees. She told me I'm not a lady." Her real name is Beulah, but she was born on Palm Sunday, and she claims that puts her at the right hand of God. "Yet she can pee by the side of the road near Kadoka?"

Mark is sneaking a cigarette and leans toward the window to exhale. "She's eighty-nine," he whispers. "You need to give her some leeway."

Leeway seems to be all I've given Palma since we picked her up in Yankton seven hours ago—saying nothing when she pulled scissors from her bag and told me I needed a haircut, only grimacing when she asked if I thought being a librarian was a real job. Mark and I are taking our first vacation since the honeymoon one year ago when we went to Grand Island to see the crane migration, a trip partially paid for by a fellowship Mark received from the ornithology department at UNL. I've been planning this vacation for months, gathering brochures on Mount Rushmore and the Badlands, spending hours online looking up facts on bison. His mother called the day before we were scheduled to leave and asked if we wouldn't mind taking Palma along, dropping her off at Mark's grandmother's, and picking her up on the way home.

"It would only be an hour or two out of the way," she said. "What's an hour?"

When Mark is done with his cigarette we stop to switch drivers at a rest stop outside of Belle Fourche, and when I come out of the bathroom I find Mark standing by the door.

"Something's happened, Nellie," he says. "Something bad."

I imagine a problem with the radiator or some kind of valve. "Can you fix it?"

Mark grimaces and folds his hands into his shorts pockets. "I don't think so."

Palma must have died somewhere between Box Elder and Spearfish, South Dakota. We last stopped at Wall Drug, the tourist trap famed by hundreds of miles of billboards, and stood by the tacky, oversized dinosaur at the Conoco station to have our picture taken by the attendant. Palma seemed fine—complaining about the way the tourists smelled, the offensive reminders of the Native American statues, as if any of that business had been her fault—but it's obvious now she wasn't.

Mark takes control and calls his grandma, Arthula, but doesn't get an answer. She and Orvil just installed the phone and haven't gotten an answering machine yet; voice mail isn't available in their county. He tries calling his mother but gets the machine and figures it's too much to leave in a sixty-second message.

"We're only twenty minutes out of Belle Fourche," Mark says, spitting a fingernail onto the gravel. He puts his index finger back in his mouth, a nervous habit I found endearing when we were dating.

"What are you suggesting?" I say. "Are you suggesting we just keep driving with your aunt in the car, with your great aunt's body?" Neither one of us is fond of the woman—my only experience being today and at our wedding when she'd told me my brother Steve looked cross-eyed and asked if he was part Chinese—but to drive around with her corpse in the backseat seems a bit callous, possibly illegal.

"Jesus, Nellie, you make it sound like we'd be joyriding. I'm just thinking we can bring her to a hospital in town rather than waiting for an ambulance."

"It's a little late for that."

Mark gnaws a hangnail on his pinkie. "Well I don't think they just let you bury your own dead; we're going to have to call some authority."

Mark goes back into the rest area to use the phone, and I stand guard by the body. It's late afternoon, I'd guess after six, but there is nothing but sunshine and heat, miles and miles of gray, withering highway ahead. He comes back a moment later and tells me the police will be by within the hour.

"An hour?" I peer in the car expecting Palma to look ashy already, death having taken custody of the body. She looks much the same as she has all day: a pinched expression on her face, her hands wrapped possessively around her leather travel bag. A streak of dirt on the window makes her look as if she has been smudged.

"Do you want a soda?" Mark holds out a handful of shiny quarters I had prepared for the trip, not knowing if they charged toll in South Dakota.

"Diet Coke," I say, and Mark trots back inside.

He opens the door. "Nellie," he shouts. "They've got A/C."

I follow him inside, the cool air encasing me as I open my pop. We both stand by the doors of the rest stop, staring out at the Celica. We are quiet, apprehensive, as we wait for the police, and I tell myself it's a moment for prayer, a stillness created out of respect, although this isn't entirely true. Mark adjusts the collar on his shirt then fidgets with the built-in belt on his khaki shorts. "I'll be right back," he says and heads to the restroom. When the door shuts I let loose my breath, unaware until that moment I'd been holding it.

The ambulance arrives forty minutes later and out steps a boy barely old enough to drive, a towhead with acne and gangly limbs. He walks toward the tourist center then stops and jogs back to the ambulance, puts his hands against his eyes, and peers in the window before checking his pocket and pulling out the keys. Once in the building, I realize he is older than he first appeared, his blond hair thinning in the back when he takes off his cap, the pockmarked scars on his cheeks deepened into grooves with time.

"I'm sorry about this," he says, and I assume he is talking about Palma's death, but he motions to the truck outside, and I see it's a detox truck, not an ambulance. "We had a highway accident out on 58 and all emergency vehicles in the county were called that way." He puts his hat back on and quickly takes it off, fingering the brim. "Fourteen cars, eight casualties so far." It hadn't occurred to me fourteen cars might be driving in South Dakota; all we'd encountered were stretches of empty roads dotted with small towns. I think of Palma, stiffening in the backseat, and the crunched up cars out on Highway 58. No matter how severe your tragedy, someone's is always worse.

"I'm not even supposed to be in today," the officer says. "But they called me at the softball field and told me what had happened." He looks at Mark and then at me. "My partner's at the accident, I'm here alone." The officer glances again at the car and puts his hat back on, and I realize one of us is going to have to help with Palma.

"Well, let's get to work," Mark says.

The policeman vigorously shakes his head, clearly in a situation he doesn't want to be in. "I can take her feet," he says.

He opens the back door of the truck and then the back door of the Celica, and I turn back inside to the comfort of the air.

On the drive to Arthula and Orvil's Mark tells me about the cabin, as if he hadn't just transported a relative's body like a sack of feed, glossing over anything he wouldn't want to discuss. Arthula and Orvil purchased the land fifteen years ago when Orvil retired from farming and built the house over the last few summers. It is hidden off a dirt road that was destroyed every time it rained more than three inches in a week, leaving them stranded. As we pull up I see a one-story shingled cabin the size of a three-car garage, the yard large and neat, a thin row of pansies lining the house, oak trees shading every side. "The boonies if I've ever seen them," Mark says.

Orvil lumbers around the corner from the back shed with a ball of twine bigger than a basketball in his hand. When we get out of the car he sets the twine on the porch and grabs Mark by the shoulders, pulling him in for a hug. "Damn glad you could make it, Markie," he says and ruffles his hair. Mark slaps him on the back and holds on a moment longer than he normally does, perhaps to steady Orvil for the blow. Orvil releases him and steps toward me. "And how's the prettiest Cornhusker?" he asks, putting an arm around my shoulders. Orvil also grew up in Nebraska and still follows the football team religiously, perhaps pathologically.

"I'm fine, Orvil. It's great to see you." And it is. There is something steady about the large, ruddy man that seems inherent in Mark's family, that sense of largeness leading to a feeling of safety and protection.

He leans over and looks in the car. "Where's the battle-ax?" he asks. "Wasn't that the hook to get you kids up here?" We had originally planned on bypassing the visit with Orvil and Arthula in order to get another day at Sturgis. I knew Mark's mother had most likely written to them two weeks earlier to let them know the date we would be dropping her off, although she'd only asked us the night before.

Mark puts a hand on Orvil's arm. "There was a problem on the way," he says.

"What? Did the old bat die?"

Mark stifles a nervous giggle. "Yeah."

Orvil throws back his head and laughs. "Better with you than me. I'm not even strong enough to lift the body anymore. A hundred pounds of meanness is too much for me." Mark stands on looking increasingly uncomfortable, eyes shifting as if he's contemplating making a break for it.

"The police came and took her away outside of Belle Fourche," I tell Orvil; the detail about the detox truck seems too sordid to tell, too close to home. "We couldn't get a hold of you to see what you'd want us to do with the body."

Orvil stops laughing. "You're serious? You mean she's really dead?" Walking to the globe-size wad on the porch, he pulls a piece of twine out of his pocket then ties it to a loose end. "My God, I figured you were joking."

Arthula brings a tray of iced teas into the living room and sets it on the stump used as a coffee table, the edges and top cut and sanded to expose rings of age. Most of the furniture Orvil has made from hand in the shed out back, including the rocker Arthula eases into. She has a Kleenex tucked into a rubber band around her wrist, her arms solid but covered in the skin and fat of old age.

Mark is next to me on the loveseat, holding my hand in his lap. "I'm sure she was a nice woman," I say. "I'm sorry I didn't get to know her better."

Arthula laughs, her arms shaking in the sleeveless tank top with an airbrushed picture of a waterfall on the front. "You must not have gotten to know her at all," she says. "Palma sure wasn't nice, but she was my sister, and based on the laws of relativity, I loved her."

Orvil comes in from the kitchen with a decanter of brandy and three glasses decorated with dancing Smurfs and the logo for McDonald's. "I got this bottle after the Second World War," he says. "I've been saving it for an occasion."

Arthula looks at the decanter then up at Orvil. "You were never in the war," she says.

He sets down the glasses. "No, but I was alive for it, that's got to count for something." Mark squeezes my hand. I know from his mother that Orvil hasn't had a drink in over three years, since the police brought him home from Duggan's with a broken nose and a toe missing. The toe was never found—Orvil too drunk to remember how or where he'd lost it—but presumably it was bitten off by the man he was fighting, or a stray animal in the parking lot, and swallowed whole. I wonder if the man who arrested him was the same towheaded policeman who took away Palma, although I doubt he was out of high school three years ago. Orvil passes the glasses with two fingers worth in the bottom. "I thought you and the kiddies would like a shot to calm you down."

Mark nods his thanks and hands the first glass to me. I take a tentative sip and set the glass on the stump; Arthula hands me a coaster from a plastic bag by the rocker. "Palma tried," she says.

Orvil sits in the other rocker next to Arthula. The chairs are identical except for the backboard of Orvil's where there is a large gouge running from the top to halfway down the back—an incident with the chainsaw.

"Tried what?" I ask.

Arthula sets her brandy down, ignoring my question. "She was bitter and mean, I don't question that, but people seem to have forgotten she was young once. She was married for seventy-two days back in the early thirties. Lost her husband to a drunk driver during the days of Prohibition." She scrubs her fingernails with the Kleenex under the rubber band. "No one remembers that."

"Seventy-two days?" I can't imagine anyone wanting to marry the woman who'd peed near Kadoka without even the decency to hide in the ditch.

"It was a mercy killing," Orvil says. "That man was spared."

Arthula unbinds and throws the Kleenex at him. "You were a mean drunk," she says, "and now you're just mean."

I clear my throat. "How'd she meet him?" It makes me uncomfortable watching them argue. It seems different out here on this gravel road off nowhere, as if it can't be defined by region just how to act or behave. After two years of marriage, Mark and I still fight quietly, tentatively, as if frightened the neighbors will hear although we're in a rented duplex with a garage in between.

Orvil puts his hand on Arthula's, and she rolls her eyes, although I think she squeezes his back. Mark puts his arm around the back of the loveseat and cuddles my head to his shoulder. I have to scrunch my back; although his legs are long he is short-chested, and I've always felt we fit short of perfectly.

"We're going to need to make arrangements," Mark says. "We need to call Mom."

"My God, I'm not calling Caroline," Arthula says. "I can't bear it. You call her, she's your mother."

Mark's fingers tense on my hand. "She's your daughter."

"Christ's sake," Orvil says. "I'll call her. Where's the phone?" He pushes the handset locator button on the phone cradle, and a beep sounds from the bedroom where the cordless is. It's the one piece of high-tech in the cabin, a gift from Mark's mom last Christmas when she insisted they install the line. Orvil follows the beeps to the other room. "Mark, what's your mom's number?" he yells.

"Good God," Arthula says, "don't let Orvil call her. He's got the tact of an elephant."

Mark goes into the bedroom and moments later his voice comes out in soothing waves, like something piped through the halls of an accounting firm or Macy's. "Passed on" is how he puts it, and I can tell by his reaction that his mother isn't crying; they are discussing what to do with the body as calmly as where to put a toaster. Mark and his mother are pragmatic and seeing Arthula and Orvil in their seventies—a shower in the backyard, forty miles from a hospital—I wonder if it isn't a reaction, some kind of defense against the hapless luck of the generation before. I remember Mark's mother telling me that as a child Arthula left her at a street fair to see what she'd do, "to see if I could keep my wits about me," she said. "For God's sake, I was four. I didn't have any wits." She found out later Arthula had been behind her by no more than a quarter of a block, safely trailing her home.

Mark comes out of the bedroom with the phone in his hand. "We've got it settled. Mom's going to call the funeral home and make the arrangements, and we'll have this cleared up tonight. I'll call back the police and see about transportation for Palma." He says this smugly, as if he's the only responsible adult here capable of handling a funeral. "This whole thing's going to sail smoothly."

"You make it sound like she's taking a cruise," Arthula says. "That would be Palma's luck, to get a cruise in before she's gone."

"A cruise for *really* retired seniors," Orvil snorts. "Think the boat hands would know the difference?"

"Like *Love Boat*," I add. "*The Postmortem Princess*," and Orvil barks out a laugh.

Mark sits down on the loveseat next to me. "It's not a cruise."

"Shuffleboard at six!" Orvil yells.

The phone rings in Mark's lap, and he jumps, scowling at the rest of us. I feel close to Arthula and Orvil and don't want to stop and think about our indelicate, silly jokes or Palma laid out in a morgue in Belle Fourche.

Mark answers the phone. "Hello?" He sits for a moment. "Well that's a problem, then," he says and gets up and walks back into the bedroom.

The three of us sit and listen to Mark. I know his mother must be calling with a glitch in the plan. I can hear it in the slow way he enunciates his words, pausing for small sips of breath like the time I ran over the gnomes in the neighbor's yard. "Well, what do you mean they took the plot?" he says.

Orvil looks at the brandy decanter on the floor and says softly, "They'd save a fortune on entertainment. Just get some guy in a bad tuxedo telling necrophilia jokes. He'd be the hit of the cruise."

"You're a lovely crowd," I whisper, "but what a bunch of stiffs!"

Orvil heaves himself out of the rocker and sits in Mark's place. "You're a catch, you know that, Nellie?" He points to the bedroom. "Speaking of stiffs, what're you doing with that guy? You and me should steal away tonight."

"Good God," Arthula says. "She'd kill you."

Mark comes back looking hangdogged and tired. "The plot's gone," he says. "We don't have a plot."

"What plot?" Arthula asks.

"For Palma. Dad defaulted on the payments, and Wyuka Cemetery gave it to some old guy who's already using it." Mark's father died eight years ago, run over by a train in downtown Lincoln. He tried to jump the tracks on a bet from a buddy and missed by a crucial eight inches. Now Paddy is settled in Wyuka, and Caroline is married to a sensible man, Kerry, who wouldn't consider crossing a track without first checking for vibrations, or at the least, looking both ways. Mark picks up his Smurfs glass. "We don't have a place to put Palma."

Orvil settles his arm around my shoulder. "We've never had a place to put Palma."

Arthula picks another coaster out of the bag and wings it at Orvil's head, smacking him in the chest. "This is my sister we're talking about, Orv. Not some dead possum." He looks chagrined, as if he knows he's taken the joke too far, but doesn't apologize.

"Where's her husband buried?" I ask.

Arthula perks up—"Now that's an idea"—but immediately she deflates. "It's some unmarked grave in Virginia. I don't even know the town." She sips her brandy. "She would have liked that, though. It's a nice thought, Nellie."

"She's coming out tomorrow," Mark says.

"Who?" Arthula asks, her glass splashing a bit, an alarmed look on her face.

"Mom. Your daughter."

"She's coming here?" Arthula looks around the cabin, and my eyes follow hers: exposed wood walls, the Smurf glasses, a welcome mat in the shape of a pig the only carpet. Caroline has an original Keith Jacobshagen painting in her foyer and at least five sets of silverware that I'm aware of. "Where's she going to sleep?"

"I saw an exit sign for a Super 8," I say, although even this would be a stretch for Caroline. Mark and I made reservations for this very night at a Holiday Inn in Spearfish. I would have rather camped, made love in a tent, but he seemed set on having me comfortable. I remember the green swirled bedspread and matching curtains, the individually wrapped soaps as boasted in the brochure, and am glad, suddenly, we are stuck in this cabin. As if left to the forces of nature, we'll be forced to see what will survive.

When the chicken curry and chocolate ice cream are gone, Arthula brings us pillowcases stuffed with towels and an air mattress from the shed out back. "It's all we've got for you kids," she says. "We'd give you the bed, but we're just too damn old."

"This is nice," Mark says. "It'll be like we're in college again."

Arthula sets the makeshift pillows on the loveseat. "You are in college."

Mark sighs. "It's a Ph.D. program, Grandma. Hardly college."

Arthula leans over and hugs me roughly to her chest, which is looming and loose under the tank top. "You kids sleep well," she says and then gets up with a grunt and shuts the bedroom door on her and Orvil.

Mark goes into the kitchen and comes back with our glasses a quarter full of brandy. He hands me one and sits next to me on the loveseat, moving the pillows to the floor. "I wish we had a TV," he says. Sometimes when we watch television together it makes me nervous—an apprehension that something on the show will spark a memory in our relationship or something from our past will become known. When we watched *Diner* together I cringed, sure that Mark would recognize us in the moment when Daniel Stern tells Mickey Rourke he proposed so he and his girlfriend would have something to talk about. I am sure in moments like these that Mark will turn to me, his mouth formed in a small "oh," and realize that's what we did.

He twines his hand in my hair, and I remember Orvil walking out to the car with his big ball of string. "It's nice, though," he says, "not having the TV as a distraction. It's more time for us just to talk." We both take sips and look around the room. It would be silly to ask each other about our day.

This vacation is the first break we've gotten with each other since right after the wedding, and the weeks beforehand have been filled with talks of the trip, travel arrangements, maps being put in the glove box. I realize suddenly a part of me was relieved when Caroline asked us to take Palma. Even after we dropped her off at Arthula and Orvil's, I assumed she would provide conversation, outraged chitchat about her and her obtrusive ways. "It's great, Mark," I say, "really nice to be alone," and I crink my neck to place it on his shoulder. On our honeymoon we stood wrapped in one sheet at the window of the bed-and-breakfast, the powerful wings of the birds overhead, a solitary gray V set in directed motion. Ahead of us still was the year of negotiations neither of us was anticipating: who pees in front of whom, who fights the nastiest, and who, out of the two of us, would dare say it wasn't what we imagined? I hadn't anticipated marriage could be so hard, two people who love each other thrown in a house with a garage door opener and a key to adulthood. I look over at the rockers where Arthula and Orvil had been sitting earlier and try to imagine one quiet, awkward moment between them. One moment in their fifty-year marriage where there wasn't something to say, or yell, or even a coaster to pick up and throw.

Caroline arrives and kisses me lightly on the cheek, leaving the clinging smell of face powder near my shoulder; we have formed more of an understanding than a relationship since Mark and I met two years ago. Kerry pulls the bags from the Explorer, puts them on the porch, and rests his hand on my back. "I'm sorry about this loss," he says, and I know it is the line he will repeat like a mournful, honest recording as the weekend progresses. When Mark first brought me home, Kerry would say, "So you're Nellie," whenever there was silence and look at me nodding his head, while Caroline addressed me in third person. "Would Nellie like some more peas? Would Nellie like to listen to the radio?" After two years of this kind of talk, I realize it is her way of keeping Mark a child and safe through association. She often does it to him too, asking if Mark would like a new winter coat or if Mark would consider, just this once, telling his mother he loves her. I've heard him say it—*Mom, I love you*—but she is leery, looking at him out of the corner of her eye as if assessing his motives. I told him he should write it on a three-by-five index card and have it laminated so Caroline can keep it in her wallet, pulling it out randomly in line at Dillard's or at her desk at work, to reassure herself it's true, which it is.

Arthula runs out of the cabin in a fresh tank top, the first one splashed with tomato juice and dirt. She spent most of the day pruning pansies, planting a fresh row of azaleas around an oak out front. She hugs Caroline to her bosom and says, "I'm glad to see you. I'm glad you're here." Arthula runs a hand over her hair and looks around the yard. "We've got supper started. I know you like to eat around seven."

Caroline smiles tightly. "Isn't that nice of Mom?" She takes her purse off her arm and holds it protectively against her chest before slinging it again over her shoulder. "You shouldn't go to any trouble on our account."

"It's no trouble," Arthula says. She holds out her hand as if to take Caroline's purse then drops it empty to her side. "You're my daughter. I can cook a little something early, no trouble."

"Kerry can't have dairy," Caroline says.

"It's true," Kerry adds and blows out his cheeks, his hands expanding away from his head.

"No dairy," Arthula says, shaking her head vigorously. I've never seen her so tentative, so eager to please. I wonder how it could have gone so long unnoticed, her hesitancy around her own child, and I remember at our wedding Arthula had sat nervously at the "immediate family" table, eating dinner mints as if they were peanuts, retiring to bed early with an upset stomach. Orvil had stormed the stage and led the crowd through a drunken toast, the gist of which was, "love isn't enough, here's to hoping the sex is good." He comes around the corner now with his ball of twine tucked up the front of his shirt. "Doctor," he says to Kerry, "I've got this unexplainable growth," and then drops the twine on the ground. We watch it in uncomfortable silence as a loose string unravels from the side.

In the kitchen Arthula opens a can of tuna. "We're going to have to start from scratch. I forgot about the dairy." She points with her elbow to the celery batch brought in from the garden. "Cut those real small. Caroline can't stand big bites. Ever since she was a child, she's had a fear of choking." She drains the tuna over a bowl and sets the juice on the back porch for stray cats. I wonder if, like her fear of crowds, Caroline's fear of choking is somehow related to her childhood.

I wash the celery and begin cutting, Arthula behind me wringing a towel. "Smaller," she says. "Like this," and takes the knife from my hand. In short, quick snaps she dices the celery. At the end of a stalk she stops, knife suspended. "I've failed my daughter," she says.

I peer over her shoulder. "It looks fine."

Arthula turns toward me as if startled I am there. "She doesn't even like me." She sets down the knife and puts her hands on my shoulders. "No one likes me but that nincompoop Orvil."

For the first time I imagine having a child: her hiding in the living room, a grown adult with a lactose intolerant second husband and a bitterness I'd never anticipated. "Mark and I like you."

The swinging door opens, and Caroline comes into the kitchen. "Does anyone need some help?" she asks.

Arthula turns toward her. "I forgot about the sour cream. I absolutely forgot."

Caroline shrugs and sits down at the table. "It's a psychosomatic condition. Kerry had a bad milkshake in the cafeteria at the hospital, and it's been soy products ever since."

"But I should have remembered," Arthula says, not allowing herself a reprieve.

"You should have, that's true, but it's not the end of the world." Caroline stands up, picks the knife off the counter, and walks over to the celery. She nods her head and sets down the knife, returning to the living room.

On Sunday Kerry insists on having a wake for Palma, even though we don't have the body. "That's a good idea," Orvil says. "I'll fire up the Weber. We'll make it a nice send-off."

Kerry looks around the room, unsure how to proceed. "They usually don't have hamburgers at a wake," he says.

"We had nothing but a cheese log and some crackers at Aunt Gertie's," Arthula says. "Palma should feel blessed." She turns to me. "Even the wine was terrible." Kerry seems content with the word "blessed," and with that Orvil sets off to look for the flame flicker.

Mark comes up behind me and rubs my shoulders, and I lean back slightly into the weight of his body. "Let's get a cigarette," he whispers in my ear. We both gave up smoking during the engagement—a hasty, bad decision made when we were concentrating too seriously on "till death do us part." Now smoking is a guilty pleasure left over from our early adulthood, a small sign that allows us to believe we could still stay out until 2:00 a.m. on a Tuesday, if there were just somewhere to go and we weren't already so tired so early in the week.

We meet behind the shed and Mark pulls the pack of Camel Lights from his pocket, along with a lighter that advertises FREE ICE WATER! at Wall Drug. He has never told his mother he smokes, and he keeps the cigarettes buried under maps and extra napkins in the glove box even when we are home. He lights two and hands one to me, coughing a bit. "It's not the vacation we expected."

According to the itinerary I had planned we were supposed to dine at a romantic restaurant in Deadwood, possibly at the casino owned by Kevin Costner. He bought it on a whim after filming *Dances With Wolves*, and although I want to believe he fell in love with the land, he is rarely in South Dakota, and it is most likely a tax break. "We can always go again next year," I say.

"As old as everyone is, I'm afraid to try it again. Who knows what could happen." He exhales, his mouth buried near his armpit, a trick he learned at thirteen and has believed ever since: the last place your parents will check for the smell of smoke.

"We could go to the Ozarks, maybe Hawaii."

Mark nods his head. "They've got the Corvus Hawaiiensis there. I'd love to see them." He stubs out his cigarette with his heel then picks up the butt and puts it in his pocket. "Commonly known as the Hawaiian crow, they're near extinct."

"A crow can become extinct?" It seems impossible when I look up and see dozens nesting in the trees.

"Only twenty-nine left." He crouches at the knees and lets out with a "*Ha-wah!*" that sounds like a honk then stands back up. "That's the call for the Nene, the Hawaiian goose. It's actually very similar to the Canadian's." He buries the cigarette pack deep in his pocket then untucks his shirt, averting his eyes. "I'd love to take you there."

I look at him, a shy grin creeping onto his face. "I'd like that, Mark. I'd like that a lot." He bends at the knees again, and I'm sure he's going to repeat the honk, but he merely picks up my cigarette butt and puts it in his pocket.

As I pour Frito-Lays in a bowl, Kerry comes up to me looking lost. Not so much like a puppy as something rare and slender, like an antelope or a gazelle. He is delicate like a woman, all thin wrists and neck cords whispering out of the cuffs and collar of his shirt, the only one even close to appropriately dressed in a button-down oxford and a pair of Dockers. "Where's the body?" he whispers, his hands folded like a church in front of him.

"She's in Belle Fourche," I tell him softly. "The police took her to the morgue." If it was Orvil I'd tell him she was put up at the You Don't Check Out Motel and is playing blackjack with Elvis and a former vice president. But it's not, it's Kerry, and he shakes his head solemnly and tells me, "Life's a funny thing." I know he isn't sure how to behave, having expected a funeral and gotten a barbecue, and if I were to riffle through his Bergdorf suitcase, buried at the bottom I would find a tie I'm sure he put on this morning, and only after much thought and resignation, removed when he saw Orvil and Arthula in their matching Niagara Falls tank tops. I think it's nice for Palma to have some form of respect at her funeral-slash-barbecue and am glad Kerry is here to provide it. I want to go in the house and put on his tie, but it would look silly and disrespectful next to my own tank top. Mark could pull it off with his collared golf shirt, if you ignored the clashing Bermuda shorts he had planned to wear at Mount Rushmore.

Orvil is over by the Weber making patties and shouts out, "Arthie, one or two?"

Arthula holds up her middle finger. "You know I'm on a diet." She turns to me and Kerry. "I've got high cholesterol," she says. "The way Orvil eats, it's a miracle he's not dead."

Orvil looks up, the spatula dangling from his hand. "Nell—one or two?"

"Two, Orvil," I say. I've been starving since we'd gotten here, convinced it is the open air, the freshness invading my blood.

"Hearty eater," he says. "I like that. Girls these days can barely lift a box of Kleenex."

Arthula puts the relish and Heinz 57 sauce on the picnic table. "You two are perfect for each other," I tell her and mean it as a compliment.

She sets down the napkins. "Have you met the man I'm married to? Have you even seen him?" Arthula points across the yard to Orvil who is balancing a plate of raw hamburger patties on one finger. "A woman can put up with anything if she wants to."

"Nell," Orvil barks. "How do you want this—bloody or black?"

"He does have a way with words," Arthula says.

"Medium black," I yell.

"And how 'bout Mark?"

"Bloody." I look over and see Caroline's mouth open to tell the answer, but she acquiesces, realizing that's my job now, to be able to define Mark by the way he eats his hamburger. After we'd been dating six months and only six months away from the altar, I could tell anyone Mark's favorite movie, middle name, most traumatic childhood experience, and I took this as a sign I knew him. When my girlfriend called planning a dinner party, I told her not to put walnuts in the Waldorf salad, Mark was allergic. The questions that were asked I could answer, but I admit now I have no idea what he is thinking when he sits reading the paper, toast halfway to his gaping mouth at the breakfast table Sunday mornings. And it's a mystery to me why he blushes and won't discuss sex out of bed, even when it is only the two of us, alone in the house, no one around for what seems like miles.

I walk over to Orvil who is now toasting the buns, Mark's rare patty on a withering paper plate to the side. Kerry joins us. "This is nice," he says, looking around the yard. "I'm glad we could do this for Palma, just get together as a family."

"She would have hated this," Orvil bellows. "If she'd been alive she would have despised having to talk to us. She hadn't been to a family reunion in thirty years." He takes a drink of 7-Up. "Except that it was out of everyone's way and a pain in the ass for travel, that she would have liked."

"Why was she coming to visit then?" I ask. It seems an obvious and crucial question to understanding Palma, and I'm curious although it's not a task I'm ready to undertake.

"Couldn't tell you," Orvil says. "She never really took a shine to me, hard as that is to believe."

I remember Arthula in the kitchen, the way she wielded the knife, tiny specks of celery falling in the bowl, just the way Caroline prefers them. I want to tell Orvil he's right, not everyone likes him, that it's a fine line between honesty and cruelty, and sometimes it's the little lies and gestures that are important. Telling someone you can't imagine a nicer gift than the *Peterson Field Guide to Birds* or that it's OK when they forget to tell you what money they've taken from a joint account so you overdraw on a seven-dollar check at Subway. Even that the way they chew their nails and spit them audaciously on the carpet can be seen as a quality worth holding on to.

I want to think Palma was traveling to South Dakota on a quest, to apologize to her family and take them in her shabby arms and tell them how much she loved them. I doubt this is the case, but it's these little lies, the ones we can tell ourselves when we're not looking, that sometimes make the most sense.

Kerry comes out of the cabin carrying a heavy, leather book, unmistakably a Bible. He clears his throat. "I want to read something," he says. "It's only appropriate."

"If it's not the Cubs score," Orvil says, "I don't want to hear it." Arthula slaps him on the back of the head, and he sits on a tree stump, momentarily stunned. A part of me wants to snicker, but as Kerry reads—the rest of us supine from the midday heat and Arthula's potato salad—his words come over me, like something cool, a linen sheet half dried in the shade. This talk of God is not quite right after a day of horseshoes with not a religious one in the bunch, but it's a beautiful gesture—calming—and I close my eyes and listen.

As Kerry pauses to turn the page, Orvil guffaws. "Who *wrote* this?" he says, and the spell is broken.

It is silent for a moment, Kerry's hand suspended, and then Mark's voice: "For fuck's sake, Orvil. It's the Bible; show a little respect." I turn to him, and it seems he has spoken for the first time in years. He is the last person I expect to defend Kerry—it almost being a family ritual to watch him twist in the wind—but we find our families where we can.

I want to rush to him, throw my arms around his neck, and tell him how much I love him. "Will you just let Dad finish?" he says.

The word "Dad" causes another skip in Kerry's actions, but he continues, fumbling for just a moment to find his place and then carries on with the passage, his voice becoming stronger. Orvil sits grumbling on the tree stump, chastised, but I know this is correct, to give Palma some form of send-off. I think about her husband in the unmarked grave in Virginia and imagine if he were alive how he would weep and carry on.

When Kerry is finished, he closes the book and holds it in front of him, fingers dangling as he clasps it to his chest. Caroline stands up and rests her head against his shoulder. When she raises it a moment later there is a faint smudge of face powder left against his oxford.

Arthula leans toward me. "Caroline was lucky to land that one," she says. "He's a dope, but he's earnest, and at some level you need to respect that."

Mark puts his arm around me, and we both look out across the yard—the destitute flatness of the land, with the promise of the Black Hills only an hour away. I can see how Kevin Costner fell for it. How even someone hardened by Hollywood could believe, at least for a moment, that this is what his life was meant for.

After dinner I stop in the living room, relieved to have a moment away from the ruckus—from Arthula's declarations and Kerry's earnestness and the pragmatism surrounding Caroline like a hive of gnats. I sit in a rocker in the darkening cabin and enjoy the sound of the birds outside, raised above the voices and Orvil's bad jokes. I remember the trip Mark and I took to Grand Island to see the cranes and imagine they are the birds I hear, out there now, not thinking for one moment about the long trip south coming in a few more months.

Mark comes inside, and I sit still in the rocker and watch his face slowly adjust to the dimming light. He sees me and sits down with a grunt in Orvil's chair. "They're something, aren't they?"

I am confused for a moment into thinking he also is remembering the cranes, the wings peddling into fall air, the loud sound above us, like standing under a quilt being shaken out. "You're not your family," I say, "but I can see them."

He smiles. "I hope you mean that physically, like around the eyes." Yes, I think, and ears and hips and every cell in your body, reincarnated generations into my one imperfect person.

"Maybe we can stay in here," he whispers. "Maybe they'll forget about us."

"It's too much to hope," I tell him, knowing in a moment Orvil will be calling for the prettiest girl in Nebraska.

Burn

The cabin on Lake Superior is dark. Amanda feels Nick tugging hard on her hand and hears the incessant whine of mosquitoes, like a whirling, thick fan in her ear. She stares at the cabin a moment before giving Nick a forceful tug back. He's spent the last two hours in the car flicking her arm and neck, pinching her leg, once even licking the back of her hand.

"You're not very nice," she says to him.

"No," he agrees. Nick frees his hand and wipes his palm under his nose, his index finger glistening with wetness. He is six years old and tall for his age, wiry in a quick, adultlike way. He looks much like his father—thin hands, long fingers, even his stomach bulges out like a tiny, middle-aged belly. She glances at Tom, trailing behind with the luggage.

"Need some help?" she asks, but Nick jerks on her hand.

"I'm your job," he says. "Me."

Although this is her first weekend working as a nanny, the Moores hired her two months ago, a week before the other child and Tom's wife, Connie, died. Amanda hadn't known how to ask if this meant she was still employed for the summer or if she would still be paid the salary, or perhaps half, at one child less. Tom called her a week earlier, a little slurry, and told her to meet him at their home in St. Paul at seven o'clock this Friday. "We're going on a camping trip," he said. "One of the ten thousand lakes. Doesn't that sound like fun?"

Tom pulls the keys from his pocket with a rattle, and they glow with a glimpse from the moon. "We'll need to clean out the rooms," he says. "But we can wait until morning."

"A little dust and mold won't kill us," Amanda says and wants to pinch herself at this mention of death. "I mean, no one dies from *that*." She had read in the papers that Connie and the other child, Kristin, died in a train crash. Before recognizing the names, her first thought was, Who still rides the train?

"I suppose not," Tom says, reaching again for the screen door as it swings quickly behind him and shuts with the sound of a gunshot. He pulls a wooden match from his pocket and strikes it against the wall with a loud hiss, the fire flaming in front of him hot and bright before it diminishes. He snaps his fingers, dropping the match on the damp ground. "Asthmatics," he says.

"Excuse me?" Amanda says. Nick steps on the tiny flame, extinguishing the match.

"Asthmatics," Tom repeats. "It could kill asthmatics, the mold and dust."

Amanda follows them into the cabin where the electricity is off. "It was Connie's job," Tom explains. "I'll call in the morning and get it switched on." He fumbles through a drawer in the kitchen for a flashlight and candles, lighting them precariously on every counter and table. Even in the dim light, Amanda can tell the cabin is expensive: hardwood floors more fitting to a ballroom than a lake cabin, an overstuffed sofa in denim although she can't imagine Tom ever wearing jeans. Even dressed for the weekend, it's ironed khakis with a suit coat. There's a fireplace as big as a bank safe against the north wall, a mantle above it with a picture of Tom and Connie, and one of the children, but none of them all together.

Tom takes her down the hall. "You can stay in Kristin's room," he says and sets down her ratty overnight bag and comes back with a few candles and matches. Even at the cabin, the children have separate rooms; the house is bigger than Amanda's parents'.

She can't tell if it's because she knows that the child is dead or the room itself is eerie, but she's afraid to touch anything. She lights the candles. The double bed is high with a pink-and-white quilt, matching curtains unmoving against the windows. There is a stuffed puppy on the pillows that looks like it's been mauled, half the fur matted against one side with dirt, one eye gouged out, but other than this, the room is serene, as if it were decorated for the image of a girl, not an actual child. An antique mirror and brush set lie on the dresser, a doily under the useless lamp, a wallpaper border of delicate pink roses above the chair rail. Amanda changes into her pajamas—boxers and a T-shirt; why hadn't she thought to bring a robe?—and steps on the stool to climb in the bed. She feels like she's ten feet off the ground and leans over to blow out the candles, the smell of smoke heavy in the dark. Three months ago, Luke—an anthropology professor at U of M who had studied the Maoris of New Zealand on three expeditions and with whom she had been sleeping—ended their affair. He had said he had to honor their commitment—not his and Amanda's, that flimsy thing, useless as a wet paper plate—but his and his wife's. Renae was pregnant, a month and a half along, and what was he to do, abandon her? "I made a commitment," he said to Amanda. "What kind of man would I be if I turned my back on that?"

Later that night on the phone with her mother, her mom said, "The type that has an affair, that's who." But Amanda cried for weeks, almost a month straight of tears, certain the cheating wasn't what mattered, it was that he was good enough to give her up for the love of an unborn child. Had she really been that gullible? It's amazing to her now that she'd actually felt *bad* for him and then bad for the wife—that she was married to a man who loved someone else—and finally bad for herself with the realization that he hadn't really loved her at all. Her friend Susie had sat for the Moores the summer before but was getting married, and did Amanda, like, want the job? She said yes, thankful it would take her out of Minneapolis if only over to St. Paul, Luke unable to find her.

She sniffs again, the smell of smoke still strong, and gets out of bed to open the window and light a cigarette. "Never smoke on the job," Susie had told her, "Or belch," but something tells her Tom won't notice.

Amanda sleeps fitfully, waking every hour or so to the sound of the screen door slapping against the wood frame, Nick knocking on her door, some bestial sound from outdoors like the howl of coyotes. When she rises at seven and heads to the kitchen not wanting to look slothful her first full day on the job, Tom is already up, slouching outside at the grill, cooking eggs in a pan.

"Scrambled all right?" he asks through the screen door. He looks worse for wear in the morning, pouches under his eyes, a too-big sweatshirt out of context on his skinny chest, the lines of his clavicle bone peering through the stretched-out collar. She remembers when she went for the interview he wore one of those innocuous suits that made him look exactly like everyone else, and she hadn't been able to remember a feature of what he looked like, only dull brown hair, a dull face and body. Connie, in contrast, wore color—turquoise and black, accessorized with a smart scarf and bracelet. Neither looked like they'd ever touched a child.

"I don't eat eggs very often," she says and sits at the breakfast bar, a rough slab of wood nailed to a smaller table that is too centered to have the rustic look they'd been going for.

"Would you rather have cereal?" he asks, the spatula hovering above the pan.

"No, I like eggs," she says and nods to show she really means it, although of course she doesn't. "I just don't make them very often. Eggs are great."

Nick comes into the kitchen looking innocent with slow eyelids and a passive look on his sleepy face. He stands next to Amanda's barstool, holding onto a cloth rag doll missing an arm. "Will you braid my hair today?" he asks.

Tom turns around, bits of egg flying from his spatula onto the deck. He stares at Nick, his breathing accelerated. He stares for a long moment then turns back to the eggs.

"I can't braid your hair," Amanda says. "It's not long enough."

"OK," Nick says and sits on the other stool. "What are we doing today?"

Amanda glances at Tom. *Is Nick old enough to swim?* It seems Tom could be the overprotective type, one child and a wife already buried.

Tom scoops the eggs on three plates and comes inside. "You want to go in the lake, Pal?"

Nick nods and picks up a fork and scoops the food into his mouth, Tom following suit. Amanda's never seen a grownup eat like this before, his bites quick and shovel-like with no pauses to chew, his cheeks bulging from fullness; if it were a cartoon, his arm and fork would be a blur. Nick and Tom throw down their forks at almost the same time as if it were a race, while Amanda salts before beginning with her eggs. "Get your trunks on, Pal," Tom says.

"OK, Pal," Nick replies and brings his plate to the sink.

In the empty kitchen, the silence seems more obvious. Tom shuffles his feet and clears his throat. "You like to swim, Amy?" he asks.

"Amanda," Amanda corrects. Tom looks confused for a moment. "I like to swim OK," she says. "I was a lifeguard in high school for two summers at Lake Okoboji. That's in Iowa."

"Well, you're not on duty here," Tom says. "As a nanny, obviously, but we don't expect anyone to be saving any lives."

When she interviewed for the job she stressed to Connie that she was certified in CPR, knew the Heimlich, even lied and told her she used it once at an Italian restaurant, lifting a man twice her size in the air to watch a crouton the size of a walnut fly out of his mouth. She goes to her room and puts on her suit.

Outside, the air and water are as cold as she would expect for late May, probably only fifty degrees. Nick enters the lake slowly, the tip of one foot to his knee taking a full minute until Tom comes up behind him and pushes his son down into the water, Nick popping up like a fleshy buoy, gasping from both the cold and a mouth full of dank lake water. "It's like taking off a Band-Aid," Tom says. "One quick swoop." Nick swims for a half an hour before asking his father if he can come out, his lips turning bluish in the center. The sun isn't out, and clouds have begun to gather above them, a grayish dark blue like a black eye.

"It's going to rain," Amanda says, and as if on cue, a slash of lightning flashes across the sky.

"It is," Tom says and continues staring out at the lake. After a moment he calls in his son.

Nick takes a quick bath and comes back into the living room. He's been sweet today, almost kind, and Amanda begins to think she's misjudged the rude boy who last night was probably only worn out and tired from being kept up too late, when he turns around and bites her. Not hard, more of a nip really, but enough to break the skin.

"Grrr," Tom growls at his son then begins to laugh.

"Do you have a first-aid kit?" Amanda holds out her hand, shaking it in front of herself. She shakes harder until a drop of blood pierces the surface and grows on the webby flesh between her thumb and finger.

"Oh," Tom says and waves her away. "Who wants a hot dog?"

"Me!" Nick yells and jumps up and down. "Me."

"Fritos are in the cupboard, Pal." That afternoon while Nick was napping and Amanda was reading *Self*, Tom went to Duluth for supplies. He walked into the cabin an hour later carrying two of six grocery bags from the back of the SUV filled with every junk food imaginable: Doritos, Fritos, Cheetos, peanut butter and graham crackers, Little Debbie Nutty Bars, a cake mix, although he hadn't bought milk or oil and they still had no electricity to run the oven. He'd called to have the phone connected but no other utilities. On the bottom of the last bag was a ten-pack of hot dogs and an eight-pack of buns, the closest thing to a nutritional meal.

Nick shimmies a chair across the linoleum floor, climbs up, and takes down the Fritos, opening them while still standing on the chair. "Fritos," he says. He snaps the corn chips in his tiny, thin fist and shoves them in his mouth. Amanda originally worried she'd be judged on her ability to balance a meal, that Tom would realize her expertise lay in microwaving tortillas with cheese, and she'd be out of a job.

It's pouring outside as Tom loads a plate with hot dogs from the cooler and opens the sliding door. "One or two?" he asks her. Rain scatters across the wooden deck, pelting like nickels against the windows.

She holds up the peace sign, and Nick mimics her from the chair before jumping down and following his father to the door. "Whoa, Nick," she says and lightly grabs his arm. "You need a coat."

He stares up at her blankly. "It's not that cold."

"A raincoat."

"I don't have one of those." Amanda looks at the hooks near the door; he's right, there are no raincoats, only a red and green Mexican poncho and an L. L. Bean denim oxford shirt next to a straw hat that are obviously only for decoration.

She looks around the kitchen and opens a cupboard under the sink. "We'll have to improvise." She pulls out a black plastic garbage bag and pokes a hole in the bottom for his head, two smaller holes for his arms, and slips it over him.

Nick screams under the plastic wrap, his cries muffled like a body in a bag as he flails his arms and convulses to the floor. Amanda reaches her hand in the larger hole and finds his hair then pulls the bag down, his head emerging, swollen and red from holding his breath. "I almost died," he says, tears starting in his eyes.

"No you didn't," Amanda says quickly. "You didn't almost die."

"It can happen," he says, "like that," and snaps his fingers together, the sweaty skin hardly connecting to make a noise; then he turns and runs flat into the glass door, drops once, then pushes it open with his entire body.

Tom stands over the grill with the lighter fluid, squirting it onto the already hot coals around the grilling meat. Some drops land on one of the hot dogs, which he picks up with the tongs and holds up in the rain before returning it slick and wet to the hissing grill.

That night after two cigarettes Amanda sneaks out of bed and into the cold living room to use the phone. She lifts the receiver and hears a man talking, his voice low and hoarse as if he's been crying. "You don't understand," he says. "Can't you see this? My god." She barely recognizes Tom's voice but can tell it's his by the overloud echo of listening on an extension.

Her hand hovers over the disconnect button but she doesn't press it. She knows it's wrong—her listening in to her boss's private call—but she is paralyzed, convinced if she were to hang up the click would be a giveaway she'd been listening. Should she hold the phone away? Nick comes up behind her and pinches the inside of her thigh. She jumps, the phone loosening in her hand and clamoring to the table.

"Goddamn it!" Tom yells, and she hears the voice in stereo, coming from his back bedroom and through the phone. He rushes into the living room, his hair disheveled, his sad sunken chest bare and hairless.

"It was Nick," she stutters, holding the receiver in her hand. "I came in, and he was on the phone."

"I wasn't," Nick wails, but Tom is covering ground fast, crossing the room in large, quick steps.

He wraps a hand tightly around his son's arm until his thumb overlaps with his fingers. "Don't do that again," he says, his voice low and menacing. "Don't ever do that again."

"Tom," Amanda starts, but Tom releases his son's arm and starts for his room. Nick's upper arm is covered with white indents and sharp red lines where his father's fingers pressed the flesh. Nick stands there, his flat, bony feet curling on the Indian rug.

"I'm sorry," he whispers.

Amanda sits on the couch and pulls him into her lap. His stomach is doughy but hard underneath, filled with cupcakes, Fritos, and two hot dogs. "It's not your fault," she says. "It's mine."

"I know," he says.

What kind of nanny blames the child for what she did? She was going to call Luke and Renae, just to hear the edge of panic in their voices from a phone call at 1:00 a.m. Maybe they would think it was her, the panic even higher as Luke put a hand on his wife's flat belly and reassured her once again that the affair was over. She'd loved him, my god, she had, with a passion deep and quick and unexplainable. She'd sat in his classroom for three months listening to lectures on food methods of indigenous tribes, and when he finally asked her for coffee then drinks, she'd built Luke's intelligence into integrity. He touched the inside of her wrist lightly with a finger that first night and told her he was confused, and who knows, maybe he was at the time. She'd never been with a man before, boys certainly, but never a man, and she'd assumed he would protect her. Had he not lied to her later she never would have reacted the way she did, but it made the whole relationship a sham and her a fool, and she wasn't going to let him get away with that. "Can you forgive me?" she asks Nick.

He tilts his head backward and looks at her face, his brow furrowing. She rubs his arm lightly, bends and makes kissy noises against the bruising skin. The boy giggles and wraps his thin arms around her neck. "I was supposed to be on the train with Mom and Kristin," he says. "I was supposed to die too." He stares unblinking at Amanda. "Momma," he coos like a toddler, and she tenses.

She's not used to the touch of children and is unsure what to think when his grasp loosens, and he puts a hand on her breast. Does a six-year-old know what a breast is? "You want a snack?" she says suddenly and stands up, but the boy clings to her, his arms locked once again behind her like a monkey, his legs now wrapping around her waist. "How about a snack?" But the boy burrows deeper into her neck. She grabs the box of Little Debbies from the kitchen and drops it along with Nick on his bed from a foot in the air.

She'd begun following Luke's wife two weeks after they broke up. For a fleeting second she imagined following Renae into the obstetrician's office and seeing the baby amoebalike in the gray and grainy ultrasound, the *wub wub wub* noise of the wand riding over Renae's jellied stomach as they looked at their baby. But that didn't happen. Amanda followed her to a charity auction for the Rights of Animals shelter, to Figlio's for lunch, shoe shopping at Bay Street Shoes. At the Fine Grind coffee shop in downtown St. Paul she sat close enough to Renae and a mannish-faced woman to hear the conversation, and not once was a baby mentioned.

After two weeks Amanda followed her to Mall of America then to Bloomingdales to the bath towels, a beige-y woman against bright pastels. She found a stray nametag on the counter, pinned it to her natty sweater, and approached Renae.

"May I help you?" she said. Up close Amanda always found Renae prettier than she had hoped, with delicate and pale features, the bones in her face sharp and swooping.

"Just browsing," she said and offered a slight smile. Her arms barely looked strong enough to support the purse.

"Browsing for what?"

She turned toward the wall, all those towels impeccably folded and tightly stacked. "Towels, I'd guess."

"We have a wonderful baby section." Renae turned to Amanda, a hateful, sudden look on her face. "You're pregnant," Amanda said then peered at the flatness of Renae's body, the near concave between her belt and blouse.

"Why would you think that?" Renae asked as if genuinely curious, her hand on her stomach, as if she were desperate to know the answer.

"You look . . ." Amanda stammered. "Happy."

Renae looked at Amanda's fleece pants and cardigan with the hole near the shoulder then around at the other saleswomen, all dressed in sleek black. "Say . . ."

"I know your husband," Amanda said.

"Luke?"

"Luke." She pushed herself forward, inches away from Renae's face. "We're lovers. He told me he couldn't see me anymore because of the pregnancy."

For a second Renae looked hopeful, as if maybe she were pregnant and everyone knew but her. "We've been trying for three years." Then her face fell. "Lovers?"

She looked at Renae. "No baby?"

"No baby." Renae put a hand on the rack of bath mats and leaned forward breathing heavily. "You're sleeping with my husband."

A salesperson—Salone—walked up, her lithe body tipped forward on thin black heels. "May I help you?" She caught sight of Amanda's nametag. "You're not Elena," she said, and Amanda bolted from the store.

Amanda hears someone knocking outside her door. She's certain it isn't Nick, the rapping too high on the wood. Could it be a bear? Tom turns the knob softly and the door clicks open, a shiver of light coming through from the living room. He walks in holding an unsteady candle, the flame wobbling in the air, and sits on the side of her bed. His face is a mess of wavering shadows as if it's not made of solid bone and flesh. "Amanda?" he says, his voice thick and phlegmy. She pretends to sleep, huddled against the cold air under the covers. "I miss my wife." Tom scoots back, and she pulls her legs up out of his way, curling in the fetal position. He lays his head back against the wall, pulls it forward, and hits it harder, three drops of wax landing on the quilt. He turns toward Amanda, and she smells the faint woodsy smell of whiskey, Luke's drink of choice. "I miss her hair and her smile." He sighs. "I miss her boobs. I haven't had sex in a long, long time." Amanda flutters a fake snore, and he's silent long enough she opens an eye to make sure he's not fallen asleep. "I feel bad I don't miss Kristin more. She was an ugly child and obviously liked Connie more than me."

Tom lays down behind her and puts a hand on her hip, spoons into her back on the big double bed, and falls asleep instantly, the candle dropping from his hand, the flame catching on the quilt. Amanda grabs the glass of water from her nightstand and pours it over the small fire, and it hisses out, the smell of wet smoke heavy between them.

Luke had called her later that night, angrier than she'd imagined anyone could be. Called her a bitch, a whore, a no-good fucking whore. She could imagine him on the other end of the line, spit flying into the phone as he told her she'd ruined his marriage. For a moment her body went cold, sure he would come over and try to kill her, and it almost seemed worth it, to have his hands on her again. Why not let Tom sleep, she thinks, what's a hand on the hip? It's less harmful than a dead wife and a homely child, than an anthropologist who can't dig his way out of a hole.

Amanda awakens alone at eight o'clock to the smell of coffee Tom's brewed on the grill, her breath nearly visible in the air. She walks to the kitchen and Tom's at the table, his eyes heavy as he sniffs at a mug.

"Morning," he says. It's Sunday, the end of the weekend. Amanda is glad to be getting rid of this family—Nick and his inconsistent behavior, and even more so Tom, who leaves her feeling uneasy, as if he has Nick tied to a rope and is swinging him, closer and closer, to a lion's mouth. "Do you want me to make eggs?" she asks Tom.

"Cereal's fine." Amanda opens the cupboard and grabs the Sugar Pops and eats them with her hand.

"I'll take some," Tom says, and she holds out the box. "Why don't you go wake the kid. He'll want to get in some swimming before we leave this afternoon." Amanda looks outside, the sky overcast once again and a strong wind blowing through the sturdy trees in front of the cabin. "He loves to swim."

Nick is already up when she enters his room, snuggled under the covers and wearing a hat. "I was cold," he says and sniffles twice for effect. He's right, the night cooled off considerably by the lake, and the cold has snuck into the cabin.

"Maybe your dad can turn on the furnace," she says, although she doubts it. Her friend's parents had a cabin similar to this on Mills Lac, and lighting it was an ordeal, nothing to start on the Sunday they were going to leave. "We're eating breakfast," she says.

"I don't feel so good," Nick says, and he points at his stomach. The boy vomits suddenly, violently, on his comforter, a navy-blue-and-white-stripe too adult for this child. Amanda feels the bile rise in her own throat, the stench sickly sweet like chocolate cake and battery acid. She stares at the mess. She's a failure as a nanny—she can't cook, the child has vomited, she'll be lucky if they make it out without scars.

"Here," she says and pulls the boy by his armpits out of the bed. "Go see your father," she says, then, "Wait," and wipes the brown mess from his mouth with the corner of the comforter. She looks at the underside, a solid navy against the sheets, and rather than stripping the bed, she turns the comforter upside down. What does it matter? She knows she'll never come to this cabin again, wouldn't if he doubled her salary, even tripled it. She imagines Luke at home with his wife, her pregnant belly raised in the air, then deflating as she remembers Renae's not really pregnant. Even if she were, on her sickly thin frame she'd be lucky to have a lump there yet, a small pea, like a growth of cancer. Amanda, at her worst moment, has wished there was a baby and that it had died. That'd teach Luke to lie.

She follows Nick to the kitchen and catches another whiff of vomit. Tom too? she thinks, but no, the boy has thrown up again, this time on the carpet, the stain burning into the light beige carpet.

"It seemed like a good idea when we got it," Tom says staring at the wall-to-wall carpet. "Connie thought it would blend in the sand."

"I'll get a rag," Amanda says but stands there a moment staring at the stain. Tom stares at it too then sits on the couch. Amanda sits next to him.

Nick begins wailing from the kitchen, standing precariously on a chair, his foot tipping it back as he struggles toward the cupboard holding the Ho Hos. Amanda blinks as if she's been in a trance then lifts her heavy body from the sofa and goes to the kitchen to steady the chair and grab the snack.

"Why'd you do that?" Nick asks. "I could reach them," and nips his head out to bite her again on the hand.

Tom stands up from the couch then lies down. "I'm glad sometimes it's the boy that lived. I wouldn't know what to do with a girl, how to raise her." He looks at Nick who looks back; the boy already has one Ho Ho unwrapped, waiting in his hand to be eaten. "His voice hasn't changed yet; he still sounds like Kristin. I hear him sometimes in a different room and almost think she's still alive. I don't get that with Connie. No one sounds like her." He puts a wrist over his eyes as if blocking out the sunlight. "I thought maybe you would, but you don't."

Amanda feels a pang of guilt, as if she's let Tom down. "I'm sorry."

"It's OK." He lifts a pinecone from the basket set decoratively by the fireplace and throws it hand to hand. "We'll plan on leaving today around four, that way we'll avoid the traffic in the city. We always leave at four." Amanda looks around the cabin, no games to play, no magazines left to read, nothing but to eat all that food. But she can tell from looking back at Tom, the way he checks his watch and sets his jaw, that they won't be leaving sooner. Family vacations last until four o'clock.

They nap that morning, no one having slept well the night before. It rains all morning, and around noon the wind picks up and they play gin rummy. After an hour of cards, Tom pours some warm whiskey in a highball glass, the ice having melted in the cooler. "Who's ready for happy hour? It's the weekend." Nick is confused by the rules so Tom tells him just to watch, which he does obediently as his father discards a jack of clubs. "I never had to be around them when Connie was alive. I don't know how to play with him," he says to Amanda with Nick huddled in a blanket beside her, one hand resting in her lap as he watches his father. Tom gets up and shuts the windows when the rain begins blowing into the living room then puts on his suit coat over his Minnesota Gophers sweatshirt. "I should offer you this coat," he says to Amanda, who is sneaking under the blanket with Nick, but he doesn't. "We should light a fire. A fire would be nice."

Amanda looks at her watch. "It's already two o'clock," she says. "By the time we get it going, it'll be time to leave."

"We'll hose it out, no worries."

Nick reaches into the bag of Doritos, his belly distended. "I feel bad again," he says.

"You know where the john is, Pal," Tom says. He digs around in the log rack and pulls out some wood. "That kid's sick all the time since his mother died."

"Don't you think it's all the shit he eats?" Amanda says. "I mean, the kid never stops eating."

Nick drops the bag of Doritos on the carpet and stomps on them. "I want to come live with you," Nick says and tugs on Amanda's hand. She hasn't bonded with the child at all, except for the rare moments of affection that were too over-the-top to be sincere.

"Sorry," she says, and for a second she means it. "No can do."

She takes him to the bathroom, where he throws up a wet orange tube of barely chewed chips. "Ouch," he says.

She wets a washcloth and wipes his forehead with the rag. Back in the living room, Tom's loaded eight or ten logs into the tiny fireplace and is bending over with a pack of matches. "It won't light," he says.

"A fire's a bad idea."

"Newspaper," Tom says and snaps his fingers, then, "I don't have any." He goes to the kitchen and scrounges through the drawers until he finds the warranty and instruction booklet for the microwave then grinds it into tiny paper balls. "This should do the trick." He throws one on the fire and lights it. The flame grows then fizzles out. He lights another, but nothing. He touches one of the logs. "It's not wet, I don't understand. What's the problem?" He tries another then kicks the brick fireplace with a dull thud that makes Amanda shiver with pain, although he raises his foot and kicks the wood again and again, deeper into the fireplace. "What's the fucking problem?"

"We don't really need a fire," Amanda repeats. "We'll be leaving soon." She looks at the clock. "In an hour and a half. Or now, we could just leave now," she pleads.

"I'd leave now," Nick says.

"We're not leaving without a fire," Tom says. "No matter what, I'm building this fucking fire." He strides outside and returns with the can of lighter fluid from the grill.

"I don't think you're supposed to use that," Amanda says, but he's already uncapped the liquid and is spraying it in high arcs on the wood, some up inside the walls of the fireplace, some dashing to the carpet, the curtains, on the pinecones by the hearth.

"I'll show you how to light a fire," he says and takes the matches from his pocket, his hand trembling, slick with lighter fluid. He stands for a moment then pulls off a match and strikes it.

The wood goes first, bursting into red flames, spreading like oily heat onto the carpet, an inch away from the couch. Amanda springs up, grabs Nick across the chest, and pulls him, swinging his legs in the air like dead weight.

"Outside," Amanda says and in that moment thinks about taking him for earnest, getting in the car and never looking back. She feels a shudder of triumph as she grabs the keys from the counter. "Now," she yells to Tom. "We've got to go."

"I'm coming," he says but continues staring at the fire as she runs out of the room. She turns around in the yard and looks at the cabin, the living room lit up as if with yellow and red dancers billowing in black; he forgot to open the flue. "Tom!" she yells, but he doesn't answer. Nick still in her arms, she runs and throws him in the backseat of the SUV.

Amanda moves to turn the key quickly, but her hand slips. She wipes her palm against her jeans and tries the keys again. She looks back at Nick, grabs his hand, and squeezes, but it's limp in her own. "We made it out, Pal," she whispers, but he says nothing, only stares at the flames. She wants to explain that his father is fine, that he'll make it out too, but she knows Tom is far from fine. She roars the car to life then sits there watching the door. Tom comes out a moment later walking slowly, his hand wrapped around a cell phone. He steps in the car.

"Call 911," Amanda says. She hits his chest hard with a fist. "It's not even spread from the living room yet, make the fucking call."

"No signal," he says calmly and gazes at the house. "There's nothing you can do with a fire but watch it burn."

She turns to the cabin. It's almost beautiful in its white and orange heat, and she realizes she's warm for the first time in days, since coming to this god-awful lake. Amanda knows she should do something—grab the phone from Tom and try to call the police, put the gearshift in reverse and slam down on the gas—but she only sits there. It's not her cabin, and besides, some things have to end badly for everyone for them to end at all.

Any Ordinary Uncle

In the summer of 1980 my Uncle Manny was let out of the Big House. That's how Dad put it, three scotches into the night. Released. Paroled. Set free. I was aware through conversations over the years that my dad's younger brother was in prison on charges of manslaughter, that he'd killed a girl while driving home drunk from a bar called the Do-Si-Do.

I'd met Uncle Manny eight years earlier when I was four, shortly before he was sent away, and there's a picture of me in flannel pajamas and cowboy boots, sitting on his lap, sharing an ice cream cone. In the photograph, he looks like any ordinary uncle dressed in a cardigan sweater and chinos, and we are both laughing with the ice cream smeared over the bottom halves of our faces. That summer night in 1980, my parents told my four-year-old brother, Gordon, and me that above all we were to treat him with respect. "He's your uncle," my mother said. "We've got to remember he's family."

When Uncle Manny arrived the next Saturday afternoon by taxi, after spending two days on a Greyhound coming to Illinois from Nevada, Dad rounded up the whole family and brought us to the front porch to welcome him. Gordon was on all fours sucking on a rawhide (he'd decided two months earlier if we couldn't have a dog due to Dad's allergies then the next best thing was to *become* one) while I stood next to my dad trying to look cool, as if having an ex-convict, murdering relative arrive for an extended stay was no big deal. But when the taxi door opened and Manny rolled onto our driveway and kissed the pavement, I thought for sure he must be crazy. "Free man!" he yelled, grinning, as his duffel bag tumbled after him.

He was dressed in a shabby rust-colored suit, a too-wide tie, and an old-fashioned Cubs cap with the elastic band in the back rather than a plastic adjustable tab. My dad walked over and extended a hand, and they hugged like grown men do—one hand shaking, the other whapping on the back. My dad and I were at that point where we still hugged with both arms, and I secretly liked that. Dad gripped Uncle Manny's shoulder and steered him toward the porch to meet us, as if he was just up visiting from Nevada, as if he'd just casually stopped by to say hi.

My mother emptied the top two drawers of my dresser and loaded the clothes in plastic crates to be stacked in a corner of Gordy's closet. I was sentenced to bunk-bed hell for the extent of Manny's stay. "He's a grown man, and he needs his privacy," she told me, rolling up my underwear into tiny cotton tubes. How was I to object to something like that? I was twelve then and did not want to give up my privacy for reasons obvious to any twelve-year-old boy, although the thought of voicing this to my mother was close to insane.

Uncle Manny came into my room and threw his bag in the corner, put his hands on the mattress, and pushed down on the springs. "Nice bed you've got here, Jeff." He turned around and looked at me, took off his cap, and ran his fingers through his slightly graying hair. "Bet you're not too happy about having to give it up."

"I don't care," I said, kicking at the door where the carpet was coming up.

" 'Cause I could take the couch," he said. "Even sleeping on a couch doesn't sound so bad." He put his hands on his lower back and stretched backward, looking around. "Nice room," he said and went over and picked up the plaque I'd gotten for second place in a spelling bee. "Can you spell supercalifragilisticexpialidocious?" he said.

I began flicking the light switch off and on, off and on. "That's not even a real word."

He put down the plaque and laughed. "You'd have a hell of a time telling that to Mr. Dick Van Dyke," he said and started to unpack his clothes, refolding them neatly into piles and putting them into my drawers. He mostly had white T-shirts and jeans, and if the suit he was wearing was any indication, they would all be too big. "I missed on the word 'incarceration,'" I told him. It had really been "phosphorescent," but my mother was out of the room by then, and I felt this was something I could get away with.

He looked up from his packing, four rolled balls of socks in his hands. "Well I can't spell that either, Jeff. It's bad enough I have to know what it means." He went back to unpacking, and I left the room with the light switched off.

Gordon and Manny hadn't met before Manny came to visit—Mom delivered when Manny was halfway through his sentence—but as a four-year-old, Gord liked everybody. At the grocery store Mom would be shaking cantaloupes and turn around to find he'd wandered off, sometimes to the deli section to watch the men slice meat or three aisles over to look at the dog toys. She'd round the corner, frantic, with the cantaloupe still in her hand, and find him sitting complacently on the floor or behind the register where the checkout girl would have given him a sucker and let him hit "Total." The night Manny arrived Gordon brought out his array of toys—Barbie-size action figures from *Star Wars*, a chewed-up Tonka truck, a plastic baggy full of Weebles—and laid them at Uncle Manny's feet.

Manny picked up the Darth Vader doll and turned it in his hands, lifting up the cape. "My God," he said. "What is this?" I couldn't believe he didn't know. Even in prison I figured they let people watch *Star Wars*.

"It's an action figure," I told him. "Not like a doll-doll. It's OK for boys."

He picked up the Princess Leia. "Now she's OK for boys, huh, Jeff?" He held the doll out to me. "She's a looker."

I turned away, embarrassed. Even a twelve-inch plastic woman was enough to fluster me at the time. "She shoots a gazillion stormtroopers in the first movie," I told him. "And saves the rebel base."

"Feisty too!" Manny said.

Mom came in the living room with a *Redbook* and sat on the sofa next to Dad, who was unabashedly watching Manny. It seemed odd to me that he would stare so openly at another adult.

Gordon fingered the ammunition belt on Chewbacca. "You killed someone," he said, looking at Manny. My mother's head shot up, and she turned toward my dad. "And now you're better."

My mother leaned toward Gordon, letting the magazine slide off her lap onto the floor. "Honey, it was an accident. Your Uncle Manny made a mistake." Gordon and I looked at our father who was still staring nakedly at his brother, waiting for his reaction.

"But it's true," Uncle Manny said, tracing with his thumb the entire head of Princess Leia. "All the same, it's true."

After a week of getting used to Uncle Manny—the way he did calisthenics in the room (my room) next door at 5:00 a.m., the way he sang horrible country-and-western songs non-stop while walking aimlessly through the house or mowing the lawn for my mother—Mom took him to get a haircut, dragging Gord and me with her. Manny talked amicably in the car on the ride there, reading off street signs and billboards as Gordon pointed to them from his lap. "Thirty miles per hour, Camel cigarettes, Kentucky Fried Chicken. Kentucky Fried Chicken!" he said again. "I used to love that!"

Gordon traced the small tattoo on Manny's arm. It was a grayish-green outline of the torso of a woman, faded but still visible, the face unfinished with a mouth and only one eye. In retrospect it was what I would now consider tasteful for a tattoo, but at the time I stared at the naked breasts, both elated and uneasy. My mother reached over as if to put her hand on the back of the seat and turn around to check for traffic and casually rolled down the sleeve. Manny started singing a George Jones song about a horse dying, and my mother softly joined in.

We pulled into the barber's down on Center Street where my father usually went to get his haircut. Manny settled into the chair while Mom, Gord, and I sat in folding chairs by the piles of magazines. On one of the shelves high above the shampoo and far out of my reach, I could see old issues of *Playboy* and realized this place was not like the one my mother went to on Aldrich with the ferns and hairdryers attached to the waiting-room seats. I had been here before a few times with my father, who sat silently while his hair was clipped, always refusing the lather and shave, the pomade they offered to put in his hair for free. When my father left he would put a dollar in the glass jar, which was accepted with a "Much obliged, Mr. Harris."

Uncle Manny lay back in the chair as the barber whisked the cream across his face, the smell of lather heavy in the air. I heard the barber ask Uncle Manny what he did, and Manny told him, "Just got into town, still looking for a job." They discussed any openings that might be available at the light bulb factory down on Fulton, how the price of gas was on the decline. After awhile I could just catch snippets of their conversations—whispers followed by bawdy laughs. The barber was the same one who cut my father's hair, but his demeanor was much more relaxed as I watched him lean in to whisper another joke into Manny's ear. When we left he shook Manny's hand and told him good luck with the job search, he was sure he'd have no problem.

Nineteen years later I still go to this barber, although he seems to remember me more as Manny's friend than my father's son. He only knows me as Jeff, not Mr. Harris, and has no idea I make my living as a zoning commissioner for Peoria County, but can tell you I like to be shaved right to left and have always admired a good dirty joke.

The Empire Strikes Back was the first movie Uncle Manny had seen in eight years other than the informational rehabilitation films he'd been forced to watch in prison. Gordy and I had been running around the house for weeks like crazy people. We rarely played together because of our age difference, but that time was an exception. We sat on the floor with the *Star Wars* figurines spread between us, possible plots swimming in my head along with visions of Princess Leia in her clingy, wet robe down in the garbage compactor. Uncle Manny hunkered next to us, watching with fascination. "And this little guy, he's a good guy or a bad guy?" Manny held a Jawa in his hand.

"They're not really on a side," I told him. "They work separately."

He picked up Darth Vader. "And this guy, he's like the big honcho?"

Gordon looked at the figurine in Uncle Manny's hand. "He's the *really* bad guy."

Manny stared at the scattering of stormtroopers and sandpeople. "All this for a movie," he said. "I can hardly imagine."

Our whole family went for the event, even my mother, who as a rule did not like science-fiction movies. Manny insisted on buying popcorn and Milk Duds and extra large Coca-Cola's for everyone. "A movie!" he kept saying. "It's been years!"

In the theater Gordy and I headed for the front. Mom stopped about halfway down and said, "This is far enough." She looked at our pleading faces as Gordon started to whine about being too far away and held out a bucket of popcorn to us. "Just behave," she said. Manny stood for a moment, glancing from my parents to me and Gordy, before following us down. "You kids seem to be the experts," he said. "You must know where to sit." He was the only adult in the front row and we sat in respectful silence waiting for the movie.

In my memory, there were no previews that day. It was almost as if all Hollywood knew there was no way they were going to beat this movie, that we had waited for three years, and nothing short of the second coming of Darth Vader himself was going to satisfy us. This was before the days of surround sound and digital mastering, but when the music started—louder than anything I had ever imagined—and the words began slowly scrolling up the screen, stark against the blackness of the starred space behind them, Uncle Manny shrunk slowly in his seat, hand suspended over the popcorn bucket. "Holy God," I heard him whisper.

No human sounds were heard in the theater as the movie started—no shifting of seats or passing of snacks—only that booming music. I'd waited three years for this moment, an eternity. Gordy hadn't even seen the original *Star Wars*—we didn't have a VCR back then—but I had acted out every scene I could recall, recited all the dialogue I could remember, and made up what I couldn't. Even Gordy, at four years old, observed a respectful silence. But it's Manny, leaned back in his seat with his head strained almost perpendicular to his neck, that I remember from that day.

About halfway through the movie—right when Luke Skywalker sees his own face superimposed on Darth Vader's and has to come to terms with his own possible dark side—Uncle Manny got up from his seat and walked out of the theater. I sat stunned, trying to concentrate on the plot; Gordy continued to eat the popcorn, sticking his entire head in the bucket and catching it on his tongue. When Manny didn't return by the time Luke emerged from the cave, I stood up angrily and went to find him. God knows what he could do, I thought. God knows what a convict could do.

I walked up the aisle slowly trying to find my way in the dark; it was futile to look for my parents to send them instead. I opened the door and squinted against the bright lights of the lobby, standing for a moment adjusting between the dark of the theater and the harsh fluorescent of the outside. I closed my eyes tightly seeing pockets of light, and when I opened them I saw Manny on the lobby bench, hunched over, my father's hand on his back. I moved quickly to the side and hid behind the water fountain, sensing this was something I shouldn't see.

"It's not real, Manny," I heard my father say.

Manny's voice broke. "I know that, Jimmy. Jesus, I'm not stupid. It's that someone could even make it. That that's what people want to see." I could tell he was crying—*crying!*—and I wanted desperately to be back in the theater watching the movie. "All that destruction for entertainment. That's the world I can't believe exists."

"Manny, it's been eight years. You've got to understand things have changed. Nobody wants to watch *The Sound of Music* anymore." I heard the strong sound of my father patting him on the back, a reassuring rhythm words couldn't convey. I'd known it myself, six months earlier, when I'd been beaten by Laura VanderWoude at the regional spelling bee.

I heard them stand up, my father's knees creaking, a familiar sound. I hunched down next to the hum of the water fountain as they walked past, my father's hand still on Uncle Manny's shoulder.

Mrs. Dagel was the one who brought over the flyer announcing the block party. My mother had answered the door dressed in one of my father's old button-down shirts, walking shorts, and a pair of huaraches. Mrs. Dagel had on a neon-pink knit sundress with a braided orange belt. I guessed her to be anywhere from twenty-five to forty with her bright pink lipstick and her hair piled high on her head—one of those fashions my wife would later refer to as "mall hair"—and I was very conscious of how different she looked from my mother. When she arrived at the door she didn't look like a suburban housewife but like something exotic and unexpected, like finding a pomegranate among the oranges at the supermarket. When she handed my mother the flyer I saw her nail polish matched her lipstick and dress, although it was chipping badly at the edges.

My mother ran her hands clumsily through her hair as she listened to Mrs. Dagel drone on about the block party. "We still need any tables you've got—picnic, card—we're going to need something to put all the food on." Mrs. Dagel smiled at my mother, and I noticed her lipstick had smudged on her teeth, giving the impression it had melted in the heat. She took a swooping look inside the foyer and living room, barely stopping on me in the hallway. "And that houseguest of yours I've seen around town, what's his name? Manny? You be sure to bring him too."

It was obvious from the start Mrs. Dagel liked Uncle Manny. He sauntered out of the house and into the blocked off street with a Pepsi in his hand, wearing a muscle shirt and a pair of my father's jams. He looked different from the other men—all middle-aged husbands and one effeminate man from over on Douglas Street who in 1980 did not feel safe enough to be openly gay. Manny looked uncomfortable in his clothes, especially when set against the others in their plaid, pleated shorts and solid pastel golf shirts. He came over and casually laid his hand across my shoulders, compensating for what I believe was his shyness with a cocky attitude he'd most likely picked up in prison. "Jeff, it looks like we've got ourselves a par-tay." I was self-conscious knowing wherever Manny was, people were looking, and I wanted to crawl in a hole when Mrs. Dagel walked over with a tray of little cupcakes decorated with birthday clowns and pink elephants. She worked part time at the Piggly Wiggly bakery and got leftovers at a discount.

She tapped one finger on Manny's chest. "And you," she said. "I don't think I've met you before. I'm Carla Dagel, four blocks down."

He took her hand and turned it over, kissed her on the inside of the palm. "Manfred C. Harris, ma'am." He twisted her hand back over, front side up. "I thought I'd better flip that hand down. It looked like I might be in danger of cutting my lip on that rock." He closed one eye slowly in a wink.

Mrs. Dagel laughed and held her hand out, watching the sunlight glisten on her diamond. "This little thing couldn't cut a piece of paper," she said. She cocked her head and looked from the ring to Manny. "You met my husband yet?"

Manny put his arm around my back, and I could feel the sweat from his armpit against my shoulder. "Happy fellow, I imagine," he said. "But I haven't had the pleasure."

"Well, Manfred," she said. "Today just isn't your lucky day. He's down working at the office for most of the weekend." She handed me the tray of cupcakes and took a cigarette pack out of her pocket. Her jeans were so tight I swore I could read "Winston Lights" even before she wiggled out the box. Manny took the lighter from her hands, lit her cigarette, and handed the lighter back.

We stood for a moment in silence, Mrs. Dagel smoking her cigarette, the smoke catching on a soft breeze heading my way and smelling adult. Manny cleared his throat and tightened the grip on my shoulder. "Carla, you know this fine man, Jeffrey Harris?"

"Ummm," she said, and wandered off, undulating, leaving me with Uncle Manny and the tray full of sweets.

Manny came into the house late that night. I was awake still thinking about the evening: the way Mrs. Dagel had looked in her tight denim jeans, how she touched Manny's arm whenever they were talking, which was frequently. I heard him make his way to his room, the sounds of him softly singing a country song, the bed creaking as he lay down. I wondered for just a moment if Mrs. Dagel was with him. After a few quiet minutes there was a knock on my door. "Jeff, you awake?"

Gordy snored above me. "Yeah," I whispered. Manny came in and sat next to me on the mattress. "You been with Mrs. Dagel?" I asked, although I was pretty sure he had.

"Yeah," he said. I could see his outline clearly, having lain awake in the dark for the past hour. He was still wearing the muscle shirt, and I could see the goose pimples on his biceps. "We went over to her house. She said I could come in for a drink, but I swore I wasn't going to drink anymore, not after last time." I recognized the sweet scent of scotch I sometimes smelled on my father's breath when he kissed me good night. "I only had two drinks, Jeff. I'm not drunk." I knew this to be true by the way he sat on the bed, sitting still but with his shoulders slumped. There was another odor too, damp and sharp along with the scotch, that I would not be able to place for a few more years. "But I'm a weak man, Jeff. I do things I shouldn't do, no matter how much I tell myself I'm not going to."

I wondered why he was telling this to me and not my father or another adult. I had no idea how to react, or what to say that would make him feel better about the man he was. "Uncle Manny," I said, "you're doing OK."

"Yeah?" he said. I heard Gordy roll over in his sleep, felt the bunk shift from Manny standing up.

"Yeah."

He walked to the door, and I saw his face clearly in the light from the hallway, wet tracks of tears on his face. "You're doing pretty good too, Jeff," he said.

The next day my parents were going to be gone until late evening, at a barbecue across town with one of my father's colleagues. I stayed in bed until ten that morning, afraid when I came downstairs Uncle

Manny would treat me differently. He didn't mention coming into my room the previous night but instead made me fried eggs and hash and told me that's what he had eaten for breakfast almost every day for the past eight years. "It's still not too bad," he said. "You'd think I'd be sick of it, but there are some things you just grow so used to that you can't even think about hating them."

It was Uncle Manny's idea to paint the fire hydrant. We'd been sitting on the porch playing poker while Gordy scooted across the yard on all fours, sniffing trees. He had just galloped away from the redwood and over to the fire hydrant on the corner when Manny was struck with the idea. He told me all about the block of wood he'd seen in *Better Homes and Gardens*—one of the magazines the warden would bring in after his wife had finished with it—that was shaped like a fire hydrant and painted like Uncle Sam, displayed on a porch for the Fourth of July. Uncle Manny had looked to the corner deep in thought, his hand going limp just enough so I could see he had a pair of tens. "We could do better than a block of wood," he said.

The plan was to go to Ace Hardware down on main street and get some paint—red, white, blue, and maybe a flesh color for the face—and paint the hydrant on the corner. Manny and I headed downtown on our bikes, him borrowing my dad's with Gordy sitting on the handlebars. He told me he liked to ride bikes since he hadn't been outside for so long, but I knew they hadn't given him his license back after he'd killed that girl, and I wasn't sure what he was going to do come winter.

At Ace Hardware, Lynn Sanders sat at the register sorting paper clips. Her father owned the store. When we came in she gracefully slid from the stool and followed us to the weather-resistant paints. It made me extremely nervous being even so much as in the same aisle as her, and I was glad when she finally picked out some paint samples and left. When we approached the register, she stared straight at me for a moment before rolling her eyes and going to the back where her mother usually sat watching TV, waiting to help the female customers who came in for domestic supplies. Uncle Manny watched her walk off and looked at me before I could look away from her. "She's a pretty girl, that one," he said. "You like her, I can tell."

I was petrified of Lynn Sanders, her and her paint samples and freckles and her brown, permed hair. I could feel the heat surge into my face as Lynn's dad put the paint in a paper sack with a smile on his face. "She's stuck up," I whispered. "Everyone says she dates ninth-graders."

"And you, you won't even say hello," Manny exclaimed, loud as could be. "I wouldn't date you either. She followed you to those paint samples, young man. She was hoping you'd ask her a question."

I was mortified to be having this conversation at Ace Hardware in front of Mr. Sanders, Lynn no more than twenty feet away watching *Days of Our Lives* in the back with her mother. "She doesn't even like me," I told him. "She doesn't even know who I am."

Uncle Manny took the bag from Mr. Sanders and we walked out to our bikes on the curb, Gordy trailing behind. I turned around and looked at the store hoping for a final glimpse of Lynn. Or even better, to not see her, so I could believe she was still in the back, as frightened to talk to me as I was to her. All I could see was the glare from the tin-siding display and the reflection of Manny, Gordy, and me through the window, standing on the street with our bag of paint. Manny took my backpack and loaded it with the cans and strapped it on his back. "You can't keep letting opportunities pass you by, my boy."

Five years later when Lynn Sanders and I lost our virginity in the backseat of her father's Volvo, I'd wanted desperately to tell Uncle Manny he'd been right about the paint samples. By then he was gone, living somewhere in the Southwest, sending postcards every Christmas from random cities, never with a return address or any hope of a forwarding number.

Gord and I stripped to the waist as Manny laid out newspaper in the garage to put the cans on. Uncle Manny had taken off his shirt inside, and I noticed his chest was pale but solid. I could see the sketch of muscles on his forearms and biceps, along with the faded, half-outline of the woman's torso. He caught me looking at his arm and ran a finger over the tattoo. "It hurt like hell," he said. "I could never get it finished. After a while the guy who started it got paroled, and I felt I'd lost my opportunity." Without my mother to stop me, I traced the outline of her breasts and her hair and her one eye. Manny stood still as I ran my fingers over his skin. "I call her Alice," he said, his voice lowered to a whisper, catching on the name. "Don't tell anyone this, Jeff, but sometimes I talk to her. Just tell her how my day was and what I've done." It would be years later, after my father passed away and I was cleaning out the basement, that I would find the box marked "Manny." It had some mementos from their childhood, such as a glow-in-the-dark yo-yo and a broken Slinky, along with articles from the arrest and trial. It was then I found out the girl he had killed was named Alice Mairs.

Manny ran his hands up his arms and bent down to pick up the can of blue paint. "Your father'd have a shit fit if we spilled, wouldn't he, Jeff?" He tipped the can upside down with the lid still tight.

Gordy laughed and squealed from the scare as he put his hands to his mouth. "Yeah, a shit fit," I said, and Manny slapped me on the rear, also laughing now.

After the paints were stirred, we brought out the old brushes Mom stored in the freezer and pulled them, along with the cans, in Gordy's Red Flyer to the corner. "We should start with the hat," Manny said. "Work our way down." He stood for a moment staring at the hydrant. "I'm not sure about those knob things. I can't remember what those were in the magazine. Must be arms. What do you think, Jeff? Arms?"

I looked at the hydrant. "Shit, yeah," I said. "Arms." Manny laughed again and kicked me lightly on the leg.

While we worked it grew cooler in the shade cast by the fir trees my father had planted as a windbreak along the north side. Gordy fell asleep before we finished, rooting a spot under one of the trees, his knees held tightly to his chest. Few cars drove by in our neighborhood, but most that did slowed down to admire our paint job or at least to try and figure out what we were doing. I thought at the time people most likely would assume we were father and son. When we were almost finished, Mrs. Dagel came screeching around the corner in her white Bonneville headed toward the Quickee Mart, smoking a cigarette. Manny stood tall, sucked in his stomach, and saluted with the paint brush in his hand. I could hear her laughter coming out the window as she tooted her horn.

We finished around eight, the beginning of dusk in the summer. We woke Gordy and all walked across the street to survey our handiwork. It was lopsided at best, unrecognizable at worst. Manny tilted his head to the side. "Well, we got the colors right, boys. You've got to say that much." The original red of the fire hydrant shone through on the face, giving Uncle Sam a ruddy, sunburnt color. The striped suit he wore was so wobbly it looked as if we were seeing it through the heat rising from the street. In a flash of brilliance, Manny had decided to paint stars on the hat and they came out looking like the birds had already gotten to it. Gordy was delighted all the same by the bright colors, the sun gleaming off the hydrant from the west as it was beginning to set. Gord fell down on all fours and began galloping across the street, Manny with his hand on my shoulder, a feeling of camaraderie I'd never experienced before with an adult.

I think it was the sound I heard first—the shifting of gears—or maybe first I felt the tightening of Manny's hand on my shoulder. In memory I can see the Bonneville blocks away, and it's a panic that freezes me, causes my stomach to tighten and convulse, almost paralyzing in its clarity. In reality I know that can't be how it happened. There were the trees from the windbreak blocking the view around the corner, and of course Mrs. Dagel who, had she been driving down a straight road, would have had time to react. It's a hard line to draw, years later, between what happened that evening and what I believe I remember. Mrs. Dagel did hit her brakes but not quite in time. Gordy screamed once, I do remember that, but it must have been before the impact. Perhaps he turned his head just in time to see the grill approaching, or heard the brakes himself. Mrs. Dagel came around the corner at her usual breakneck speed, and with the sun in her eyes, was unable to see Gordy scurrying low across the street. The car hit his body with a dull thud I hear, still, at odd times of the day—when someone sets down a load of books in the library or my wife pounds out chicken breasts for dinner.

Gordy survived, with severe lacerations on his back, thighs, and face, and a broken femur. There was some concern at the time that the bone had been broken at the growth plate due to his age, but with the speed Mrs. Dagel had been driving, he'd been lucky enough to have the thigh break at the point of impact. Gordon is now twenty-four, engaged to a Phi Beta Kappa and beginning the Ph.D. program in linguistics at the University of Michigan. He walks with a slight limp recognizable only to immediate family.

But that evening, we didn't know what the outcome would be. As Mrs. Dagel whipped around the corner, pummeling Gordy with her Bonneville, all we saw was an immobile four-year-old on the pavement, a stain of blood on the fender. As the car heaved to a stop, I felt Uncle Manny's hand deepen into my shoulder, pushing me to the ground as he shot himself into the street. He fell at Gordon's side shouting directions—"Carla get a blanket," "Jeff call 911." Those eight years in prison had given him plenty of time to consider the correct procedure for assisting the victim of a car crash. The proper reaction was to keep the body still, elevate the head and uninjured leg, apply pressure to the wound, and keep the victim conscious. Eight years to realize the magnitude of leaving the body limp and tangled in the street as he continued down the road—hitting the torso once more with the back tires—so drunk he was unable to recall thirty seconds before he had fatally wounded a nineteen-year-old girl, home on spring break from the University of Nevada.

Uncle Manny stayed hunkered down on the pavement whispering to Gordy, brushing back the hair from his forehead. His voice was a soft cadence of baseball scores and news, repeated from the radio humming though the open windows of Mrs. Dagel's car, combining with the sound of the cicadas on the cooling night air. "Mets 5, Cubs 6, sale on Pepsi-Cola at Wally's Grocery Mart, Carter to visit Afghanistan again in the fall." The last moment I remember clearly from the accident scene is Uncle Manny singing "White Lightnin'" softly into Gordy's flaccid ear.

Manny rode in the ambulance with Gordy, after securing me a ride with Mr. Craig, our neighbor next door who had never liked children. My parents came home twenty minutes later to an empty house and a note I'd written, reading, "DON'T PANIC!!! but Gord's been hurt. call st. johns, ask for emergency." And, of course, they panicked. When they arrived at the hospital my father was barely able to control his body, arms flailing as he talked to the doctors, demanding that he be let in to see his child. My mother stood stoically by the ashtray. With somewhat of a shock, I realized I was seeing her, not only as my mother but also as a woman suffering the possible loss of her son. I noticed the way the bones of her skinny wrists jutted out as she tapped her cigarette on the side of the can, the lipstick smearing the right side of her face where she had obviously been wiping away tears. As Uncle Manny rounded the corner with a tray of coffees and congealed pudding he had rescued from the cafeteria, one of those bony wrists snapped out and slapped him, hard, across the face. Manny looked at me, and I turned away.

Uncle Manny left two weeks later, three days after Gordon was released from the children's ward and allowed to come home. Gordy's cast was the coolest I'd seen—ranging from his toes to his hip—and was already covered in the flowery scribble of my mother, the thick, block writing of my father. Gordy still played dog but quietly now and without much enthusiasm, usually just sitting in front of the TV with his foot propped up, a squeeze toy or rawhide resting in his lap.

I told my parents how the accident happened innocently enough, but they had seen Manny and Carla at the block party and had too much time to convince themselves that it was due to negligence on someone's part. My father cajoled the police chief into dropping the destruction of government property charges against Manny—claiming the patriotic spirit made him do it—so he wouldn't be in violation of his parole. My mother, who in the beginning had told us to show

Manny respect, would not even address him by his name or allow herself to look at him.

The morning Manny left, he looked much as he did the day he came: dressed in a suit—this one a castaway of my father's—his hair grown out a bit, the duffel bag slung over his shoulder. We all saw him off on the porch, even my mother, who stood close to my father with her hand on his elbow. She had baked Manny a cheesecake, an awkward peace offering to carry on the Greyhound for the next two days, but accepted all the same.

We all waved as he got in the taxi to ride away, to a job offer he said a buddy had lined up for him just north of Taos, New Mexico. Gordy sat on the steps with his rawhide at the foot of his cast, having forgotten, as children will, the pain my parents thought Manny had caused him now that the incident was done. I reached out my hand to touch Gordy's shoulder, and he whimpered once, softly, as the taxi drove away, although I don't think he truly realized Uncle Manny would not be coming back.

In This Weather

Every Saturday morning Marlene's boyfriend, Greg, snuck out of his house to serve her Lund's cinnamon rolls in bed. His wife thought he had taken up jogging—that he ran for three hours every weekend and was training for the Twin Cities marathon—but by the time Greg arrived at Marlene's house, only two miles away, he was already winded, his hair soaked and frozen with sweat. She would take him into her bed, still damp from the run, and they'd make love at least once before eating the rolls, the icing already congealing on top of the pastries.

Six months into the affair, Marlene stood at the breakfast bar drinking orange juice while Greg put back on his shoes. The phone rang, and she walked to the living room already knowing it would be Carl, her next-door neighbor. "Is your friend over, the handy one?" Carl asked. Every Saturday he called like clockwork with a project—a washing machine hose that had come unscrewed or a tile in the bathroom that had miraculously dislodged.

She switched the phone to her other ear and pretended to stab at her heart then pointed across the room at the window while Greg laughed and put his hands to his throat. "He's out now," she told Carl. "Running errands."

"But I just saw him on the sofa."

Marlene peered out the window and saw the moon of Carl's face in his own window through the bed sheet he used as a curtain. He waved.

"Well he must be here, then," she said and clanked the receiver on the end table.

Greg walked over to the phone. "What is it, Carl?" He paused. "Can't that wait?" He "uh-huhhed" his way to the end of the conversation then hung up the phone and licked the frosting from her cheek. "It'll just take a minute."

"I'll see you in a half-hour if a minute." Marlene nodded toward Carl's house. "What's it look like in there anyway?" Greg put on his coat then opened his mouth. "Never mind, I don't want to know." They heard a loud but muffled sound like a car backfiring, and Greg closed the door behind him. When she'd moved into the neighborhood a year ago, she'd thought Carl's house looked like a shack, an honest-to-God shack, a square with an unfinished porch and peeling paint.

A few moments later Greg burst through the doorway holding Carl's cordless phone. "Did you steal that?" Marlene asked. She looked at Greg's face, white as the phone in his hand, splotches of red starting in his cheeks from the cold. "What is it?"

"He shot himself," Greg said. "In the bathtub."

"What do you mean he shot himself?"

Greg pointed at his face with the cordless, his voice rising. "I mean he's in the bathtub, he has no head." He stabbed himself at the hairline.

"Jesus." Marlene bent at the waist and put her head between her legs.

Greg looked down at the phone as if trying to remember how it had ended up in his hand. "I called the police."

There was the sound of a car outside—a low whistle followed by a pop—and Marlene jumped as if fearing another gunshot, that Carl hadn't finished the job.

She ran to the window and looked out. "It's his daughter, Janice."

"Carl has a daughter?"

"In-law." She pushed Greg. "You've got to stop her."

Greg ran onto the porch with Marlene behind him. "Janice!"

Janice raised a mittened hand and started toward the porch, the monotonous whistle of the siren in the distance. "Is the old coot bothering you?" she asked. "I'm just here for the mail."

"It hasn't come yet," Marlene said.

"Janice, wait." Greg ran off the porch.

The cop car ground to a halt, the siren dying abruptly. An officer got out belly first and stepped through the snow toward Greg. "Sir, are you the one who called?"

Janice's eyes widened. "I didn't do anything."

"Ma'am," the cop said and pointed a finger at Janice, stopping her like an obedient dog.

"Yes, I called." Greg held out a hand. "I'm Greg Jacombsa, and this is my friend, Marlene Shaw. I just stopped by to see my friend." The cop looked at them, and Greg motioned to Janice. "This is Janice." He whispered, "The daughter-in-law."

The cop shook Greg's hand. "Officer Raymond." He took a notebook out of his coat pocket and wrote something down. "I guess we'd better get inside."

Janice and Marlene went as far as the living room, while Greg and the officer headed to the bathroom. The house looked much as she expected—a black-and-green-plaid couch backed against a wall with orange lamps the size of half-grown children on each end table, the wheel from an old boat stuck on a wall. The faint smell of urine tinged with copper and gun powder wafted in from the back rooms, and Marlene remembered that Carl had numerous problems house-training Cheech, his rat terrier. The rings of the shower curtain rang against the rod. "God Jesus," Officer Raymond said.

Janice looked at Marlene's face. "What's going on?" She was probably no older than twenty, with loose, long hair piled on top of her head. Peeking out of her shirt was a red bra strap like an unexpected smile.

"There's been an accident." Marlene took Janice's hand and pulled her toward the sagging couch. "Something terrible."

Janice grabbed Marlene's hand, a grip so hard Marlene winced. "Lee?"

"Not Lee." Janice's face slackened with relief. "Carl."

Janice pushed her bangs further up on her forehead. "God, I should have known that one."

There was the sound of something smacking the tile in the bathroom and then the officer's low mumble. "It was an accident," Greg said. "I slipped for Christ's sake."

"What happened?" Janice asked.

Marlene held onto her hand. "Carl shot himself. With a gun."

"Which gun?"

Marlene blinked and looked around the room. There was a map of the United States above the sofa, smattered with pushpins, a jagged line heading south. "I don't know."

Janice pulled the ponytail out of her hair. "Carl's been threatening for years to shoot himself in the head with a .22. It was always, 'Lee, you marry that girl, I'm going to shoot myself in the head with a .22,' or 'Janice, you don't get that son potty-trained soon, I'm going to shoot myself in the head with a .22.' I mean, I never figured he'd do it."

Marlene sat there stupid. "Well, he did."

Marlene had transferred to the Twin Cities a year ago for her job with Modern Solutions, a last-resort resource for companies in trouble. Her boss in Cincinnati had told her she was needed in Minneapolis, a fast-growing metropolis, as if she were some surveying superhero who could rescue the job. Her task was to work with various companies to find where the problems lay—in morale, office politics, initiative—then help them fix the problems. She'd spend weeks giving surveys to everyone from custodial staff on up, then analyze the data and present it to the directors. Often when she went into meetings the executives would dismiss her, as if hiring her had been enough of a sign they were willing to change. When this happened, she'd keep them locked in a boardroom for days, charging overtime and asking open-ended questions based on the results she'd found—*If your company were stranded on a desert island, what three resources would you take?* The questions rarely differed from company to company, and the men—they were almost always men—would shift uncomfortably in their swiveling chairs until one, desperate to please her with the right answer so they could get on with their work, would clear his throat. "Our humanity?"

The women in her own office were the same as Cincinnati: cold at first and once warmed up, boring. She had tried to make friends with the women, had even baked Connie Dunekacke in personnel a lemon cake for her birthday, but next to the bagels and store-bought cookies the other employees brought, her efforts looked like a desperate bribe.

Marlene had met Greg at Champps, a sports bar downtown decorated with Vikings jerseys and cut-out models for Miller Lite. It was embarrassing at thirty-four, she thought, to meet a man at a bar, but after six months in a strange city she was happy to meet anyone anywhere.

He had told her up front that he was married, and when they made plans to go to lunch it was as no more than friends, but three weeks later they slept together. She never asked Greg if he'd planned from the beginning to sleep with her, being both flattered that their friendship was really a seduction and sickened that she was with a man who would so purposefully cheat on his wife. She never would have guessed she'd be a mistress, but their affair somehow made Greg vulnerable, almost desperate for love. She liked knowing more about Greg than his own wife. When he left on Saturday mornings, she'd curl into the still warm covers and tell herself how nice it was to roll over to any side of the bed as if she owned a small country.

Carl had started bothering her four months ago when his wife disappeared in the middle of the night, not leaving so much as a personal note, only a grocery list of essentials she never figured Carl would think to buy: Windex, E and C vitamins, a twenty-pound bag of rice. He'd wait with Cheech at his side while Marlene got out of the car at the end of the day, a bag of take-out in her hand, ready to tell her about the cost of new tires or the dog's diuretic habits or how he'd gotten another postcard from Alice. "She's in Atlanta now," he'd tell her, "must be seeing a Braves game," while Marlene stood in her driveway with a carton of shrimp lo mein, shivering and nodding her head.

A half hour later three more officers had tramped through the snow and into Carl's house. Marlene watched from her front living room window while Greg made fresh coffee and fetched the bourbon from the pantry. "She was so calm, I couldn't believe it," Marlene said. She held a spoon to her head and said in a squeaky voice, "If you make that coffee too weak, I'll shoot myself in the head with a .22, I mean it." Janice was laid out in the spare room, a damp towel on her head. "Her father-in-law? Doesn't that seem a little cold?" Greg slopped another finger of bourbon into the coffee cup and handed it to Marlene. He'd called Helen shortly after he found Carl's body and told her there'd been an accident on his jogging route. Marlene took a sip of coffee and winced.

"She's probably just in shock. I found out she's not really his daughter-in-law anyway, more just a girlfriend-in-law."

"Still, she knew him."

Greg clanked his mug on the table. "I'm just saying." There was a low moan from the spare room followed by a thud.

Janice came into the living room a few moments later. "Are the cops still there?" She glanced out the window then eyed the coffee. "Can I have some?" Marlene got another mug from the cupboard while Greg unscrewed the cap on the bourbon.

"How old are you?" he asked.

Janice looked at the bottle. "Twenty-one." Marlene took the bourbon from his hand and poured it in the coffee, adding two spoonfuls of sugar to take off the edge.

Janice gulped half the cup and set it down on the counter. "Well, Lee's not going to know what to do about this," she said.

Marlene had met Lee only once, a month after she moved in. He'd been at his father's patching windows on the porch and held out his hand, the skin callused like scales on an extinct animal. The handshake left Marlene's hand feeling dry for hours. "Where is he?"

"Got me," Janice said. "He's been gone four days now. I haven't seen hide nor hair." She stuck her hand in the cup and swiped the sugar on the bottom then stuck a finger in her mouth and giggled. "Hairy hide."

"Do you know how to get a hold of him?" Greg asked.

"He's been showing up for work, or I'd be getting calls from the garage. Every time I drive by during his shift the car's there, so I know he's going in." She set down the mug and looked from Marlene to Greg. "He even took the car, can you believe that? I had to steal it back just to come here today."

Greg held up a hand. "What garage?"

"Jimmy's on Marquette and Eighteenth." She turned her head to Marlene, eyes wide. "I'm not calling him."

Marlene put an arm around Janice's shoulder and raised an eyebrow to Greg behind her back. "You don't have to. No one's going to make you do anything you don't want."

"I know that," Janice said, her back straightening. "I should've known he'd just take off like this," she said. "Like mother, like son." She smoothed a hand over the counter like it was a highway. "Alice's been gone four months, and look what happened. Where's this going to leave me?"

After Janice and Greg left, Marlene spent the rest of the morning wandering through her house. She'd read the paper for a few moments before walking to the kitchen and, forgetting why she'd gone there, picking up a dust rag to clean a shelf. She looked out the window at one point and saw Carl's body being removed on a stretcher—no signs of blood on the snow, just black plastic covering the weight. Greg called her around one. "How're you doing?"

Marlene sniffled. "They took the body away."

He sighed into the phone, and she could tell from the lack of echo that he was upstairs, not hidden away in a corner of the basement. "Do you want me to come over?" he asked.

"Yes." Marlene sat down on the couch and looked out the window at Carl's house. "Where's Helen?"

Greg cleared his throat, and she wondered for a moment if he was trying to remember. "She's at a community meeting. She should be gone another hour." How can I compete with a woman who goes to community meetings? Marlene thought. Marlene was a good person, she knew, giving money for the past three years to the Cancer Society when no one in her family had ever died from the disease. "I can't stay long, but I'll be over."

Ten minutes later Greg showed up, and Marlene collapsed into his arms. It was dramatic but seemed warranted—a dead man's house next door and no one to comfort her. She moved her eyes up and could see nothing but a head, the collar of a sweater. Looming like this, Greg could have been anyone, Carl for that matter. At the thought of Carl she rolled away. Janice had told them earlier that no one had any idea how to get a hold of Alice. Rather than notifying them directly, she sent postcards from the cities she visited, thirty-two in all, with messages to Carl to keep an eye on Cheech, to clean up that compost heap he called a backyard, and to get on with his life.

"I just don't know how I'm going to get through this," Marlene said. "I don't know how I can sleep here." She was close to tears and almost laughed to think she was supposed to rescue anyone, company or otherwise, forty hours a week at work.

"Do you want me to stay the night?" Greg asked.

Her heart tugged, almost a physical ache, as she thought of Greg staying until morning. "You think you could?"

He jiggled the change in his pocket. "I'm not sure how exactly. It'd take a lot of maneuvering." He reached out and touched her chin. "But if you need me."

Marlene gave him another squeeze. "I'll be fine," she said. She told herself the offer had been enough, and as she peered up to kiss his chin she wondered if he thought the same.

He kissed her in turn on the forehead. "I need to go." She walked him to the door and watched him climb in his car, struggling to situate himself as he sat on the back of his parka, rubbing his hands together before he touched the steering wheel. She looked at the clock on the wall. It seemed unlikely that the car could have gotten so cold in the mere twenty-three minutes he'd been inside.

Janice showed up the next day with a pot roast and a small child. The boy had gaps between his tiny teeth and hair so blond it seemed translucent. She held out the roast. "It's a thank-you for taking care of everything yesterday. I get a twenty-percent discount on quick-sale meats at Cub Foods."

Marlene held the screen door open and followed them into the kitchen, where Janice set the roast down with a thud. "This is Leo," she said and gave the boy a gentle nudge with her knee. Marlene bent down and smiled at the child; she had little experience with children and often found herself treating them as very small adults she knew she was condescending to. Leo raised his head and opened his mouth as Janice pulled him back. "Leo's a biter," she said and motioned to the wrapped meat. "Greg and you were really great to handle everything with the cops yesterday. It's a good thing Lee wasn't here when they showed up." She pointed her chin at the ground and looked up with an eyebrow raised.

"He's in trouble with the law?" Marlene asked.

"It wouldn't surprise me," Janice said and sat down at the breakfast bar bringing Leo onto her knee.

"How did he take the news?"

"He hasn't heard yet, not in so many words." Janice picked a napkin out of the holder and folded it into a tiny square. "When I called the garage yesterday, I put a T-shirt over the phone to sound all ominous-like, saying he'd better come home quick. I just didn't think I should tell him over the phone." She took a pack of cigarettes and a lighter out of her coat pocket and handed them to Leo. "Is it OK?"

For a moment, Marlene thought she intended for Leo to smoke, but Leo took a cigarette out of the middle of the pack and handed it to Janice then took the lighter and held the flame near his mother's face. She bent in and lit the cigarette and Marlene went to the cupboard for an ashtray. She rarely smoked in the house, had been quitting now for months, but when Janice held up the pack she took one.

"It's sweet, don't you think, that Carl called Greg before . . . you know." Janice put a finger to her head like the barrel of a gun and exhaled a long thin line that Marlene followed over her head like a cloud.

"Sweet?" She remembered Greg in the living room, his face like bone. In the six months they'd been together, she had never seen him so shaken.

Janice leaned in as if they were in a crowded room. "A lot of people don't know this, but Lee's a big softy, can't take the sight of blood. Can't even watch those *Halloween* movies without tossing up his lunch." She took another drag. "I'm about the only one who knows that about him, me and Carl. So I guess just me now."

Marlene got up and put the meat in the fridge.

"That roast is for something else too," Janice said. Marlene looked up. "I mean, I have another favor." Marlene shut the fridge door as Leo took the cellophane off the pack and put it over his lips, breathing in and out, fogging the plastic. "It's just that the idea of going over to that house gives me the willies." Janice shivered, an affected moving of the shoulders. "Would you mind going with?"

The thought of going back to Carl's sent a flutter of nausea through Marlene's stomach—the smell of old pennies, the reverberating ring of the shower curtain. "Why do you need to go at all?"

"They need a suit for Carl, for one thing, and some info on how we're going to pay for this shindig." She put her hand under Leo's chin and squeezed his cheeks. "Would you want us going in alone?"

Marlene fished a pair of rubber gloves from underneath the sink. "I'm only staying ten minutes," she said. "Not a second more."

Janice jumped from the barstool and took Leo's hand. "In and out, swear to Christ."

When Janice fit the key in Carl's door, they heard a low moan like a mourning wail. "God, it's Cheech," Marlene said, and Janice twisted the key and swung open the door. Marlene ran through the kitchen toward the stairs to the basement.

Cheech was behind a baby gate, his hind-end wiggling so hard she thought he'd spin in circles. He was an ugly dog with matted white-and-brown fur, his body near gaunt from being alone just two days. He let out a hoarse bark and put his paws on top of the gate. "Cheechie," she said, and the dog barked again as she took off the gloves and reached down to lift him up. He wiggled from her grasp and licked the calf of her jeans twice before bolting past her to the living room. He looked around, his tail still going, barked twice at Leo, and jumped to a well-worn place on the back of the sofa next to the window.

"I never understood how Carl could like that dog so much," Janice said. "I mean, he's really ugly."

Marlene hadn't understood either, but it seemed obvious now, the dog in the window waiting for Carl to come home. She saw a leash on the end table by the door and clicked it to his collar. "We'll be back in a second."

Outside Cheech peed instantly, barely off the steps, and Marlene blew into her uncovered hands, her breath hovering in the air. Looking up, she was amazed how different the neighborhood appeared from one porch over, everything centered further to the left. She looked at her own house—the eaves drooping in the front, a mess of weeds hidden by the embankment near Carl's house. Despite the difference in the rest of the neighborhood, from Carl's porch, her house looked similar to how his did from hers.

Their neighbor—Marlene thought her name was Tina—came around the corner and Cheech lunged, desperate for more attention.

Tina skittered back around the corner before peering at Marlene and laughing. "I thought you'd be Carl," she said, then came over and put a hand down for Cheech to smell. "All I saw was the dog."

Marlene had done the same many times, even going so far as to circle the block in her car if she saw Carl outside with the dog. She wondered if a part of Carl's depression wasn't caused by her, all those times she had seen him out with Cheech, glad the mangy dog barked so loudly that she had an excuse to go inside. Would it have killed her to ask how he was getting on without Alice? To see if he wanted to split her shrimp lo mein? In her mind now she could see it—she and Carl eating dinner on their respective porches, two lonesome people against the world.

"Carl's dead," Marlene said, taking pleasure in the horrified look on Tina's face, the guilt as she tried to remember what she'd just said. "He left me the dog."

"I'm so sorry to hear that," Tina stuttered. "Not about the dog, Carl." She bent down and tried to soothe Cheech, who was choking himself trying to get to a squirrel.

"We're all sorry," Marlene said.

"Has anyone told . . ." Tina smiled awkwardly at Marlene. "Mrs. Carl?"

"Alice is gone," Marlene said. "She never even liked the dog." Marlene looked at Cheech then back at the house. She could see Janice through the front window shuffling a stack of papers. She looked like a thief moving quickly through the pages, glancing around the room every few moments to make sure Leo was near. Marlene glanced at her own house and wondered what she would look like if she were in there—sitting on the sofa under the window reading a book or maybe walking to the kitchen for a glass of water. Either way, anyone looking in would know the house was silent by the stillness of her shoulders, no movement to music or voices they couldn't hear outside the walls.

Marlene heard a low rumble in the distance and bent down to quiet the dog who was rushing circles in the snow, catching her in the leash. For months any loud sound in the neighborhood would remind her of the gunshot.

Lee drove up in a maroon Caprice Classic, low to the ground with speakers vibrating in the back. "Nice talking to you," Tina said quickly and started for her house on the corner. Janice ran out to the porch with Leo behind her and met Lee a foot away from the car. "You shit-for-brains rat bastard." She hit him with a closed fist on the top of his skull as he climbed out.

"Jesus," Lee cried and covered his face, falling in the snow in only a T-shirt. She hit him again, this time in the chest. "Honey, stop it." Marlene ran to the porch with Cheech and stood next to Leo, unsure what to do. Should she call the police? Run inside and close the door? Janice stepped back until Lee looked up then swung again. He grabbed her arms and held them down until Janice went limp. "Do you have any idea what I've been through?" Janice asked. "Do you? You're lucky your dad's the only one who's dead."

Marlene could see the muscles on Lee's forearms under the goose bumps from ten yards away. He stepped back and Janice lunged for him. "I didn't mean that, Lee. Swear to Christ." At first Marlene thought she was attacking him again, going for the open face, but Janice's body began to rock with sobs, and Lee put his arms around her.

"Baby, it's OK. I'm here." He wrapped his grease-stained hands around her head, his dirty nails popping out of the shaggy, blond hair. "What happened to my dad?"

Marlene watched the couple unable to look away.

Later that evening Marlene sat in bed with Cheech and tried to concentrate on the portfolio Claudia had given her on Friday. The company was a national sporting goods chain specializing in outdoor rafting and climbing equipment. Their training manual had a special section for women employees: *It is important to understand sports analogies even if you do not use them.* The executives who read the countless surveys seemed to take comfort in the fact that the employees at Modern Solutions were all women, as if what the business world needed was just a feminine touch and a shoulder to cry on. She thought of Greg, safe at home, leaving her with the wreckage of Carl's death and a quick afternoon visit to compensate.

She moved a pillow to the side and set Cheech at the head of the bed, pulled the quilt up until half of his wiry fur was covered. He snapped out of the bed, trotted into the living room and jumped on the back of her sofa, circled once, and laid down facing the street. She wondered how much Cheech knew, if he was in some kind of canine mourning or would continue for months to stare out the window with hope.

Marlene swung her legs out of bed and felt for her slippers then thought better of it and put on her jeans and tennis shoes. She pulled Cheech from the sofa, expecting a low growl, but he sat complacently as she bundled him in a T-shirt and put him in the car.

Driving down Aldrich Street, even in the dark, she could recognize the house—a limestone ranch-style with white shutters. In the yard were two iron Labradors, the paint chipped from sitting in the elements for years. She couldn't see them, but she knew they were there. She'd driven by this house at least once a week the past few months, looking for some clue that kept Greg here, a tangible sign that said he'd never be hers.

She pulled a U-turn at the end of the block then shut off her lights and stopped in front of the house. Greg's car was in the driveway, a light on in what she knew was the living room. He had told her about the fights he and Helen had had over that room—the navy-and-green sofa, to curtain or not to curtain. He had told her over dinner at a restaurant in the suburbs and had used a falsetto voice to indicate Helen—"but blinds look so *cheap*"—and Marlene had laughed along, eager for any news of the enemy.

Marlene got out of the car and walked toward the front door. It was still outlined with unlit Christmas lights, and the porch was dusted in new snow, the Labradors two useless sentries in the yard. She rang the bell then glanced back at her car, wondering if she shouldn't just turn around and drive Cheech to his new home, cuddle in her bed with man's best friend. There was a shuffling noise inside. It's the ninth inning, she thought, sink or swim.

The door opened, and there was Helen looking not much different from the photo Marlene had found in Greg's wallet. In the picture her hair was highlighted by the lights and held back in a barrette as she smiled for the camera, Greg behind her with a hand on her shoulder. "Hello," Helen said. Her face looked tired, more lined around the eyes and mouth, but she still looked young, kinder than Marlene would have imagined. "May I help you?"

Marlene opened her mouth—to say what, she didn't know—and then Greg came through the hallway from the kitchen. He looked up from a magazine, and his eyes locked with Marlene's as the magazine slid from his hand and hit the carpet, pages rattling. She remembered how he looked coming back from Carl's with the phone in his hand, the look on his face as if he had pulled the trigger. She broke her gaze with Greg and looked in Helen's square face. "I'm taking a survey," she said.

Helen wrapped her arms around her chest and looked out past the porch at the barely falling snow. "We're fixing dinner right now," she said. "Maybe you could stop by tomorrow?"

Marlene glanced at Greg. He bent over to pick up the magazine, his face the color of oatmeal, and she thought for the first time that he looked old. Usually when she saw him, he was wearing a suit coat or his nylon jogging suit, but at home, dressed in sweatpants and a flannel shirt, he looked middle-aged, maybe older. "What are you cooking?" she asked. "I haven't had dinner yet, maybe I could just come in." She glanced at Greg who had rolled the magazine into a tube. "Wouldn't that be a kick if you just invited me in for dinner, a stranger here at your door for a survey." She held Greg's gaze. "What do you think?"

Helen looked back at her husband.

"It's . . ." he stammered then looked at Helen. "If she hasn't eaten."

Helen's hand fluttered to her hair like an exotic bird, or maybe a larger insect. "I think it's a bit odd," she said.

Marlene laughed, a sound like steam escaping a kettle. "Oh, I could tell you about odd," she said and ducked past Helen to take off her scarf. "I see all kinds of things on this route. Your neighbors, three houses down, they've got a small child who answered the door and tried to bite me." Marlene leaned into Helen baring her teeth, "Grruf."

"The Hagens?" she asked.

"Maybe it was four houses."

Helen peeked around the door before shutting it, and Greg took Marlene by the elbow. "I'll show you where to put your coat," he said loudly and steered her toward the kitchen, his grip tightening through the goose liner of her jacket. "Just what the hell," he hissed.

Marlene took off her coat and handed it to Greg. He wanted her to do this, had wanted some kind of ultimatum. That's what Carl had done, had sent a message to Alice, but in typical Carl fashion, had gone too far.

"One time," she yelled to Helen in the hall, "I found a dead body in a house." She was speaking too loudly, Helen almost in the kitchen to meet them. "He killed himself because his wife left him, can you imagine? Killing yourself for *that*?" Helen glanced at Greg, an uneasy look on her face. "I suppose you can," Marlene said. "You two look really happy. In my survey," she announced, "I'd give you a nine out of ten." She looked around the kitchen then walked to the living room. "Do you want to know how I can tell?" she called back.

Helen had her arm entwined with Greg's, his jawbone clenching and releasing under the skin as they followed her to the living room. Helen slipped her arm out and moved toward Marlene as if genuinely curious. "How?"

Marlene looked around the spacious room before settling on the windows. "A couple that was on the verge of separating would never have purchased such beautiful curtains." She poked at the thick beige fabric.

"We just bought those three months ago," Helen said slowly, her eyes never leaving Marlene. "What else?"

Marlene put her head to the side. "Well, the fact you're home together on a Sunday night seems like a good sign. I'd be worried if there were a lot of extracurricular activities, though. Say, if one of you took up a 'sport' "—she made quotation marks with her fingers—"on the side, like golfing." She peeled back the curtain and was shocked when a face appeared. It took her a moment to recognize herself; the skin pulled too tight, her hair dampened and flat from the snow. "Of course," she laughed shrilly. "No one's going to be golfing in this weather."

Helen walked over and looked out the icy window. Marlene was surprised to see how similar they looked in the reflection, both with brown shoulder-length hair and hollowed eyes, as if they were the same person or would be in a few more years. "What about jogging?"

Marlene touched one index finger to her nose and pointed the other at Helen. "Exactly."

Helen turned around and raised a hand again to her hair, stopped halfway up, and wrapped her arms around herself. She looked at Marlene then back at her husband. "Greg, what is this?" she asked. Her voice was hollow, similar to the reflection they had shared a moment before.

"Yes," Marlene echoed. "What is this?"

Every Sad Detail

Jasper reads the letter again and figures he's got two days to find a place before his ex-wife comes to visit. How his living situation became so dismal so fast is more than Jasper can fathom. One day he's set up in the swankiest neighborhood in Lincoln, Nebraska, with a therapeutic indoor swimming pool and a backyard like a golf course, and the next day, zilch. He's been living in his truck now for eighteen days. And not a fancy truck with a sleeper and a mini-fridge but an '84 pick-up that Carol has always hated. The idea of her coming and staying the night—her head crunched low as she sits in the truck bed eating chicken filet sandwiches warmed at the U-Stop microwave—is more than Jasper can bear.

Carol doesn't say in the letter why she's coming, only that they'll be there Saturday and to please call by Wednesday to let her know it's all right. Jasper wonders who the other part of "we" is, although he has a pretty good idea it's Gary, the man she's mentioned in the last few letters whom she'd met at a country-western bar in Kansas City. Jasper was there a few years ago, one of those new country jobs with a jazzed-up lighting system for the dance floor and deer antlers at every turn; half the people in there wouldn't know Lester Flatt from Earl Scruggs.

He looks at his watch. It's already after noon, but he buys a paper to start looking for an apartment.

Jasper'd been working as a home companion up until three weeks ago when Damon, the man he'd worked for, died. Lance, his buddy from the Kawasaki plant, had gotten him the job as a favor and at first Jasper was leery, knowing how a favor could go, but Lance swore it was on the up and up. "You live with the old guy in his house, make sure he doesn't take a spill and break something important, and you basically get run of the joint. I'd take it myself, but the wife." Sarah, Lance's wife, found him the job on a special listing posted in the hospital where she's an X-ray technician, and Jasper figured she still had a soft spot for him after their affair broke up his marriage.

He drives out to meet a landlord on Seventeenth and Garfield. The ad boasts a balcony, A/C, and a dishwasher, but when he pulls up he finds it's a ramshackle apartment complex no different than the other three he's visited this afternoon. A large-ish woman with a clipboard meets him at the stairwell running the height of the building like a fire escape and points to a parking lot full of cars as depressing as his own. "Ten dollars a month," she says. "Off-street parking's not included." Inside, a brown-and-beige carpet is cut out around the doorway and expands like a dead lawn to the breakfast bar ten feet away. He can't imagine bringing Carol to an apartment worse then the one they rented when they were first married, eight years ago. They had mice and used to wake in the early mornings to the snaps of the trap, Carol clinging instinctively to his arm in her sleep when the sound went off.

"I'm going to have to think about it," he tells the woman.

She shrugs. "Suit yourself."

In his pickup he heads to U-Stop and grabs Carol's letter from the dashboard. Her handwriting hasn't changed, the same optimistic loop she used to write drafts of his psychology papers in senior year. If only he hadn't been such a schmuck, he thinks, he'd be looking at notes in that handwriting every day.

At U-Stop he calls from a pay phone and Carol answers on the fifth ring. "It's me," he says.

He can hear something rustling in the background and wonders if Gary's there. She coughs. "Jasp, we haven't spoken on a phone in over six months, you can't just say that anymore."

"You knew, though," he points out.

"How are you?"

"Good," he says. "You?" A woman at one of the two booths openly watches him, listening to the conversation as she smokes a cigarette.

"Keepin' on keepin' on," Carol says. It's an old saying they used for years, and the memory of it makes Jasper smile.

"Keepin' on," he echoes.

"You must've gotten my letter," Carol says. "You were supposed to call me yesterday." Then, "Hold on a sec." He hears the receiver clunk and looks over at the woman who jabs out her cigarette. She's in her late fifties and has some kind of growth on her neck, a smooth round lump the size of a jawbreaker, shiny and red as a new burn. He's tempted to laugh or nod so she won't know he's listening to dead air but turns his back to her instead. He hears Carol blowing her nose in the background, and then her voice is immediate again. "Allergies," she says. "So, is that going to work if we come on Saturday?"

"Since when do you have allergies?"

"Since always." She sniffles. "Are you going to be around?"

"That depends," Jasper says. "Who's all coming?" He knows he's walking a thin line and couldn't explain himself why he's doing it, but it feels good knowing Carol needs a favor.

"Gary and me. We're coming for the Husker game." She sighs. "If it's a problem, just say so, we can get a hotel."

"No, I've got more room than I need. I'd be happy to see you."

"We'll probably just come over after the game then, not bug you during the day."

"Great, I'm looking forward to it." There's an awkward pause, and Jasper glances behind his back to see if the smoking woman has noticed. "You want me to make dinner?"

Carol laughs, another old sound that rings in Jasper's memory. "God, no," she says. "I just need your address."

Jasper goes cold for a second and stammers. "I don't have it with me."

"Your address?"

"I moved at the beginning of the month and don't have it memorized. I could give you directions from the stadium, but it's complicated." He hears the flick of a lighter behind him and smells the stream of smoke as the woman exhales.

"Call me tomorrow, will you?" She gives him another number, probably Gary's, and hangs up after saying good-bye. Jasper walks back to the cooler for a burrito and a bag of corn chips and considers buying a six-pack but decides against it, knowing the beer will get warm in the bed of his truck.

At the cash register, he looks over at the woman in the booth. "That was my wife," he tells her. "She's coming home Saturday." The woman rotates her head slowly toward Jasper's face. Her eyes jump in the sockets, not completely focused. Despite the Harvey's Casino sweatshirt, she looks like some kind of soothsayer with her welt and pinball eyes, and he wonders what she'd tell him about this weekend, about whether or not Carol will stay the night with Gary and then keep on, or whether she'll take one look at him, her one-time husband, and decide never to leave.

"You left a quarter in the phone," she says, her voice heavy with cigarettes as she lifts a Styrofoam coffee cup to her red-lined mouth.

Jasper walks over to the phone, pushes the tiny metal door, and sure enough, the coin is waiting for him.

Jasper pulls up to Lance's and parks on the street, hoping in person he'll seem more desperate. Sarah answers the door with Samantha on her hip and leans out onto the porch to give Jasper a kiss on the cheek. "I'm sorry to hear about Damon," she says. Sarah is a plain-faced woman with a good heart, and Jasper is glad for her sake, not just his own, that Lance never found out about the affair.

Jasper nods. "Lance home?"

"Should be soon," Sarah says. Jasper looks around the living room and thinks if he can hide the toys in the attic, take down a few pictures, Carol'll never know the difference.

In the kitchen, Jasper sits down, and Sarah sets a cup of coffee in front of him after putting Samantha on a blanket on the floor. There's little tension left between them, only a tittering of guilt and secrets that have made their friendship stronger. Jasper is glad Sarah has some secrets from Lance, because he knows Lance has plenty himself. She's the only person Jasper can imagine telling that he and Damon had posed as lovers for Damon's family.

Lance's car farts in the driveway, and he walks in a moment later. "Here's trouble," he says when he sees Jasper at the table, then reaches for a beer from the fridge and sets it next to Jasper's coffee cup. He sits across from him then gets up and gives Sarah a kiss before sitting back down.

"I need a favor," Jasper says.

Lance reaches for some potato chips on the counter and holds the bag out to Jasper after taking a handful. "Go figure."

Jasper shakes his head. "You two going to be around this weekend?" he asks.

"Game's on," Lance says through a mouthful of chips. Jasper knows how much it bothers Sarah when Lance speaks with his mouth full. They used to lie in bed in the afternoons, taking turns listing the sins committed by their spouses; it's this more than anything that makes him feel guilty.

He explains his plan to them, how he'll move in Saturday afternoon, play host to Carol for a night, and be out by Sunday. "I'd pay for the hotel room," he adds. He still has a chunk of money socked away from living with Damon.

Lance lets out a guffaw. "She's got you, buddy. No can do." He puts more chips in his mouth and washes them down with the beer. "You could never get this place to look like a bachelor pad in two days. And anyway, the thought of being locked in a hotel room with my kids—," he shudders. Samantha starts crying as if to accentuate the point, and Lance swoops her off the floor.

"We could try," Sarah says weakly. Jasper knew it was a stupid plan; Carol has been there at least a dozen times and has a memory like an elephant. He begins to imagine Gary, who he assumes is a hulking cowboy, laughing at his pickup as Carol hightails it back to K.C. He puts his head on the table, and Sarah pats his shoulder.

"You want to stay here tonight?" Lance asks.

Jasper shakes his head. "Got a date."

They all know it's not true, but Lance purrs for show. "Tomcat."

At the door Sarah takes his elbow. "We'll think of something," she says. It's touching, and for a moment Jasper wonders if it wasn't all worth it—losing Carol, ruining his life—to know that for a bit both he and Sarah were appreciated.

Jasper eases his pickup into a spot under the "O" Street viaduct. He's been parking here for the last week, sleeping in the truck-bed, thankful it's only September and not February. Before that he was out at Holmes Lake where he could bathe in the lake, but the cops drove by before dawn every morning, telling him he had to move. He munches on the corn chips left over from the gas station and turns his flashlight on the want ads. It's useless. Even with the money he's saved he couldn't find a decent apartment and furnish it by Saturday. Carol would walk in the door and instantly know something was wrong with his life—no pictures on the walls, no personal touches.

He's never told her about Damon and couldn't say why, although he has a feeling it has to do with pride. He wants her to believe he'd been promoted as planned to shift manager at the Kawasaki plant and is keepin' on keepin' on. But in truth, he hit a low when she left, drank until he lost his job and apartment, and in a state of self-pity, blamed that on her too. She still addresses his letters to the plant, and Lance picks them up, forwarding them first to Damon's and now to general mail.

He thinks about Damon. In the last few weeks he hasn't had a chance to miss him, but the ache is there now, heavy on his chest. When he first took the job, it was awkward caring for another man, and a stranger at that. It would have been different if it was his own father or his grandfather, but he can't imagine that either—both farmers, self-sufficient as they come. Sarah had coached him to lie in the interview, to tell Damon he had some experience with home health care and that he was pre-med in college. "You can't smoke in the house," Damon said. "My emphysema. But I don't care about the garage." Most of the time Damon had joined him, huddled in blankets next to the Oldsmobile. Jasper had tried in the beginning to stay aloof, but Damon refused to let him, asking Jasper at every turn to perform intimate tasks, bathing him and feeding him as if he were a child. It was obvious to Jasper that Damon was gay, possibly the first gay person he knew. Definitely the first one he'd bathed.

His mind drifts to Carol, how they used to bathe together when they were first a couple. "Conservation," she called it. In his memory it's just miles of soft skin, the smoothness of every swoop from her collar to her hipbone, and with this, he falls asleep.

Jasper wakes to a tapping on the roof and wonders for a moment if it's raining. A gruff voice says, "Police," and his heart races until he recognizes the voice as Lance's. Jasper pulls himself up, by instinct now not hitting his head, and looks out the window of the truck bed. "I've got an idea," Lance says and shakes a bag from McDonald's.

Jasper crawls out of the truck, and Lance hands him an Egg McMuffin and a cup of coffee. He's dressed in his plant overalls, and for a second Jasper feels self-conscious in his flannel pants and sweatshirt, another day of loafing. "You can stay at Kelli's place. She's in the Black Hills until Sunday night." Kelli is Sarah's sister, a sorority girl who legally changed the ending of her name from a "y" to an "i" three years ago.

"You serious?" Jasper is overwhelmed and wants to hug Lance, affection he wouldn't have thought possible with another man before Damon.

"Sarah called her cell phone this morning and left a message saying you'd be there. Just don't break anything. She's always liked you, God knows why." Jasper wonders if he's talking about Sarah or Kelli.

"I appreciate this, you know that."

Lance shoves a whole hash brown in his mouth and gets back on his motorcycle. "Here," he says and throws Jasper the keys.

Driving to Kelli's, Jasper feels like he's been given a second chance, as if this will be his real apartment, his start at a life. When he opens the door, the light feeling dissipates, displaced by a girlish apartment and the realization Carol won't believe it's his for a second. There are dried flowers hanging from the ceiling, ruffly curtains on every window, a poster of the UNL men's swim team in Speedos taped to a kitchen wall. Sarah knocks on the half-open door and walks in, Samantha on her arm and four-year-old Travis trailing behind. "It's hopeless," Jasper says.

"Nah," she says and looks around. "We'll have it together in no time."

He follows her to the parking lot, and she hands him Samantha, a wiggling weight in his arms. She opens the trunk of her car and inside are boxes of stuff: a Green Bay Packers fleece blanket, a plastic singing fish marooned on a plaque that he bought for Lance as a gag for Christmas.

They haul the boxes into the apartment, and when Jasper looks around again he realizes that most of Kelli's personal possessions are movable—candles and picture frames—and that the furniture is most likely hand-me-downs from her parents, solid pieces that are neither too feminine nor masculine.

Sarah and Jasper spend the next three hours refereeing the children and switching Kelli's things with the items in the boxes, all but the Packers blanket, which would tip off Carol, Jasper being a Vikings fan since birth. When they're done, the apartment looks so inviting Jasper almost believes he does live here, and it's as easy as three hours of labor to step into a life he wants to live. He calls the second number Carol gave him—it is Gary's—and leaves an address after the beep.

"I'm sorry she left," Sarah says as they walk to their cars and Jasper offers her a sloping smile.

"Yeah, me too."

Jasper knows when it comes down to it, he fucked up. He wouldn't go so far as to say he'd suspected Carol would be *proud* of him for confessing, but he had hoped she'd be more lenient if he was enough of a man to come clean when he didn't have to. She came home from work on a Tuesday, and he followed her into the bedroom, planning just to watch her change out of her slacks and blouse and into his sweatpants and T-shirt, and instead sat on the bed and told her everything. How he'd gone to Lance's to fix the skylight in the living room and next thing he knew he and Sarah were somehow intertwined on the carpet, Travis and Samantha both down for their naps and Lance out of town at a Kansas State basketball game. Carol stood there tiny and vulnerable in her flowered panties and a mismatched bra. "It just happened? You expect me to believe you just blacked out and came to having sex with Sarah?"

And then the clincher: he told her these blackouts lasted two weeks, and she was gone by Wednesday morning.

Jasper knows he loves Carol and has never completely figured out why he cheated. Part of it had to do with the way Sarah had looked at him, so specifically happy he was someone other than her husband. And part of it, he admitted, had to do with her being someone who didn't care that he probably drank too often and too much, that he would never make manager at Kawasaki, that he didn't want children, at least not until he was done being a child himself. Someone who didn't look at him day after day across the breakfast table, knowing he was the person she was stuck with for life.

Jasper sleeps late on Saturday, his first solid bed in twenty nights. He spends most of the afternoon watching the Huskers on Kelli's TV and orienting himself in the kitchen to the items he might need: coffeepot, plates, a pan for eggs in the morning. He looks through the fridge packed with tofu and sprouts. Maybe this will be more evidence to Carol that he's turned himself around.

Jasper wonders for a moment how deceitful it is to pass off Kelli's apartment as his own or if he can convince himself this is *more* honest then his real life, this life he wants to lead. When Damon's kids came to visit, Damon would dress up in his Brooks Brothers suits, although he spent most days rattling around the house in jogging pants. The oldest daughter, Marianne, had walked in when Jasper was dressing Damon: Damon laid out on the bed, Jasper bent over him working the leather of his belt. "For God's sake," Marianne said, a look of disgust on her middle-aged face. When Jasper and Damon came into the kitchen arm-in-arm from the walk downstairs, Jasper left his arm around Damon's shoulder comfortably, an unspoken sign he was on

Damon's side. They hadn't let anyone other than Damon's children believe they were lovers—Jasper didn't want half the town thinking he'd gone queer—but it seemed significant that the ones Damon lied to were the ones that mattered most.

When the game is over Jasper lies down on the pastel couch, now covered in a navy fleece blanket, and awakens an hour later to pounding on the door. "Police," Carol yells in a deep voice. It's the second time in two days Jasper has awakened to this warning, and he wonders if he really is doing something he could be arrested for.

He opens the door, and there's Carol holding a pizza box, still skinny as a twelve-year-old, with a blond braid thick as a forearm down to the crack of her butt. Behind her is Gary, a looming man with a thick head of hair and a belt buckle of Herbie Husker. He looks like a caricature of good looking with everything too prominent—his muscles, his forehead, his chin.

"We've been out here for ten minutes," she says. "Thought we might have the wrong place."

"No, this is it," Jasper says and awkwardly bends to kiss her cheek.

Gary clears his throat. "Oh," she says and turns. "Gary, Jasper. Jasp, Gary."

"Nice to meet you," Gary says and holds out his hand; Jasper nods and shakes it.

Carol walks into the kitchen and sets down their dinner then takes a look around. "Nice place," she says. She laughs when she sees the poster of the swim team. "Since when do you like anything but football?"

Sarah had convinced him to leave the poster up, saying that it added character to the kitchen, and now he regrets it. "I'm broadening my horizons," he says.

"To swimming?" She opens the pizza box and turns to him. "It's good to see you." She smiles, and for a moment it feels so right having her here in his kitchen that he can imagine her in the morning with a cup of coffee after sex, the same red T-shirt hanging halfway to her knees over underwear and socks. "Let's see the rest of the place."

He takes her and Gary on a tour of the apartment—the sunny bathroom, the bed as big as a Buick in back. "You can put your stuff here," he says.

Gary sets two overnight bags on the bed. "Thanks again for your hospitality," he says. "Not a lot of men would let the new fellow come to stay." Jasper resists telling him not to pee in the corner marking his territory.

"So you like country music," Jasper says. "You ever listen to Ralph Stanley?"

"I've got *Sunday Morning* on vinyl." Gary mauls a hand through his hair, a challenging look on his face.

Carol grabs both of their elbows. "Jasp thinks he's the only one who appreciates country music because he got caught with a woman and had another one leave him. Be nice boys." She pulls them into the living room. "Let the little lady get you some drinks." She comes back with three cans of Budweiser and hands them out. "To the Huskers," she says and takes a gulp, then rubs her flat belly. With a twist of wicker, Gary sits down in the papasan chair, teeters back, and grabs an end table to steady himself. He looks emasculated in the womblike chair, and Jasper lifts his can to keep from laughing. He warned himself not to get too drunk, to let Carol see what a responsible citizen he's become, but the beer tastes good, and he drinks a third of the can before coming up for air. He goes to the kitchen, pulls three paper plates out of the left cabinet, and brings in the pizza.

Carol takes a picture he has missed from a shelf underneath the end table, and Jasper worries he's going to have to explain a sorority picture full of girls, or who Kelli is and why she's kissing another guy.

"Honestly, Jasp, if you could be a little more discreet. Is this still going on?"

He looks at her with what he hopes is an innocent expression, and she pushes the picture in his face. It's Lance and Sarah with the kids at the Sunken Gardens, Samantha in Sarah's arms while Lance twirls Travis like an airplane. "It's just a picture," he explains. "Lance gave it to me for Christmas."

Carol holds the picture out to Gary, who looks at it, nodding. She points to Sarah. "This is the woman Jasp had an affair with, and this"—she shifts her finger to Lance—"is his best friend."

"Sounds like a sticky situation," Gary says.

"Well, it was," Jasper agrees.

"I don't want the dirty details," Carol says. "It's all for the best." She reaches for a piece of pizza, and Jasper gets up for another beer. Gary rattles his empty can, so Jasper grabs two more.

"What do you do, Gar?" Jasper says. He looks at the belt buckle again—solid as a piece of steel, thighs underneath his jeans like crocodiles.

"Gary," Carol says. "With a 'y.' "

"Gary," Jasper says.

"I'm in phonics." He says it like he's in a swimming pool or in a truck bed night after night, like it's an actual place and not a job. Jasper has no idea what "in phonics" means, so he nods his head and looks at his ex-wife. "How's your job?"

"Good," she says. And right before the next sentence, Jasper knows he's worked his way into a pickle: "How's the plant?"

"Good," Jasper says. "It's good. Anyone want anything?"

"I'm fine," Gary says.

"You ever get that job as shift manager?" Carol asks.

"You could say I'm between positions," Jasper explains, nodding slowly. "Not quite the old line but not quite manager." She looks at him. "I'm working more with people these days."

She points to the picture again and says to Gary, "Jasper was always a people person."

Jasper hadn't realized he would get browbeaten about the affair. For Carol it's still fresh, her last image of him, while he's seen Sarah nearly every day until she faded back to being just Lance's wife and a close friend to talk to. "Are we going to fight tonight?" Jasper asks, sitting on the sofa. "I just want to know what to expect."

Carol pats his knee. "No, we're going to do our best to play nice."

They finish the pizza and spend the next few hours in polite conversation—everything from the Huskers to the intelligence of different dog breeds—anything but the situation at hand. Gary has been fighting since nine o'clock to stay awake, a losing battle, and he slumps even further into the papasan chair, nothing but legs and a head visible from the couch. Jasper is disappointed that he turned out to be a nice guy, kind to Carol, and even though Jasper dislikes Gary, he knows it's not his place. It's disconcerting to be sitting on the couch with his wife, just like six months ago, only her lover next to them. Like most things in his life, he has no idea how this has happened and no conscious idea how to rectify it.

At a commercial in the ten o'clock news, Carol turns to him. "I know your secret," she whispers and takes another sip of beer. Jasper tenses with a rush of nausea as he realizes he'll have to sleep on a couch she knows isn't his as she climbs into bed with Cowboy. "I think it's sweet," she adds. "I never would have guessed you could do something like that."

Jasper sits still for a moment. "Do what?"

"Care for old people."

Jasper hadn't thought of this before—Damon as a way to get laid—and is instantly ashamed of himself. He looks over at Gary. "How long have you two been together?" He doesn't really want to know but wants Carol to see he's matured enough to ask her.

"Long enough," she says and shrugs, glancing at Gary, his eyelids fluttering in his head. "He's asked me to move in."

"Are you going to?" He can't imagine an answer that'll make him feel better.

"We haven't decided yet. My lease is up in a month."

Jasper goes into the kitchen and grabs another can and sits on the sofa before switching to another channel. He realizes it's a wide line between maturity and where he actually is, although he sits silently with the remote control in his lap, knowing the incorrect response is to keep drinking.

"Aren't you going to say anything?" Carol says. "Technically we're still married, at least for a few more months." Jasper turns to the Weather Channel and gets an update on the rain fronts in Nashville, Tennessee. "You can't even give me this," Carol says. "You can't even be upset for a second."

"I'm upset," he says and opens the beer, dimly aware one of his problems may be that he's given up too easily. It already seems she's made the decision, and what can he do but go along with it? Carol rises from the couch and pokes Gary in the arm—"we're going to bed"—and there's a rattle of keys outside the door before Kelli pokes her head in and says, "South Dakota was a snore. I hope it's OK I came back early."

Jasper coughs a spray of beer into his hand and lunges for the hallway. Kelli's face is shiny with makeup, not at all as if she has been camping, and Jasper remembers Lance saying she always liked him. Kelli looks over and sees Carol on the couch, Gary crooked uncomfortably in the chair. "Is this not OK?" she asks.

Jasper walks the rest of the way to the door, "Just a surprise." He gives Kelli a hug, a quick peck on the cheek. "Hi."

Kelli widens her eyes and hugs him back. "Hello."

Carol glances over at Jasper with her lips drawn tight and forms her arms into a cradle and rocks it. Kelli smiles at Carol, who pretends to brush her shoulder.

"I'm Carol," she says, holding out her hand. "The ex-wife."

"Oh," Kelli says, her voice rising before she bites her lip.

Jasper grabs Kelli's hand to pull her down the hallway. In the bedroom he shuts the door. "I need a favor," he says.

Kelli sits on the bed and pulls a pillow into her lap. "Who's the big guy?"

"Carol's boyfriend." She gives him a quizzical look, and Jasper clears his throat. "Is it OK if I tell her you're my girlfriend?"

Kelli leans back on her hands and shrugs her head to the side. "Do you want me to be?"

Jasper smiles, amazed at how easy it can be.

Kelli jumps pertly from the bed and kisses him on the cheek, leaving a pink, wet smear that smells of raspberries. "No problem." She opens the door before Jasper can explain further and walks into the living room, sits on the couch, and pats the cushion next to her. She looks at him with the adoration only someone in her early twenties can muster.

Jasper sits next to her, and Carol moves from the doorway to sit on Gary's lap in the papasan chair; Jasper watches her kiss him and is certain he sees a flash of tongue. He moves closer to Kelli and puts his arm around her as she snuggles into his armpit.

"Sorry I was so confused before," Kelli says. "Jasper forgot to mention you were coming."

"I understand," Carol says. "One time Jasper forgot he had a wife."

Kelli looks at Jasper as if disappointed, hurt to know her boyfriend could be that type of man. "Is that true?" She looks back at Carol. "I think we met once, at a barbecue at Sarah's."

It suddenly dawns on Carol, and she turns to Jasper. "Her sister?" She gets up from the chair, pushing off Gary's belly. Carol's eyes are rimmed red from drinking and the allergies, and Jasper wonders for the first time how hard it was for her to leave. "We're going to bed. I'm not staying up for any more of this."

"Let's hit the hay," Gary says, and Jasper knows he can't let them go, can't watch Carol walk out of the room with another man.

"Not yet," Jasper says. "No one's even tired." Gary puts an arm around Carol. "How about some music?" Jasper says and runs over to the boom box, turns the radio on, and slides the tuner to 96 KIX, the country radio station they'd listened to through college, all those hours they spent dancing around their apartment or making love to Willie Nelson. "Come on," he says, moving his hips in what he knows is a desperate gimmick. "Let's dance." Even Kelli looks at him with a confused expression, as if she can't imagine why this man is gyrating in her living room.

"Jasp, we're tired," Carol says. "The evening's over."

"One dance won't hurt," Gary says and curls an arm around her shoulder. "Then we're off to bed."

"I'll get more drinks," Jasper says. "Another round for everybody."

He runs to the kitchen and opens the fridge, Kelli behind him. She stands by the open door, the silhouette of her slim hips blocking his view as he tries to see into the next room.

Kelli looks over her shoulder at Carol and Gary as Gary swings her through the air, almost knocking over an end table, her toes six inches from the ground. "You still love her," Kelli whispers and touches Jasper on the shoulder as he comes up with the fresh cans of beer.

"Of course," he says, then looks at Kelli, eyes big as a kitten's. "Of course." In her overly adult makeup and starched hair she looks so young she almost reminds him of Carol—not the one in the living room but the one in his memory—and he wishes he were twenty-three again, alone with Kelli, or maybe the old Carol, or maybe just twenty-three. "I'm sorry," he says.

Kelli squinches her nose and flutters her eyelids, and Jasper realizes it's the idea of anyone in love that's got her moony, not him. "Come on," she says and tugs at his arm as she reaches for the four full beers in his hands. In the tiny living room, she pushes Carol and Gary apart and hands them their beers, then throws her arms around Jasper's neck, surprising him with a bump of her pelvis.

Carol rolls her eyes and then leans in close to Gary. "Let's do it," she says. "Let's move in together."

Gary stops dancing and holds Carol out at arm's length as Kelli smiles into Jasper's neck. "Why?" Gary says.

"What do you mean 'why'?" Carol says.

Gary looks over at Jasper, then back at Carol. "Just how good of a sport do you expect me to be here?" And with that, Gary taps Jasper on the shoulder, takes Kelli's empty hand, and spins her into his arms.

Jasper and Carol watch Gary hold up an arm for Kelli to twirl beneath. Jasper knows he should come clean, confess every sad detail, that he's living in his truck, unemployed and alone, that even he can tell Gary would be a better man for her. He could sing it even, like a slow, twangy country song that's so much worse, because she'd know it was true. He thinks briefly of Damon and the lies they told his family—it left Damon with his pride, but in the end, really, what was that?

"I've got something to tell you," he says.

Carol moans, a low sound. "Confessions is not a good game for us." She looks from Gary to him with an expression so weepy and crumpled it's like she's standing in her underwear back in their bedroom, trying to decide if Jasper is the man she wants to forgive. He wants to say something honest, atone for his sins and show she didn't waste eight years, but that's not what comes out, and even he can't believe he does it, but he does: he pulls Carol to him and says, "Kelli's not the woman I'm in love with," then reaches an arm behind her shoulder and leans in for a kiss. Jasper hears a guttural sound issue from Gary's throat, whether a battle cry or a mating call, he couldn't say for sure. Carol puts a hand on the nape of his neck and kisses him back without protest, but it's a sad kiss, like those at the end of their marriage, which he knows now for certain was ending long before he forced her to walk out.

Carol pulls away and raises her hand in a delayed reaction as if to slap him, but it hovers in the air before falling lamely to her side. "We should go," she says.

"I'd say so," Gary says and walks quickly to the back bedroom to get their bags. In the living room he holds out a hand to Jasper. "It was interesting meeting you," he says. Jasper is pleased Carol must have said something respectable about him before they made the trip, at least enough for Gary to know it would be a wrong decision to hit him.

"Likewise." He walks Gary and Carol to the Cherokee parked next to his '84 Chevy, a sad heap of metal he'd be glad to never see again. Carol looks over at Jasper's pickup and shakes her head. "I can't believe that thing's still running," she says and climbs into the Jeep.

Gary starts the engine and revs it, louder and for a longer period than is necessary. It wouldn't be so difficult, Jasper thinks, to wake up in the morning to a cup of coffee, maybe some orange juice, and start a new life. To think that tomorrow he could put on a pair of shoes, go down to the U-Stop for a paper, find a place to rent, and just rent it. He sees this in his mind's eye, superimposed with the image of Carol's head leaning against Gary's shoulder, Gary's arm tucked in the window as they pull into the street.

The Last Girlfriend

Over the years Anita and Joan had begun to look alike, much like dogs and their owners. Three years ago they'd actually been mistaken for twins by a drunk man at a bar with bad lighting; they joked about it for weeks, how they were slowly merging together like a long lost, separated egg. Now getting off the plane, disoriented by the cabin pressure and over an hour of turbulence, Joan was convinced not only would she not see *herself* but would hardly recognize the woman mistaken for her. She was so sure, looking around the waiting area, that she was surprised to see a woman who so much resembled Anita holding a sign above her head that read, "Joanie," and scrawled in the corner, "loves Chachi." The woman ran toward her in big whooping steps, the sign flapping in such an erratic manner that Joan looked furtively at the doorway she'd just exited, as if she could climb back on the plane, fly back to Minnesota, and restore not only the two hour loss but the past six months and the inevitable feeling Anita had moved not only to a new time zone but to a new life.

Anita crushed Joan in a hug, both of Joan's arms bolted to her sides as she continued looking around for a woman who looked less like Anita. This woman, the Anita in front of her, looked familiar but seemed larger somehow, as if she'd gained height not weight, and was far more substantial than Joan remembered. "I'm surprised they let you in wearing denim," Anita said. "It's like no one in this state has heard of jeans."

Anita had moved to California six months earlier, taking off on the red-eye after the reception. At the wedding Joan stood next to her at the altar thinking how glad she was the bridesmaid's dress was a tasteful black, elegant and understated, how hopeful she was she'd be wearing it again. As Ralph and Anita repeated their vows, she thought how odd it would feel, the shimmer of tulle against her thighs as she danced with a groomsman, hopefully the second to the end, a cousin flown in from Vermont for the occasion.

Ralph came up carrying Anita's purse and tentatively hugged Joan. "She's been in a state," he said, "ever since your phone call."

Joan put her arms around Ralph's thin neck. It was amazing, she'd thought when she met him, that a neck so tiny could support his face. "I like drama," Joan said.

"You're in good company," Ralph replied.

Anita swatted Ralph's butt with the Joanie loves Chachi sign. "Ralph wouldn't know drama if it bit him in the ass."

He grinned at Anita. "I'd know if you bit me in the ass, what's the difference."

Joan glanced again at the door, but the hallway had disappeared, leaving only a gaping hole. The flight attendant who had been so willing to fly them into the face of death with her coiffed bangs and a refreshment cart closed the door with one efficient snap, wrapped her fingers around the handle of a neat, black carry-on bag, and wheeled it into the crowd, disappearing.

Four days ago Joan had called Anita in California when Dean left. "It is absolutely over, I kid you not." She exhaled loudly into the receiver. "Finito."

Anita had heard this before in the numerous nights they'd spent on the phone only three miles apart. Joan wished the phone lines from Minneapolis to L.A. weren't so clear, as if the distant static would remind Anita again how far away she was. "What happened?" Anita sighed. Joan couldn't blame her for being skeptical, having heard so many times before that this breakup would stick, as if they were putting something together rather than tearing it apart.

"It's another woman," Joan said. "An old girlfriend from college."

"For Christ's sake, that was twelve years ago," Anita said. "Leave it to Dean to fall in love in college." Joan and Anita had met at Moorhead State and lived together most of the four years, except when Anita fell in love with a guitar player and moved out, although in retrospect they realized she was more like his landlord than his girlfriend.

Joan paused and gulped. "It's true, Ita. We've never broken up over an outside party before. Usually all our problems come from the inside."

"Well that's that," Anita said. "And good riddance. You need to come out here and see me." Anita could do that, move past a year-and-a-half relationship as easily as picking out a melon, and Joan had taken the invitation at face value, calling her back an hour later to say she'd booked the flight. Now waiting at the baggage claim, both women stared silently at the mouth of the conveyer belt as if conversation would wreck their concentration. Joan remembered now that Anita was that kind of Midwestern nice, making invitations without meaning them, offering her heart when it was already on loan to someone else.

Anita met Ralph eight months earlier at a Safeway in Rancho Cordova, California, where she had flown for her job inspecting bakeries. "It's like that Ginsberg poem," Anita told Joan over the phone when she called, as promised, from the Ramada Hotel. "You know, 'A Supermarket in California.' "

And it was, it seemed: "Aisles full of husbands!" Ralph was a husband, soon to be ex, an ugly divorce impending that had him staying in a friend's apartment over a garage. At the grocery mart where he was picking out bread for his dinner—a rye with caraway seeds—Anita poked nosily into his cart and told him that would never go with the processed box of fettuccini. "Fettuccini in a box, can you imagine?" she'd asked Joan that night over the phone. Now at the airport, Joan wondered how their love had blossomed from *that*, a badly planned meal and a need to mother. Anita pointed at a plaid monstrosity making its way around the belt. "Whose?" she said.

Joan looked around and saw a man with sans-a-belt slacks and a walkman. "His," she said.

Anita grinned and pointed at a woman in the corner in Mickey Mouse stretch pants and a Goofy T-shirt. "Or hers." She grabbed Joan's hand and squeezed. "I've missed you, I really have. It's weird out here in California." Her face shaped into a lopsided smile. "It's like everyone's stupid from the sun."

"I've missed you too, Ita. It's like everyone's stupid from the cold." Joan saw Ralph in the crowd, back from getting the car, with his hand above his eyes fielding the florescent glare. Joan pointed. "Could be his," she said, and Anita glanced over.

"Too easy," she said and stood up waving one arm until Ralph saw her, a smile easing across his face at the sight.

Joan followed Ralph up the stairs. "Here you go," he said and set her suitcase on the bed. The room was like Anita's had been in Minneapolis only slightly skewed, like seeing a picture of yourself you no longer recognize or remember having taken. Joan thought it was like the photos of herself in high school when she was fat, fatter than most people would believe possible looking at her now. She'd shown the pictures to Dean a few months after they'd begun dating, dragging the shoebox of pictures from under her bed. "Here," she said. "Look at these."

Dean refused to look, saying it didn't matter, but when she forced them into his hands, flexing his fingers around the yellowing photographs so he had no choice but to look, he'd taken them, peering down. He let out a long, low whistle. "You *were* pretty fat." He blew out his cheeks and laughed. "I'm kidding," he said and pulled her into a hug, the pictures dropping to the floor. Joan felt she should have known right then they'd never make it: never trust a man who could lie when you were naked and vulnerable, proof of your ugly self in his hands.

"You need anything else?" Ralph asked. His face was slightly sweaty from the walk upstairs, and he took a handkerchief from his pocket and swiped his forehead like it was a chalkboard.

"I think I'm fine." She felt like she should tip the concierge.

Ralph cleared his throat. "I know how worried Anita was when you called. She's really glad you came." He patted her suitcase. "Me too. We never really got a chance to talk at the wedding."

She wanted so badly to dislike Ralph, but a smile erupted from his face, and she smiled back. "It was a nice ceremony." Joan had sat at one of the tables with Dean who refused to dance and instead created a pyramid with cocktail napkins and place cards. But at least he had been there, a body in the chair. Two months later Anita sent a photo back to Minnesota of Joan and Dean sitting at the table visibly bored, their uneaten pieces of wedding cake between them. "This is your future," it said in Anita's hard, black scrawl. "Get out while you still can." Her handwriting always looked like it had been exercised with a charcoal pencil by a third-grader.

"Anita was beautiful, that's for sure," Ralph said. "I've never seen anyone dance quite like that." He flayed his arms back in stiff jerks. Joan laughed and Ralph clicked his heels together with stiff posture. "Dinner at eight, madam."

He saluted her before turning around, and Joan thought about all the dates she and Anita had had over the years, ending with them on the phone coming up with nicknames and cruel jokes about the men they had gone out with, even the ones they liked. "Heil Hitler," she whispered, "you won't believe this one," but Anita was downstairs starting dinner. Joan had a feeling it was probably for the best; she didn't imagine this new Anita would laugh.

The next morning Joan found a note taped in black crayon to her mirror, "out back painting, come see me." Joan put on a sweatshirt and went downstairs, stopping in the kitchen for coffee on the way outside.

"You going to help with the garage?" Ralph's voice startled her, and she followed the sound to the living room. "I can't believe I'm going to get it painted for such cheap labor." He put down the paper and grinned.

Joan felt disarmed in her boxers and sweatshirt, with Ralph looking so passive and friendly in his overstuffed chair. She could tell by looking outside it was almost ten, the time change and breakup having suspended her sense of balance. "I'm hoping I missed the hard part having slept so late."

"You must have needed it," Ralph said.

Joan walked over to the mantle and set down her coffee next to a porcelain figurine three inches tall and nine inches long, painted a clean bone-white with small black triangles. It was an exotic and eerie animal curved like a painfully flattened bell, with a red scale above its tail and gold for eyes.

"It's the anteater," Ralph said, getting up from his chair and nodding toward the figurine. "I started collecting them about ten years ago. My ancestors are from Hungary." Joan looked back at the figurine. Was Hungary full of anteaters? "They're Herends," Ralph explained, his eyes focused on the anteater. "Manufactured over there since the early 1800s." He swung his arm widely, encompassing the room. "I have others," he said, and the speckled animals seemed to appear out of nowhere: an ostrich on the piano, a short, fat duck with a gold bill by the window sill. "I like to keep them out where I can enjoy them." Ralph smiled and put his hands in his khaki pockets. "No use keeping them locked in a cabinet."

Joan moved to touch the anteater's head, and Ralph's left hand shot out, his face folding into a nervous smile. "We don't normally touch them," he said, putting his hand back down. "But go ahead."

Joan looked at Ralph's face, his eyes amazingly blank. "I don't have to," she said. "I was just curious about the weight." It looked heavy sitting on the mantle next to a bouquet of dried flowers.

"Here." Ralph picked up the statue delicately, cradling the head like a newborn. He placed the anteater in her hand, and the weight was satisfying; the claws that had looked so menacing sitting on the wood were a polished, smooth surface that cupped in Joan's palm. "Forty-six ounces."

She looked at Ralph, his hands shadowing hers as she held out the animal for him to take. He stared at it for a long moment before his hands moved to guide the anteater back to the mantle, holding onto hers until he heard the reassuring click. It took all Joan's concentration to not drop the animal when Ralph's clammy hands touched hers, the skin soft like a toddler as if he'd never touched anything harder than a plastic book.

"They're nice," Joan said, still looking at the anteater, the gold eyes fixed and shiny.

Ralph blinked twice before turning toward her. "They're just a doodad I collect," he said. "Just a knickknack." Joan imagined her hand flying out to tap the anteater, just to see his reaction.

Anita came into the living room carrying paintbrushes wrapped in plastic baggies. "Morning, Sleepy. I made us lunch reservations, just the girls."

Ralph looked at her hands, speckled with colored paints. "I thought you were painting it white," he said.

She stood on tiptoes and kissed his nose. "I decided to brighten it up a bit."

Ralph glanced at Joan then back at Anita. "What's 'a bit'?"

Anita put the paintbrushes behind her back. "Jesus, Ralph. It's a little color; it won't kill you."

Ralph forced a laugh. "I don't mind a little color; I'm just curious what you did after we agreed on white."

"See what it's like to have a husband?" Anita said to Joan. "Do you see this?"

Ralph sat back in his chair. "I'm just curious, that's all. I'm sure I'll love it." He smiled at Joan. "I'm sure."

On the way to Vindaci's Anita prattled on about the calamari and mussels, telling Joan she'd never had seafood like this, ever ever ever, as if all that was flown into Minneapolis were Van de Kamp's fish sticks. Even the way Anita spoke, without the long vowels, seemed foreign and vaguely Californian.

At the restaurant, Anita dabbed a napkin in her water glass and rubbed the yellow paint from her bone-thin wrist. "So tell me about Dean."

"It's really a good thing I got rid of him," Joan said. "I can see that now." She spoke as if the breakup had happened years ago, a distant memory that made her stronger. "I'm excited to be single again, concentrate on my work." Joan was an assistant manager for Carmel Cosmetics, the result of a four-year liberal arts degree, although she could see little connection between this and the humanities. Women came in with their daughters, preparing them for the prom, and stood to the side, bored, while Joan lectured on the horrors of soap, applying twenty-seven-dollar eyeliner that was no different than the Max Factor the girls had been shoplifting from K-Mart since they were twelve. She felt like she was on a job interview right now, explaining to people the life she hoped they perceived. "It'll be good to concentrate on me."

Anita squeezed lemon into her water. "One to ten, how bad do you miss him?"

Joan smiled brightly. "Miss who?" Truth was, sitting across from Anita she did feel better, could barely remember why Dean had seemed like a good idea in the first place, and she chose instead to concentrate on the bad traits: the way he gnawed apples with his front teeth, scraping off the skin before eating the meat; how he folded the Sunday paper into a tiny hat and wore it around the apartment well into the afternoon. The first time he did this Joan laughed so hard he continued until the paper became a headline for everything stupid and childish about their relationship, all that educated mess folded and unreadable. She realized now he'd been no more ready for commitment than he was to surrender the hat, and when she was honest with herself, she was willing to go so far as to say she missed the idea of Dean much more than Dean himself. Joan dropped her napkin in her lap and leaned forward. "I'd rather hear about Ralph."

Anita opened her mouth to speak but sat for a moment, the lemon in her hand. "Oh, Ralph's Ralph," she finally said. "What can you expect from a man named Ralph?" The young waiter brought their food and placed it in front of them without giving either woman a glance. Anita looked at her trout. "I've never seen a fish so wonderful." Joan glanced at the coiled and gilded scales now a shale-gray in the restaurant's drab lighting. She didn't remember Anita even liking fish that much.

Joan took the bun off her chicken sandwich and salted. "What do you two do for fun?"

"Fun?" Anita gulped down a spear of asparagus. "We do married things now. Shop at Home Depot. It's wonderful, truly." She poked the trout where the head would be, not looking at Joan. "Sometimes it's weird, though, to imagine I'll be with him forever. I'll never have to regret having sex on a first date again or doing something stupid like getting stoned with Joel Mishak and ending up on the interstate in my underwear." She looked out the restaurant window. "I haven't been stoned forever."

Joan rolled her eyes. "You haven't been stoned since college."

"Well, I know that. But it seems less likely now it's ever going to happen again."

Joan chewed a water chestnut, speaking with her mouth full. "Maybe you'll get cancer."

Anita let out a quick, short laugh, and the old couple next to them hovered possessively around a basket of rolls, glancing sideways at their table as if afraid Anita would try to steal one. "Our neighbor had a double bypass last year and lost thirty-five pounds," she said. "Maybe I could get one of those too." Anita stuck her fork in the trout and lifted it from the plate. "Have you ever seen a fish like this?" The elderly couple sat stock still, their conversation halting abruptly. Anita dropped the fish to the plate with a thud, the lemon wedge scuttling to the floor. "It's nice, just different than I imagined. Ralph and I didn't really spend much time together before the wedding. You know, the romance of long distance. It's nice though, really." Anita smiled widely, all teeth displayed. "Now back to *you*," she said. "I've invited a friend to dinner." Joan remembered how in college if she met a gay man she instantly introduced him to her friend Michael; desperation and low numbers seemed as good a reason for compatibility as any. "Tab's a guy at the shop next door to me. He's a printmaker, a really nice guy." She wiped her hands on her napkin, eyes averted. "Cute."

Joan looked at her skeptically. "Don't get nervous," Anita said. "It's not a set-up, I just thought it would be nice if you could meet some of my friends here."

"Have you ever invited him to dinner before?"

Anita put her hand up and waved to the waiter. "Well, no, but I've been meaning to. It seemed like as good a time as any."

"What's with the animals?" Joan asked suddenly. She'd been thinking about the figurines since morning, when Ralph had shooed her away from the anteater.

Anita looked up quizzically. "Oh." She laughed and pointed at her coffee cup when the waiter went by. "You mean the Herends? Ralph's crazy about them, and I mean crazy." She took a finger and circled it around her ear, her eyes rolling around seemingly separate from each other. "He buys one every year or so, I guess." She leaned in. "You should see our bedroom. He's got one rigged to the nightstand that looks like a constipated bird. It's supposed to be a wild duck."

"Rigged?"

"Yeah, all the ones that aren't in the living room are rooted by wires coming up from the furniture. Ralph thinks I'm a klutz and might break one." Anita tossed from side to side, as if drunk. She motioned her arms back in circles and knocked her coffee cup off the table. "Shit," she laughed. "You can see why he's worried."

Joan was alone in the living room, looking at the duckbill. When they got home from the restaurant, she'd feigned a headache and spent the three hours before dinner in the guest room. Ralph had been waiting in the driveway in front of the brightly painted, nearly psychedelic, garage door. Anita had tried a splash-paint method with primary colors that looked like the massacre of a clown. Joan heard sounds from downstairs all afternoon—indiscriminate sounds, a laugh and a thud—and had convinced herself Ralph and Anita were having sex. Buckled against the door with her head to the carpet, she was convinced they did it all the time.

The doorbell rang. "Will you get that?" Anita yelled. Joan opened the front door to a man in a T-shirt that read, "Go with God: the Weather's Better." He pointed to the shirt. "You get it?" The man's face looked younger than the girls' at the makeup counter and for a moment Joan was convinced Anita had forgone the husband and brought her a child. She stared at the shirt; there was a small, red stain near his nipple that she could tell had gone through numerous washings.

"It's part of a series I'm doing," he added.

"A series?"

He held out his hand. "I'm Tab."

Anita came around the corner. "It's good to see you," she said, taking his elbow and placing a kiss on his cheek. Joan could see by the flush of color and his widened eyes that Tab had probably never had a conversation with Anita until this week, much less a kiss.

"It's good to see you too, Anita. I brought you something." He held out a cutting board in the shape of a loaf of bread. He pointed to the top where it said "The Bread Zone," the name of Anita's shop. "I whittled that myself."

Anita smiled, toothy and white, and moved to the side to introduce Joan.

"Tell us more about your business, Tab," Anita said and held up the wine bottle. Tab nodded as she refilled his glass. Throughout dinner it'd become clear to Joan that Tab preferred Anita; most people did. It was obvious in the way he gobbled up the bread like an eager goat, laughed at her story of painting the garage door.

"Well," Tab said. He scratched his chin with his knuckles like the sound of sandpaper rubbing together. "There's not much to tell. I just make T-shirts."

Anita reached across the table and slapped his wrist. "There's got to be more than that."

Ralph shifted in his seat. "They're T-shirts, Ita. How much can there be?"

"Well everybody wears T-shirts, Ralph." She smiled at him, her cheeks mooned and stiff. "So I guess there'd be quite a bit."

Joan looked at Anita bent over her fish soup to take a delicate sip. She knew every trick Anita had for flirting: the deliberate way she hunched her shoulders to accentuate her collarbone, even the gentle wrist slap that had been an old standby. *Why, she likes him*, Joan thought and felt a surge of possessiveness toward Tab. She glanced at Ralph and wondered if he saw it too, wondered if they'd be left to the dishes as Anita gave Tab a tour of the house. She imagined her hands accidentally slipping through the faucet water to touch his wet skin with suds. *I'm not really like this*, she told herself, at the same time she imagined bending over Ralph's bowl with her ample bosom, asking him if he'd like more bouillabaisse, Anita sitting flat-chested and rejected on the other side of the table.

Tab cleared his throat. "Well, there're collared shirts, that's kind of new."

Anita glanced at him, her forehead raised and hesitant. "Collared shirts?"

"It's really nothing," Tab said.

Ralph took a drink of wine. "No please," he said, making a circlelike motion with his hand. "Go on."

"Well," Tab said. "It's just lately I've gotten some accounts with Nikki's, where I bowl, and some of the leagues have started placing orders. Before I only did cotton T-shirts, but now we're doing a poly-blend snap-button with embroidery for names." He picked at a hangnail. "Like the old-fashioned bowling shirts."

"Oh, so you bowl too?" Ralph smiled at Anita, lifting up the breadboard. "Isn't that great? Tab whittles *and* bowls."

Tab perked up. "You bowl?"

Ralph shook his head. "No, but I've been telling Anita we should take it up. Isn't that right, Anita?"

Anita jutted out her chin, her mouth open. "Shut up, Ralph."

Ralph laughed, then stopped abruptly and stared at Anita. "Oh, you shut up," he said, an unreadable look on his aggressively doughy face. "Now," he said, turning dramatically to Tab and picking up the breadboard. "Tell me about this whittling."

Tab wiped his mouth with a napkin, another dribble of wine making its way to his shirt. "Well, it's just something I've been doing since I was a kid, just a hobby. It works well to pass time between press sets at the shop."

"Since you were a kid, huh? When was that, four years ago?" He laughed before becoming hauntingly serious again, leaning in toward Tab. "My wife likes you," he said.

Tab glanced quickly at Anita. "She's a nice lady."

"You and my wife have a lot in common," Ralph said. "You're both the artsy type." He went limp-wristed as if imitating a homosexual, something cruel Joan had assumed all along he was capable of. It was obvious now Ralph was drunk and had probably been drinking most of the afternoon when Joan had assumed they were having sex. "Just look at my fucking garage door."

"It's our garage door now, Ralph," Anita said. "Not just yours."

Ralph laughed again, a short, fat bark. "And what's the most"—he stuck his finger in the air to accentuate the word—"*most* difficult piece you've whittled?" A part of Joan wanted to slap Ralph, see his face widen in surprise as she defended his wife and her friend.

"Ralph . . ." Anita said, but Ralph waved her away.

Tab looked at Anita and back to Ralph, his face opening up as if he had realized something important. "I don't know, Ralph, maybe the Sistine Chapel or the Last Supper. Say, I didn't come here tonight to get insulted," he said. "If you don't like my hobbies, then you shouldn't have invited me into your home." Joan felt her heart thump.

Ralph ran his open palm over his forehead before bending his head low, nearly trailing his hair through the bouillabaisse, three sets of eyes upon him. He sighed. "I'm being an asshole."

"No shit," Tab said. Anita laughed, and Tab looked over with a weak smile. "He is being an asshole."

Joan nodded. "I like whittling."

"I love my wife," Ralph said. He pushed his cheeks together hard and spoke in a smothered voice, "A big fat asshole."

Anita threw her napkin at her husband. "Good God, that's the truth." Ralph grabbed her arm and pulled her out of her chair and into his lap, making rude noises into her hair with his smushed cheeks until she began to laugh. "The things you do 'cause you love me," Anita said. "I don't know, Ralph, I almost wish you hated me." Tab and Joan looked at the walls and floor, anywhere but at the couple in front of them. "Who wants a cigarette?" Anita asked, rubbing Ralph's head. "This party needs some cigarettes."

"We'll get some," Joan said, bolting from her chair. She had bought a pack on the way to the Minneapolis airport, praying for the best. She and Anita smoked together when drunk for as far back as she could remember, Anita managing to never get addicted while Joan was up to half a pack a day by the time Anita moved. Tab followed Joan into the living room, where he bent over his windbreaker and pulled out a lighter and cigarettes, handing one to Joan. She took the lighter from him and lit his cigarette, her hands lingering on his, eyes connected. He coughed and pulled away quickly as he exhaled. "My last girlfriend started me smoking." Joan smiled encouragingly; she thought Tab was cute like a koala bear, clinging to a tree with a blank expression. "When she left she forgot three packs in the freezer, and I took it up because the smell reminded me of her." He suddenly seemed romantic, talking about this past girlfriend and the bad habits she'd left him with. She wondered if Dean would ever do anything so stupid. She was drunk, she realized, Tab morphing into a blurry version of the perfect man.

"It's too bad she wasn't into eating more vegetables or balancing the checkbook, something more useful."

Tab looked at Joan, his nose crinkled in confusion. "She's allergic to broccoli."

"Maybe she was allergic to you," she said and moved closer, putting her hands against his chest and sniffing behind his ear.

Tab backed away. "We broke up not too long ago," he fumbled. "Only a couple of months." He nearly tripped over the end table in the foyer. "I thought we were going to get married." He held the cigarette awkwardly in front of him, a long ash wobbling on the end. Joan looked at him backed in the corner: desperate and young and undeniably uninterested. She wondered if she would be Dean's last girlfriend, the next one at the altar turning into his wife. She'd never expected that Anita would marry Ralph, but there they were.

Tab's ash dropped to the carpet. "I even bought her a ring."

She looked at Tab, practically curled into the fetal position in the corner, and thought how nice it would be to come to L.A. and find a husband, settle in next door to Anita with the men outside at the charcoal grill, preparing perfect seafood. "I don't think we're compatible," she said as if Tab had asked her on a date. It wasn't Dean she missed; it was Anita.

Tab stood there with his mouth open, something forming behind his skull like slow-moving machinery. He closed his mouth and looked at her a long moment. "That's too bad," he said. "You seem like a real nice girl."

"Where are the damn cigarettes?" Anita yelled from the dining room. Tab took off at the sound of her voice as if running toward shelter. In the dining room Anita was still on Ralph's lap, an arm secured around the chair.

"I'm sorry, Tab," Ralph said. "I really am. Sometimes love makes you crazy."

Tab glanced nervously at Joan. "It's OK, I understand. My last girlfriend turned me into a fucking nut." Anita smiled brightly at her guests, reassuring them it was OK, her hands rubbing Ralph's head as if checking for ripeness.

The overflowing ashtray sat on the coffee table, rings of ashes lining the outside. Joan sat watching Anita and Ralph; she wondered what had been said in the dining room to repair Anita's flirting and Ralph's rudeness, but it was obvious now it was behind them. Joan felt uncomfortable, like when she was in high school and couples would pair off and make out in front of her, necking like fiends before the parents came home. She knew once Tab left, Ralph and Anita would go to their room while she was sequestered to her own and have even more sex than they'd had that afternoon. Anita would not sneak in to talk to her, would never again make fun of Ralph, the boyfriend who sang "Every Woman in the World" to her at a restaurant as a fumbling attempt to seem romantic enough to fuck. She could almost hear Anita laughing into the phone as she squeaked out the song as if her voice were changing.

Tab stumbled as he got off the couch and went to the mantle. "Cool, an anteater," he said. He picked up the figurine with one hand, turning it right then left before replacing it with a thud. Joan looked expectantly at Ralph, but he let out a gush of air and merely watched Tab suspiciously as he moved away from the fireplace.

Anita stood in the doorway now with another bottle of red wine, although Joan was unaware of her, her own eyes transfixed on the anteater. "They're from Belgium," she told Tab.

"Hungary," Ralph corrected.

Tab's fingers fluttered to his belly, a confused look on his face.

"No," Ralph motioned to the mantle. "The figurines, they're from Hungary."

There was the nagging feeling in the back of Joan's mind that Anita and Ralph had *not* had sex all afternoon, had most likely not even been in the same room, but she'd spent too long convincing herself otherwise. "It doesn't matter where they're from," Joan said, looking at Ralph. "Anita doesn't like them." Anita's head shot up from the wine, the cork in her hand.

Ralph giggled nervously. "That's not true." He looked at Anita, his forehead furrowed. "You wouldn't have said that."

Anita looked at Joan with a surprised open mouth. "I don't think I said exactly *that*," Anita explained. "I don't think I said I didn't like them." She poured wine into a shaky glass, and Ralph continued to look at her. "Sometimes when it's dark in here they can look kind of creepy—"

"Creepy?" Ralph said, his face folding in.

"She doesn't like them," Joan explained. "That's the point."

Anita looked at her uncomfortably as if they were meeting for the first time and she had realized quickly and without a doubt they wouldn't like each other.

Joan walked to the mantle and picked up the anteater, the curved gold claws and snout heavy in her hands. She turned to the group. "I'm keeping this." A consolation prize, she thought. An anteater. *If Ralph gets Anita, then I get this.*

"You can take it," Anita said, "it's fine. It's just a silly thing."

Joan turned back toward the mantle, slipped the Herend in her pocket, and waited for Ralph's response.

Circus Bezerk

Ned and I spend weekends rearranging wall-hangings, trying to fill the empty space. For the past decade we'd both lived in apartments and now don't know what to do in a home with five closets, much less a basement. Shortly after we moved in I read an article in the *Star Tribune* variety section about Feng Shui consultants, how they come into your house to distribute the energy flow, warn you to keep the toilet seat down for fear something useful will float away. Ned and I've been together for years, and I know he will scoff at this idea.

Mr. Jensen, the previous owner, a thick old man dressed always in white T-shirts and a camouflage hat, keeps driving past our house. We recognize him from pictures left on the walls during our first walk-through, from the old Plymouth parked in the garage. He stops occasionally and stares at the house. Ned and I stay in the kitchen, hovering by the window, trying to figure out what he could possibly want. "He can't let go," is Ned's theory. Mr. Arbuck, our Realtor, told us that Mrs. Jensen died eight months before the house was foreclosed by the bank. With a hankie tucked to his angled nose he whispered in our direction, "*An accident.*"

We meet Mr. Jensen one Saturday afternoon when he catches us doing yard work in the garden. He parks the car across the street and continues to watch, making us uncomfortable, like we've been apprehended playing dress up, smoking our parents' cigarettes. Ned looks at me and shrugs before crossing the street with a glass of iced tea.

"I lived here," is all he says, taking the tea from Ned. Something in the way he pronounces it, with an air of finality, it's almost as if he still does.

"Would you like to come in?" I hear Ned ask.

He looks back at Ned from under the hat. "No," he says and puts the car in gear. He drives off with our glass, missing Ned's foot by inches.

I bring up the idea of the Feng Shui consultant to Ned, tell him how a woman at work is convinced it's the reason her sanity has lasted so long, why her children never suffered the croup. He counteracts with one of his frequent proposals, and although he has a steady job with a nice benefits program, I tell him I'm not ready for that. I'm still looking at this house with the thinly guised, adult notion of an investment. He brings up children. Tells me with a grin that maybe we just have too much space.

In bed that night I consider lying, telling him I had an ovarian cyst years ago, and it isn't possible for me to conceive, but Ned is a sensible and good man. He'd hold my hand and tell me it'll be fine, and within a year we'd end up with a small black son that had been abandoned somewhere in Arizona.

In the morning I leave library books about Feng Shui on his plate. "Why not, it's a new home, and I don't feel like it's ours yet, no matter how many walls we knock down."

He sips his coffee. "It's nonsense, Jane, like a home decorator–slash–psychic hotline."

I set down the coffeepot. "I get the creeps from Mr. Jensen. It's like he still thinks he lives here. I get the feeling he's out there right now." Sometimes at night when Ned and I make love I swear I hear noises in the garage, and although it might be crazy, I feel Mr. Jensen out there in his army hat, waiting to drive through the wall.

When Ned first proposed, it was over dinner at Figlio, where our waiter slipped the ring through the cherry stem on top of my sorbet. Ned got down on one knee and the restaurant grew quiet, flush with wine, as he said the words: "Marry me." It threw me that I didn't have a choice, that he hadn't asked in the form of a question, and even the wait staff knew before I did I was expected to marry Ned. I looked around the restaurant at the other couples all staring at us, at Ned bent on the floor, two women going so far as to have tears in their eyes. And then I looked again at Ned, who was also looking around at the other tables. I reached for his elbow and pulled him to his feet, put my arms around his neck, and kissed him on the mouth. He backed up and peered in my empty, somber face and winced before turning to the restaurant with a false grin and an arm around my waist to save face.

Over the next few years he kept proposing—in heart-shaped hotel rooms, on a ski trip to Aspen, and finally at the meat department of Rainbow Foods, pumping gas at the corner Kwik Shop. My girlfriends, the few I've kept in touch with since college, can't believe that I haven't said yes yet, or maybe are amazed he keeps asking. They look at me caustically as if I've eaten up the last nice guy in Minneapolis and now have the nerve to complain about how full I've become.

In an argument after a proposal eight months ago, Ned brought up the house, almost bitterly as an alternative, and I said yes. It was that or say good-bye, which I knew wasn't the right answer either. When we unpacked all our possessions from our separate apartments, I never saw the ring, and I wonder if he keeps it hidden, maybe in a safety deposit box, or if even Ned has given up and returned it. I wonder, too, if it's occurred to Ned that I keep saying no now out of habit, and if maybe only out of habit he keeps asking.

The ad in the yellow pages reads: "Feng Shui: Ancient placement expelling negativity, admitting auspiciousness. Competitive Rates!" Finally Ned agrees, telling me he'll do what he has to do to keep the little woman happy, and I go along with his condescending roles because it gets me what I want. When Margot comes to the house, I'm surprised at how young she is, twenty if a day. I'd expected someone shrouded and wise, not blond wearing a T-shirt that reads, "COOL CHICK." She watches us eat our breakfast, takes pictures of the living room and master bedroom, checks in the cupboard under the bathroom sink. Ned continues to say she's a waste of money, one of those kids with a New Age scam, but when she's over Ned is quiet, and I can tell he's checking her for a glow.

After two months in the house we invite Josh and Nancy, our couple friends, over for dinner. They bring their son, Adam, and set up a portable crib in the living room next to the wingback chair we purchased at an auction. Adam looks so odd and small and non-human that I wonder how Nancy deals with him all day. "There're some days when I consider just getting in the car and driving to Tahiti," she says. "But then he goes down for a nap, and I know I'll be fine."

I point out that you can't drive to Tahiti, you need to cross an ocean, and she looks back at me with a face so blank, it's like I've taken away her only hope.

Ned makes his world-famous vodka collins, and because four people in a room feels like a party, we drink too much. Josh burns his hand on the Weber grill and laughs, says how much it would suck to be a cow.

After dinner Nancy and I drive to the store for more ice and cigarettes. "I think Josh is fucking around," she says, barely missing the median in the road turning into the grocery store. Nancy and I don't talk on the phone or go antiquing together, we're not that kind of friends, and I have no idea, given this information, how she expects me to respond. She nearly hits a grocery cart, and we fumble out of the car.

When we leave the store, Nancy drops the bag of ice she's holding. Her hands fly up to her face. "Oh my God," she screams and runs back into the store for our shopping cart before either of us remember we left Adam at home. In that split second when my stomach hollows out, I know just what it must be like to be a parent.

We drink until late in the night. I observe Josh through Nancy's eyes, as a possible adulterer and untrustworthy husband. Ned lies on the floor entertaining Adam with socks he's tied together like a doll. Josh watches him from the couch and says, "Ned, I think fatherhood suits you." I tell Josh straight out that I don't like his face, and the rest of the evening dissolves.

Outside I give Nancy a bone-crushing, good-bye hug. She looks back at me when I release her, eyes spacious and wide open, like it's been that much distance since a person has initiated touching her.

Back in the house I look at the mess: bottles everywhere, three full ashtrays on the table, dishes from dinner littering our spacious, white counters. I turn my back—it'll be there in the morning—but Ned starts cleaning, and I feel resigned to help. The room starts spinning, and instead I lie on the kitchen floor and close my eyes.

I can hear the clinking of glass, smell the cigarette butts. "Why'd you say that to Josh?" Ned asks. "Where'd that come from?"

"I just don't like his face." I think I might throw up.

"Well Jesus, Jane, they're our best friends. You don't just say that."

"He's your best friend, not mine." I roll over onto my knees, keep my head on the ground. "Nancy thinks he's having an affair."

Ned continues cleaning.

"Is he? Is he having an affair?"

He drops an empty bottle into the recycling, and it's the sound of bad energy. I open one eye and see the sunburn that's started to peel on his arm. "How long has it been going on?"

He puts down the rag he's using and puts his elbows on the breakfast bar, his head in his hands. "A couple of months. It's some girl from the accounting department at work."

"And how long have you known?" The ceiling fan's making me dizzy; I shut my eyes and try to concentrate on the whirling noise.

"A few weeks."

"And you think this is OK?"

"Jane, he told me in confidence, what was I supposed to do? Tell Nance? You know I can't do that."

"So this is how sacred marriage is to you?" I say. "This is the type of man you expect me to marry?"

"That's not true, and you know it. For Christ's sake, you know I don't approve of this. I'm his best friend, not him."

There are a few moments of silence, no noise but the fan, until I hear Ned turn on the dishwasher and leave the room. When I open my eyes and look around I have no idea where I can possibly be.

The next morning I hear Ned roll out of bed at his normal 6:45. I fall back asleep and dream of things murky and lonesome and dark. The only tangible memory when I crawl out of bed—and it isn't so much a memory as a feeling—the only tangible feeling is that of drowning.

Ned cooks me breakfast, the smell of eggs and grease permeating the house. There's a metallic taste in my mouth, pain in my head. "You drank a lot last night," he says and sets a mug in front of me.

I pick up a plain English muffin and dip it in the coffee; the bread tastes soggy and dark like my dreams. "We always drink a lot with Josh and Nance."

Ned sits down with his plate but doesn't begin eating. "Do you remember what I told you? About the affair?" It comes back like a blanket falling over my head. "That I would never do that?" He takes my hand and brings it to his face, getting crumbs on the collar of his shirt.

I know it's true; Ned doesn't have the stomach for betrayal. I feel sometimes I could map out Ned's future on graph paper, staying in the designated lines for marriage and children and, of course, this house, with no room for affairs or surprises. And although I certainly don't want Ned out sleeping with women from the accounting department, there's something about the curlicues on Josh's chart that read like passion.

Margot agrees to come over every Wednesday morning to consult on the house. She tells us the entire process will take up to four months, and I can feel Ned's eyes roll into the back of his head as she begins dissecting the house into sections, starting with the top floor and working her way down. Her plan, she says, is to try and cover a room a day, but important rooms such as the bathroom, kitchen, and our bedroom will take extra sessions. She wears flowing, floral skirts that I'm only allowed to wear to work on Fridays.

Margot tells me that a lot of the bad energy seems to be generating near the top of the stairs, and I wonder if Mrs. Jensen fell down, and that's how she died.

"Something's going on up there," she says. "I'd bet there's a leak near the roof."

"It rained last week," I explain, "and not a drop."

She looks up and scratches her long, young neck. "Jane, I mean an energy leak." I feel foolish; I want her to like me.

She tells me we should switch our room to the smaller bedroom, that there's a beam running sideways inside the ceiling of the one where we sleep that's causing some kind of problem. Ned calls City Plan Review and asks them to look at the blueprints. "I'll be damned," Ned says. "She's right."

We haven't seen Mr. Jensen in over a month, and I'm beginning to worry. "What if he died?" I say.

Ned pulls apart the *Star Tribune*. "He probably just went to visit his kids in Florida. Old men like that always have kids in Florida."

"Mr. Jensen might have the keys to our home," I say.

He folds over the sports section and begins reading. "The locks were all changed when we moved in, you know that."

"I mean the secrets to the house, not the actual keys." I want to sound like Margot, in her flowing skirts and long ratty hair.

There's a full-page color advertisement on the back of the paper for the circus—pictures of an awed audience, an elephant balanced on one leg, four Rockette-style dancers surrounding a clown who looks as if he can't believe his luck. I poke at the ad. "Let's go," I say. "Tonight."

Ned folds the paper in and looks at the back. "The circus?" He opens the paper and begins reading again. "It's amazing with those acts," he says, "that no one has ever been sued."

The first cold weekend in September, Josh and Nancy invite us over for Josh's world-famous New Orleans chili. Two months have passed since we were all together, and I tell Ned I won't drink a lot, although we both know it isn't true.

When we arrive, Adam's already asleep upstairs, but there's evidence of him everywhere: small squeaking toys by the door, his playpen, a soft, pastel blanket on the sofa. Josh greets us with a paper bag over his head, tells me he's hiding his ugly mug, and puts an arm around my shoulder. I squeeze back halfheartedly and keep my back stiff out of loyalty to Nancy.

In the kitchen Ned grabs four beers out of the fridge and passes them around. Nancy refuses, and I know instantly, with the intuition of a womb, that she's pregnant. Josh makes the announcement, standing behind her with his hand on her shoulder. The two men clasp hands, slap each other on the back like primates. Both look over at me, silent in the chair.

"How come it is whenever men find a recipe they can make they call it 'world-famous'? Who else has really tasted it?" Ned gazes at me queerly, and I say congratulations, and when we're alone I promise to behave.

Nancy and I go upstairs to check on Adam; already she's holding her stomach, although she's only two months along. I put my hand underneath my sweater and feel nothing but another instinct passing. Adam's asleep, and she nudges him until he gurgles, thumb secure in his mouth. When we turn to go, I realize it isn't my place to say anything regarding the affair, which I know through Ned is still going on. "I didn't even know you two were trying."

She turns off Adam's light. "It just sort of happened. But it's good. It's a good thing, Jane." I give her a quick hug before she pulls away, and I make a mental note to ask Margot if she can consult on the nursery for a baby shower gift.

Again we drink too much. Everyone except Nancy, who is silent and pregnant in the corner. I stumble to the front hall closet and take out an umbrella, tell her it's to put in her drink when she gets to Tahiti.

Once alone in the car, Ned turns to me. "I didn't know about the baby," he says. I hear him fumble with the keys, the engine start. "I assume he's going to break it off with Sharon, but he hasn't said anything. God, Jane. I don't know what to tell you. He loves Nancy, I know that much."

I lean my head back into the comfortable curve of the seat. "Loving her isn't the problem."

"What is it then? What's the problem?"

He really wants to know; Ned needs an answer to this question as badly as I do. I keep my eyes shut but can imagine the way his hair is falling on his forehead, the way his chin points out when he's had too much to drink. "I don't know," I tell him, and I'm no longer thinking of Josh and Nancy and Sharon and the baby. "I just wish we could stay where we are. Why do we have to keep moving forward?"

Ned looks out the car window at the dim street and manicured lawns. "We don't live here," he says, and I don't have the energy to explain.

I begin staying home from work on Wednesdays, telling my boss, as an excuse, that I don't trust Margot alone in the house. I follow her from room to room, searching for clues as to what could be wrong. "The energy in the kitchen isn't kicking right—it's stopping at the breakfast bar, not getting past the sink."

I write it down. "But why?"

"You might consider moving the stove to the south wall. And take down those metal pots hanging from the ceiling." She drags on her cigarette. "Nothing good's coming off those pots."

After awhile she starts staying on a bit, telling me she doesn't want to go home. "My boyfriend's studying for the bar," she says. "Christ, what a bear." We smoke Camel Lights and drink kiwi tea. I tell her about my conflicts with Ned, about his plans for marriage, then a boy, then a girl.

"I can relate," she says. "Tanner wants to get a dog. I keep telling him, I'm a cat person, Tan. No dogs."

I tell her how Ned won't bring me to the circus. How in thirty-two years I've never been, and isn't that just the sort of whimsical thing a mate is supposed to support?

"Jesus, men don't get it," she says. "There's nothing better than a circus."

Mr. Jensen finally makes an appearance in late October. I see him drive by, badly in need of new snow tires. He makes a turn around the block and drops something off on the front porch, and I wait for him to round the corner before I open the door to find our iced tea glass embedded in the snow. Back inside the house I want to cry. I can tell how much he must have loved his wife. I can feel it in the house.

Ned tells me Josh and Sharon are over. Josh brought her into his office and told her, as politely as possible, that although he cared for her, he could never leave his wife. Ned says when she left the office for good, carrying the photos she'd set up at her desk and a coffee mug she'd stolen from the lunchroom, there were tears streaked down as far as her chin. "Honey, it's over," he says and pulls me in for a hug as if *we've* survived a calamity in our own relationship.

With my head scrunched against his chest, I'm still thinking of Sharon lugging her box of mementos home. The hours and weeks in front of her as she tries to recover, and that's just from a few months with an asshole like Josh.

For Margot's last appointment, I buy her wildly expensive jade wind chimes. She makes one last run through the house, telling me that she thinks it's "as good as it's going to get," but I can still call with questions, and if I want, she'll come back for a follow-up consultation in six months. I say that'd be fine, but I know she's done all she can.

When I bring out the wind chimes, Margot looks at them, back at me, back at the chimes. "They're beautiful."

She set down her ratty straw bag and fishes to the bottom, pulling out two tickets. *Circus Bezerk: Variety Theater*. "Here." She puts them in my hand. "It's like a vaudeville show, not one of the big ones like Ringling's or anything like that." She looks sheepish and out of control for the first time since I've met her.

It occurs to me Margot might not have any more answers than me. I hug her and am glad when she hugs me back.

Ned and I get ready for the circus that night. "Couldn't we at least borrow Adam, so we don't look ridiculous?" he asks, and I ignore him and the comment, snorting the whole way to the circus whenever he tries to talk to me. Sometimes I think I'm mean to him just because he lets me get away with it. In the parking lot I grab his hand and pull on his arm like an impatient child, sucking my thumb like Adam until he laughs and pats me on the head.

The circus is performed in an old theater in the warehouse district, across from the trendy sushi restaurants and upscale martini bars. Inside it's mystical and plush, the walls lined with red velvet looking like the inside of a lung or some other vital organ. The audience is decidedly adult, and Ned looks relieved as we're directed to our seats by a mime.

The emcee comes out to announce the first act looking gothic and serious in a black tuxedo and bone-white skin. The Ashton Risleys, a blond family of four, come out dressed in matching fire-red sequined jumpsuits. The father lies on his back on a bench and begins to twist a pole with his feet. There's a seat on each end and when he stops, the two towheaded children jump up and begin flying though the air at a dangerously rapid speed. Ned grabs my hand and squeezes, and I squeeze back. When the father slows down, both children spring off and somersault, landing with their arms raised, toes meeting. We all clap loudly. The son begins somersaulting on a small trampoline, folding within himself like a sheet. He catapults onto his father's spinning feet and is hurdled back into the air, touching down on his father's toes with every turn. Ned and I are holding hands so tightly it hurts. The father gives his son one more great shove, and he jumps to the trampoline and off onto his feet, arms spread wide once again. I look over at Ned with a feeling of amazement. *Is this how families are supposed to be?* I think. *Is this what I'm up against?*

The next act is a male contortionist, the Great Valentin. They begin playing slithery music I associate with cobras coming out of baskets, and he twists onto his platform. We watch his legs move very slowly over his head while he lies on his torso. His feet snake underneath his armpits. My back begins to hurt, my entire body aches. Ned has a look of wonderment on his face.

There are many more acts: the foot juggler Larisa Ivanova from Russia, who keeps three dulled axes and a ball going all at the same time; Charley Charles, who rides a bike that can fit in the palm of his hand; the energetic Chin brothers who spin plates on thin poles. At the end of their act they throw plastic eggs attached by strings at the audience, and only they know because it's rigged that the eggs won't break.

I'm thankful when the last act arrives. Miss Ping Su climbs up one of the high-wire poles and places her delicate foot on the wire; her coordination is uncanny, and she's as fluid as milk as she begins balancing from one foot to the next. A man stands to the side with a stack of bowls. She bends her left knee backward, torso erect, moving nothing but her left arm to place one of the bowls on the bottom of her upturned foot. With a quick movement she springs the bowl over her back and onto her head, her right foot secure on the wire. When she straightens her leg she wavers, one foot seeming out of control, while the other curls around the wire. Ned shudders, visibly shudders, and I look away, knowing it's part of the act.

"It's like some kind of magic," he says, "only with feet." But it's not—it's years of practicing so Miss Ping Su can wow an audience full of adults willing to believe the illusion. I want to tell Ned that we can't go on, that I don't want children, and I don't want marriage, and I wish that Mrs. Jensen hadn't killed herself in the house. She continues with the bowls for what seems like hours.

I begin to recall something Ned told me one time, before Mr. Jensen and his antiquated house, before Margot and her beatific energy. He told me that he would be willing to die for me. This was back in college, back when the sweat of him against me was still new. We were in bed that night, I remember it was around finals, and it probably had been snowing for days. He was on top of me, and I could barely see his face, mainly just the outline of his eyes, when I heard him say it: "I would die for you."

At the time I thought it was passion; I thought that Ned, like me, was caught up in the crazy love-making only college kids know. I want to think that when I rolled him on his back and sat bare-assed on his chest to say those words in return that I meant it. And I did, but not in the day to day, the minute to minute—not as a lifer. Who's to say Ned isn't equally to blame, more in love with the words than the woman?

Ned is no longer watching the show but is staring at me as if something in my face is transforming. I'm barely conscious of his fingers in my own, barely aware that they're there. I look at Miss Ping Su. There's a stack of eight bowls on her head and at least five more waiting in the man's hands, and as she continues to throw the bowls onto her head with her feet, I know now for certain there is nowhere for us to go.

Goldfish

Martha corners me at work on Thursday and hands me the invitation. "The shower's five o'clock, Saturday," she says. "Really, Holly, I hope you can make it." Martha has been wearing a birthing belly for the past two months, hauling around thirty extra pounds of sand and foam to let her partner know she loves her; Sally's the one actually having the baby. Martha stands with one arm resting solidly between the fake breasts and belly, the other arm—the one with the invitation—extends no further than her stomach. She looks around the museum gift shop to make sure we're standing alone. "There's someone I'd like you to meet," she says.

I'm doing month-end inventory and write down that we have sixteen hammerhead shark teeth for sale before moving to the tomahawk key chains. "I'm not looking to meet anyone right now," I tell her. Martha adjusts her fake stomach, heaving the thirty pounds slightly to the right so it is parallel again to her body. It's disconcerting, watching the pregnant belly sway unattached from the mother.

"Lem's not looking either," she continues. "But I think you guys would really connect."

I put my clipboard down at my side, my pen behind my ear. "Why?" I ask. "Why do you think we'd connect?" Since I left Henry numerous friends have approached me with men they think I should meet: a car salesman from Pakistan, a bartender who followed the Dead. Martha's impossible to say no to, and I wonder if I'm going to have to resort to faking an illness, send an e-mail late Friday night about a head cold I will have developed.

Martha looks offended, as if she can't believe I would question someone in her condition. "He's an interesting guy, you're an interesting girl." She shrugs her shoulders. "Lem's sensitive, he spends his time with pet fish. Don't all girls like sensitive?"

"And Lem?" I ask. "What kind of a name is Lem?"

"French-Lithuanian," she says and then as if holding the trump card: "He's my brother." She knows she's gained points since I've made fun of his name. And her brother, how can I argue with that? I can't tell her I won't like a brother she will undoubtedly say is just like her. I turn to Martha. She's attractive—dark and squat—and I can tell her features would be more suited to a man. I raise my clipboard and write down "12 toms." "He's the father," she says nonchalantly, and the clipboard goes back down.

"Whose father?"

"Our baby's," she answers. "Mine and Sally's. He donated the sperm."

I think briefly about Henry and whether or not he's been dating. I consider Lem, the sperm-donating brother who's obsessed with fish, and cough, a hacking cough, into my hand.

"It won't work," Martha says. "I already told him you were coming."

On Saturday, despite being May, it's only fifty-three degrees outside. It was Henry's job to check the weather, to come into the bathroom as I got out of the shower, steam rising, and tell me it was going to be fifty-six to sixty-two with a twenty-five percent chance of rain. For the past two months I've worn tank tops when there should have been sweatshirts, linen when there should have been down. It's comforting in its own way to stand shivering in Martha's driveway, feeling like I have a solid reason to miss Henry.

A poster matching the invitations is taped to the mailbox with arrows pointing through the front door, living room, and kitchen. Out the backdoor are picnic tables covered in pink tulle, gifts piled up on a ping-pong table. Martha waddles across the grass, stopping every now and again to place her hand on a guest's arm to thank her for coming. It's odd seeing Martha in this role—polite and charming to her visitors—although supposedly this is her job description working retail at the museum. She turns toward the screen door and sees me holding a Diaper Genie wrapped in shiny, green Christmas foil—the only paper I had on hand that didn't specifically state a holiday. Martha waves and starts for the kitchen.

I open the door and come down the steps, holding out the gift. "It's for the baby," I say stupidly.

Martha looks at the present. "You shouldn't have." She sets the obnoxious kelly-green gift on a table next to the appropriate presents, presents with tiny teddy bears and rattles tied up in elaborate, pastel ribbons. "I'll remember which one is from you," she says and smiles kindly, as if this is a compliment, as if anyone wants to be remembered for the present that looks like it was wrapped by a prostitute. She takes my arm and holds on with both hands, my elbow held hostage against the side of her sand belly. "You haven't met Sall before, have you?" she asks.

I shake my head no. Martha keeps a picture in her wallet that I have seen on occasion, but it was taken while camping, and Sally's features were blurred and hooded.

Martha laughs and points to a woman over by the hedge. "There she is," she says, "the fat one."

From her backside, I'm barely able to tell Sally is pregnant; she's nothing but slim hips and shimmery blond hair, not an inch over 5'2". She's talking to a woman dressed in scrubs and shaking her head politely. When Sally turns around, first with the belly and then the rest of her own body, I'm caught off guard by her womanly features; she's almost doll-like in her delicacy. Martha puts her head on my shoulder and sighs dramatically. "That's my Sally Alley," she says, making no sense, like all other people in love. I remember when I used to call Henry "Hot Dog Henry" because he ordered one at Dairy Queen the first summer we were dating. It was a hundred degrees outside, and all sane people were eating ice cream, and I thought how cute it was he ordered a hot dog. *A hot dog!* I'd thought, and in hindsight, really, what's so cute about that?

"She's beautiful," I state.

"And a doctor to boot." Martha laughs. "My sugar-mama." She tugs my arm and starts pulling me toward Sally for introductions.

Up close there's an indistinctness to Sally's face that reminds me of all pretty, blond girls roaming the halls of high schools—surprisingly beautiful but commonplace. She holds out her hand and shakes mine solidly. "Martha was hoping you'd make it," she says. "Have you had a chance to meet Lem?"

"Holly really did come for the baby," Martha says, but she looks around the backyard, and I follow her eyes. Her gaze doesn't stop anywhere in particular, and I know he must not be here yet, or at least he isn't outside.

"He's a character," Sally says. "I can tell you two will get along." She blinks her huge, blue, cow eyes at me and turns toward Martha. "Rogette's here from Pulmo Rehab. I'm going to have to say hello." She kisses her lover on the cheek and heads to Rogette, reluctant to leave Martha even for a second. Martha stands there watching Sally for another moment before excusing herself to get a sweater.

Looking around the backyard, I'm amazed by how few couples there are. Many women are mingling and talking in familiar little groups, the occasional man standing awkwardly by the fence, or escaping inside to wander the main floor of the house in peace. I go through the buffet table, timing the hors d'oeuvres by the number of minutes I'd like to remain. I wonder how long I can count on the food to help me look occupied, how long until a stranger comes up and talks to me out of pity, or worse, approaches to tell me again how compatible I am with Lem. I stand with my plate by the plastic Fisher Price swing set that was installed in the backyard earlier this week. Martha told me on Friday it was a gift from her brother. After Sally and the baby passed safely into the second trimester, Lem showered the prenatal child with gifts—a set of Russian dolls housed within themselves, blow-up fish for the bathtub, ten matchbox cars with a blue carrying case. I stare at my food and think how nice it would be to have Henry here with me,

Henry who would put a onesie on his head and do an impersonation of Dustin Hoffman in *Ishtar*. Everyone would laugh even though they haven't seen the movie; Henry's that good with a crowd.

I am aware suddenly of the intimacy among many of the women—a casual hand on the back, the leaning in when another woman speaks—and it becomes apparent to me I'm surrounded by couples. I feel foolish I hadn't noticed it before, but it's one of those things when you finally see it—like a cloud in the shape of a heart or a machete—you can imagine no other way.

Glancing around again I spot Lem. He's over by the punch bowl, the absolute image of Martha—only taller—with her short, dark hair and immense, symmetrical eyebrows. They're standing together and look like they're arguing; Lem runs his hands through his hair, Martha presses her hands to her hips on both sides of the belly. It's obvious they're brother and sister, that they've struck these poses for years.

Martha and Lem look at me in unison, and I turn toward the woman on my left who is smoking long thin brown cigarettes. I ask if I can have one and roll my eyes like I'm desperate, although I've never smoked before.

She pulls the pack of Mores from her purse and taps one out. "They're horrible," she says, "but they're all I had in the glove box. These baby showers are too much for me." She's in her early forties and appears alone, but I'm suspicious of everyone now. Suspicious there will be partners hiding behind the ping-pong table, couples lurking in back of the hibiscus.

"I don't usually smoke," I say as she holds out the lighter, and she hangs on a moment extra as if evaluating whether or not I'm worth the cigarette. "Well, I'm trying to quit," I add.

"We all are," she says and lights it for me. The cigarette tastes dry and dusty, and I resist taking the smoke into my lungs. We stand looking around, the only two people who aren't in rapt conversation.

She clears her throat. "Do you know Sally or Martha?"

"The mother or the mother?" I say, and she smiles tersely. "I work with Martha," I explain.

She slips the lighter back in her pocket. "I work at the hospital with Sally," and we both look over at Sally, who eats a cream-cheese-stuffed olive as Martha rubs the small of her back. "We used to date," the woman adds. "Back in med school." She looks at the blooming couple and shakes her head. "Sall couldn't have made a better choice than Martha." She smiles slightly and turns away to say hello to Rogette from Pulmo Rehab as she walks by.

The cigarette makes me dizzy, and I excuse myself to no one in particular to go inside for some water. Empty jars of baby food are drying in the sink, left over from Martha's lunches the past few weeks. I open the fridge. There's a six-pack of Hamms in the back, and I grab one, although I'm sure this is inappropriate. The last time I went to a party alone was back in college before I'd met Henry, a kegger at a fraternity house that cost six dollars to get through the door. I met him a few weeks later in a biology class, where he made the legs of the frog he was dissecting dance.

Lem comes into the kitchen with wet rings expanding under the weight of his arms. He smells pleasant, though, what I imagine hay and farm life to smell like. Seeing my can of Hamms on the table, he clutches his heart dramatically and stumbles to the refrigerator. He takes out the rest of the six-pack and pops open a can, sits in a chair across the table, and folds his arms, staring straight at me. "You're Holly," he says loudly.

"You're Lem." I take another gulp of beer. Lem is too dramatic and sweaty for the middle of the day in a friendly kitchen with teapot wallpaper.

He bows still sitting at the table. "According to my sister, we're supposed to get married. I think she plans to have us in love by the time the presents are open, engaged by the time we go home."

I look at him like he's crazy, and in the second it takes me to digest this, I'm fearful it'll happen, that I'll get swept into Lem's huge arms and have no time to protest until the wedding invitations are sent out, and I've lost my window of opportunity. "We'll have 2.5 children," he says, "and drive a minivan for the Girl Scout troop. We can grow old and fat together." He folds his fingers in a cat's cradle. "It's not a bad option."

I take a sip of beer. "And a dog," I tell him. "All happy families have dogs."

"Big dogs!" he exclaims and then is silent, his hairy hand scratching the side of his head. "I don't know how I'm going to break this to my girlfriend, Charlene. She was still in the running with the kids, but she's allergic to most domestic pets. We don't even have a hamster, just fish."

This mention of a girlfriend feels like a betrayal, although it obviously isn't. He holds out the rest of the six-pack, and I take another beer. "Does Martha know about Charlene?"

"Yeah, she knows." He lowers his voice to a whisper. "Little sister doesn't approve."

Martha seems the least likely to cast stones, with an impregnated girlfriend and her own notions of love. "What's there not to approve of?"

Lem waves his hand in the air. "Char's a little young."

"How young?" From the cowboy boots and subdued polo shirt, I guess Lem to be anywhere from thirty-one to thirty-six.

"Nineteen," he says and raps his knuckle three times on the wood table. "Char's in ballet, so she looks younger than she is, but Martha doesn't listen to sense." He mock salutes me. "A lesbian and a pedophile, our parents are real proud."

We sit drinking beer, and Lem glances at me to see if I have a story to tell, but I wouldn't know where to begin explaining four years of sex and friendship that ended with a depressing, last-ditch vacation filled with bleak talk of the future and numerous bottles of rum. I remember the solid feel of the airplane taking off as Henry and I returned to Minneapolis from Venice Beach—the flight attendants telling us to fasten our seat belts, that our cushions could be used as flotation devices. Henry kept the condo, and I moved to a development where my neighbors never hold the door for me no matter how many bags of groceries I struggle with in my arms.

Lem suddenly jumps up and does a deep knee bend, holding on to the sink for support. "You might've seen her in Tchaikovsky's *Suite Number Three* at the Guthrie last winter." He looks at me expectantly, and I apologetically shake my head no. Henry would have no more gone to the ballet than shot himself in the foot. Lem stands upright and takes another sip of beer. "Isn't that great?" he asks. "That she's in ballet? How great would it be to tell people as an adult that you're a ballerina." It's obvious from the moony look on his face that he loves her.

"I wanted to be a flight attendant," I tell him, although being a flight attendant had never occurred to me before. It seems OK lying to Lem about this minor detail. There's a freedom in knowing I won't have to own up to the conversation later, that I can say things that needn't be accounted for.

"A flight attendant!" Lem exclaims. "Well, that'd be good too." He sits down. "I always told people I just wanted to be happy. That's another one of those things you could only get away with saying as a kid."

We sit for fifteen minutes in a silence I suppose should be comfortable, but of course it isn't. "So tell me about these fish." It's the only thing I can remember about flirting: act like you're interested in whatever they care about. I wonder if that's what I did with Henry, and it served me right to have spent four years with a man who thought his own childlike need to get his way was the most important thing in our relationship.

"Fish," Lem says. "Is that a line?" and laughs, snorting at his own dumb joke. He pirouettes toward the doorway, opens the screen door and looks outside, then shuts it again. "Char and I've got the most amazing aquariums—everything from Blue Gouramis to Tangerine Peacocks, but the goldfish are the most amazing. We're going to transport them into a larger tank to see how big they can get. They're in the carp family, you see, so they could end up monstrous."

"The world according to carp."

Lem tosses his can in the sink. "Do you want to see them?" He looks like a little boy with his first pet to show off, or like Henry when we first fell in love.

"Goldfish, yeah, that sounds great," and I know I'm doing it again, saying just what a man wants to hear.

"You're sure?" Lem asks.

"Of course!" Old habits, like old relationships, die hard.

Outside the sky is darkening like a bruise, and I can smell the evening coming despite the dulling effect alcohol is supposed to have. The streamers in the trees catch on the current and float, as lifelike as human limbs. I want to tell Lem I've forgotten about him having a girlfriend, but the very voicing of this would prove I haven't. At the ping-pong table, I pick up a cloth diaper and put it on my head. It hangs like a flap of dead skin, and Lem smiles at me with twice the teeth of a normal person. Martha and Sally are sitting on a picnic bench, cuddling. I look at Lem and realize Sally's blond, blue-eyedness doesn't stand a chance; the baby will undoubtedly look like Martha.

We skedaddle over, both acting drunker than we are. "We're leaving," Lem says. "Together. You're absolutely right about us being compatible. She's the new love of my life."

I grab his hand and swing it through the air. "We're going somewhere exotic, to see the fish. It'll be like an early honeymoon."

Martha stops rubbing Sally's belly and looks at us both. I wonder how we seem, a makeshift duo drunk in the backyard. With the evening light and the six-pack of Hamms, I'm sure we would pass for a couple. "You're both shits," Martha says. "You probably deserve each other."

Lem bows and kisses my hand, leans over and makes farting noises with his mouth against both of their bellies. Martha smiles. "A couple of shits," she says.

Lem leaves me in the hallway of his apartment building as he goes to park the car. I don't feel drunk anymore, not even enough to exaggerate it, and I notice the stains on the beige carpet, a light bulb burned out by the stairs.

An old man comes out of 14C in his bathrobe and looks at me. "I'm waiting for a friend," I tell him, feeling foolish standing alone with all the apartment doors closed.

"I'll be your friend," he says.

"No, I have a friend," I stammer. "He's parking the car. We're going to look at the fish." Everything sounds silly and problematic in this dank, stained hallway, and I don't want to explain myself anymore.

He smiles, a big grin with no bottom teeth. "Lem loves those fish," he says, and Lem reappears on cue.

"Leave her alone, Morris, she's too young for you."

Morris laughs, his chin wobbling without the teeth. "By the looks of Charlene, she's too old for you. When's Char get back?"

"Tuesday," Lem says. "I'll tell her to stop by." Morris nods and shuts his door.

Lem pulls his keys from his pocket. "Come on, you're not going to believe this." In the apartment he puts his hands on my shoulders and tells me to stay in the living room—"I want to get it set up, give you the full effect"—then runs down the hallway toward a back room where there is a light humming noise. Hanging above a couch covered with a Minnesota Vikings bed sheet are posters of different ballets—*Giselle, Le Corsaire, Jardin Aux Lilas.* It's like Char doesn't live here, rather hovers on the wall.

"Come on back," Lem yells. A night-light leads me through the living room toward a soft, blue glow coming from the back. As I get closer, the humming becomes louder, and I can see the waves reflecting off the walls in undulating movement.

I step inside, and it's like nothing I've ever seen. There are fish tanks against every wall, some on stands reaching almost to the ceiling, and fish seem to swim out of the concrete and plaster. The walls and ceiling are painted an ocean green, and a blue tarp carpets the floor. The unsteadiness of walking on the plastic intensifies the feeling of being underwater. "It's like Seaworld," I whisper.

"Only better," he says.

Lem points to a half-full tank against the north wall, the biggest one in the room. "That one, that's where the goldfish are going. A hundred-and-twenty-five gallons." There are rainbow-colored rocks in the bottom catching the light off the top of the tank, looking nothing like actual rocks as they shimmer and move with color. "I'm hoping if we ever live in the country, or maybe by a park, we can set them loose in a pond." Lem walks over and touches the tank. "They'd be huge," he says. "Probably up to fifteen inches."

In the tank on the east wall are four goldfish swimming around an aquarium only half the size of the one they will be moved into. The fish are already over six inches long, bigger than I thought goldfish could ever get. "Let's move them," I say. "Let's move the fish."

Lem stares at the empty tank and begins slowly to nod his head up and down. "I could do it for Char," he says. "It'll be a surprise." He reaches into a bucket and grabs two gallon milk jugs that have been cut out at the top like scoops. We lift the covers off the two tanks and begin transferring the water into the new aquarium. The goldfish swim toward our hands, hoping for food.

After an hour of labor, I'm aware of the muscles in my back from the steady scoop of the jug into the water and the heaviness of carrying it to the other tank. We take short breaks, standing still in the room, looking at the fish. He explains there are no more than three species per tank due to territorial fights, shows me the treasure chest with a real pearl hidden inside. In one tank are fish so delicate I'm able to see every bone outlined. Lem says they're glass catfish, and I imagine they're what Char looks like dancing, thin and frail, swimming through water. I ask Lem if she travels a lot, remembering his comment to Morris that she'll be back on Tuesday.

"She's finishing up a show in Boca Raton right now," he says. "She hopes to be back for most of June." He heaves another gallon out of the tank and walks to the new aquarium, dumping the water with his back toward me. "She slept with her choreographer on a road show in St. Louis two months ago; that's why Martha doesn't like her. It really doesn't have anything to do with her age."

I'm glad he isn't facing me during this confession. I'm still used to Henry and his shallow, childlike grin, and to see it on Lem's face would be painful. "Why didn't you leave her?" I ask. It seems so obvious, the problems in other people's relationships: *woman sleeps with choreographer, man loves fish*. Lem ignores my comment, which I'm sure he's heard more than once from the glaring mouth of Martha. "Are you going to help raise the baby?"

Lem turns around and stops, the jug suspended in his hand. "The baby?" He looks hopeful for a second, and then something passes on his face, and he bends to scoop more water. "No, that baby's for Martha and Sally."

"Why did you do it?" I ask.

He laughs. "Because it made them so happy when I said yes."

When the water level in the old tank gets down to a foot, Lem says, "I think we're ready, let's get the fish," and holds out the net.

"Don't you think you'd be more qualified?" I say. It seems as silly as letting a new parent cut the umbilical cord rather than a doctor, or at the least, a nursing student.

Lem grins and places the net in my hand.

I lower the net into the aquarium and almost instantly a goldfish swims into it. I pull it awkwardly out of the tank, water flying off the net as I run across the unsteady tarp. The fish feels heavier than the water because of the movement, and the image flashes of Martha and Sally with their matching bellies, Sally's alive with motion. I'm conscious of not thinking of Henry, or rather, thinking of him and not being sad. In the water, the goldfish swims further into the screen before bumping, once, into the side of the tank. I grab Lem's hand and squeeze, sad he doesn't realize a ballerina can only break your heart. The fish takes off cautiously through the iridescent water, as if just then learning how to swim.

Source Acknowledgments

"Any Ordinary Uncle,"
Cimarron Review 138 (Winter 2002): 48–60.

"Circus Bezerk,"
The Reader, July 18, 2001, 12–15.

"Every Sad Detail,"
The Laurel Review 39, no. 1 (2005): 24–38.

"Goldfish,"
Connecticut Review 35, no. 1 (2003): 39–49.

"Honda People,"
The South Carolina Review 34, no. 2 (2002): 109–18.

"Intervention,"
in *Best New American Voices 2001*, ed. Charles Baxter
(Harcourt, 2001): 78–96.

"Intervention,"
Colorado Review 27, no. 3 (2000): 19–36.

"In This Weather,"
Green Hills Literary Lantern 15 (2004): 213–27.

"The Last Girlfriend,"
North Dakota Quarterly 70, no. 2 (2003): 127–39.

"Laws of Relativity,"
The Marlboro Review 25 (Winter/Spring 2003): 21–38.

"The Story of Gladys,"
The Baltimore Review 4, no. 2 (2000): 26–37.

"The Usual Mistakes,"
Colorado Review 30, no. 1 (2003): 67–93.